THE ABSOLVED
A NOVEL
BY
MATTHEW BINDER

BLACK SPOT BOOKS

ISBN (print): 978-1-7324007-2-6

Cover design by Najla Qamber
Edited by Melissa Ringsted
Interior design layout by Rebecca Poole
Black Spot Books

Dedicated to the city of Budapest, you treated me well.

PRAISE FOR MATTHEW BINDER

"A blistering account of an America with few jobs and no purpose. This is a funny, fast-paced novel with its finger on this country's dying pulse." – David Burr Gerrard, author of *The Epiphany Machine*

"The Absolved is a thinking person's novel. Dramatic and well written , this dystopian trip to a robotic future has everything : lust, law, medicine, betrayal, politics— even love. As humans struggle to retrieve their humanity from the robots who have taken their jobs and self worth, one man—a doctor— has the opportunity to be a hero or villain. This book will keep you up at night wondering what our future holds." – Alan Dershowitz

"With touches of Vonnegut and Huxley, Matthew Binder delivers a darkly funny look at a future we're most likely stuck with." – Seth Meyers

"In *The Absolved,* Matthew Binder has delivered us a devastating portrait of where we are imminently headed. Through his narrator Henri's fopperies, ranging from the affair to the revolution, Binder's novel is an ode to the imperfect and hilarious beauty of being human." – Hannah Lillith Assadi, author of *Sonora*

"Dysfunction—in the father and in the patriarchy that's to blame for most of this world's current ills—is the theme of Matthew Binder's novel *The Absolved*, and never have we seen it more brilliantly skewered or sadly portrayed. Hilarious as Vonnegut in *Cat's Cradle*, terrifying as Lewis in *It Can't Happen Here*, Binder offers us a parable for a future that could as well be our present, neither of which we should be proud to call our own. Eerie in its insight, lacerating in its wit, merciless in its conclusions, this is a book liable to become an instant classic. Binder points the finger in these pages, and names the names. He is an oracle for our time." – D. Foy, author of *Made to Break*

"*The Absolved* shines an unapologetic spotlight on the malaise and absurdity of an America whose soul has been sucked out by an over-dependence on artificial intelligence -- a journey that feels as poignant and honest in today›s world as it does in Binder's techno-dystopia." – John Cunningham Ph.D., AI professor, Columbia University

CHAPTER 1

I'VE JUST SUFFERED AN ACCIDENT WHILE DRIVING TO MEET Taylor, an entirely lovely woman who's not my wife. It's nothing serious—the accident, that is—just a crumpled fender and a sore elbow from the impact ... more of a nuisance than anything else. I am, after all, a busy man on a tight schedule.

There must be two dozen passersby who've stopped to stare. You'd think I just had a six car pileup from the spectacle I am.

"Go on," I tell them. "Nothing to see here. Everything's fine."

These days, ever since self-driving cars became the law, this sort of thing is rare. I almost can't remember the last time I got stuck in traffic due to a wreck, and fatalities are way down, ninety percent in six years, if I remember the statistic correctly. No more good-timing drunks on the road, at least not behind the wheel. Just like that, a scourge of suburban American society was eradicated forever. A lot of good it does me, though! Where were these marvels of human innovation when I needed them most? It's regrettable to admit, but before I had a bit of money in my pocket, I had something of a reputation for irresponsible driving. Even so, our technology is far from perfect. My car just hopped the curb and hit a streetlight.

I trace a square before me, opening my hologram.

"Insurance company," I say, and Kaylee appears, her face a composite of two of my favorite actresses.

But no sooner have we exchanged some pleasantries than she assaults me with questions. She's skeptical of my explanation for the accident. It seems she suspects I'm at fault. The insinuation is that I've tampered with the vehicle. That's a very popular thing to do these days, especially with the kids. They watch the old films in which cars meant freedom, rebellion, and sex, and they want it for themselves. People are bored of being chauffeured around, so they attempt their own retrofits, to take back some control. Kaylee has repeatedly informed me that making such a modification is a felony, punishable by fine or jail time.

She puts me on hold, and I turn on some music to pass the time. Chloe, my car's OS, is also upset. I refuse to listen to the playlists she's made. She insists she knows my tastes better than I know them myself, which, I assure her, can't possibly be true. Besides, at forty-seven years of age, I don't *do* playlists. A thousand times I've told Chloe I like albums, but without fail she tries to persuade me that they're an antiquated mode of consumption. They lack the consistency of quality and flow, she maintains, that only a machine can deliver.

On most occasions, after much opposition and reluctance, Chloe will generally acquiesce and play any of the two dozen garage rock bands from my youth that I still listen to with great piety. But today, she's forcing Rachel's music on me. Rachel has wholeheartedly embraced the technology-driven cultural shifts of the past twenty years with nary a gripe. It bothers her not one bit that it's been years and years since a tune penned by an actual human being has made any kind of splash.

"The machines are superior to man in almost every way imaginable," she once said. "Why else would we have turned over all of life's most important functions to them?"

A song written and recorded by an algorithm named Nevaeh comes blasting from the speakers. I immediately recognize the chorus, comprised of this sequence of notes: A, C#, Eb—what's come to be known as the "Melody Monetizer," because in 2032, a research project led by a team of A.I. determined that this particular arrangement is the most pleasing to the human ear, and, thusly, the most profitable. A recently released study shows that ninety-two percent of contemporary pop songs and commercial jingles now use it.

"Can't you find me any Talking Heads?"

"I'm sorry, Henri," Chloe says, "but the Talking Heads are on my *no-play* list."

"What the hell is that supposed to mean?"

"Rachel gave me a list of bands I'm no longer allowed to play for you."

"In my own car?"

"Rachel doesn't like guitar music, Henri."

"But she's not here now."

"It's out of my hands, Henri."

Kaylee returns to the line. She's completed her remote

assessment of the vehicle. The miracles these modern-day machines can perform is beyond me. It seems each new day gives us fresh ways in which they can enter what was once private. Thinking about this sends me to despair. I engage the breathing practice my yoga mentor has taught me, and repeat my mantra—"There is the nothing that is there, and the nothing that is not there"—until Kaylee informs me that I'm "not guilty." The culprit: my software had failed to update.

To meet with Taylor, I've told Rachel I'm on-call. While technically this is true, I've bribed one of the younger doctors to cover for me, promising him a weekend at Serena's beach house. This is just one of the perks of having your best friend from medical school as your boss.

I've taken a room at a hotel in Oakland, far from anyone who might know me. It's a place Taylor read about on a trendy lifestyle hologram, a spot the young techies go to drink and take drugs, swim in the pool, and enjoy their elite status.

I arrive first, check-in, and go to the room. It's really very impressive. It comes with a well-stocked bar that includes liquors of all variety. There is a bright-burning neon sign reading, "EXIGENCY," mounted on the wall, and a chandelier of loose hanging lightbulbs of different shapes and sizes. The finest touch is a claw-foot tub in the bathroom. I pour myself a whiskey on ice and sit inside of the tub.

My excitement to spend time with Taylor is of course hampered by nagging guilt. It's not like tonight is the first time I've done something like this, but it hardly gets any easier. Every time I finish with one of these flings, I convince myself that I'm through with it, that I can re-commit myself entirely to Rachel. But these sorts of situations have a funny way of sneaking up on you. I consider them my passionate curiosities. None of them really mean anything, and it's not like they diminish my love for my family. If anything, I think these dalliances may strengthen the marital bond. Every time I come home after one of these bouts, I see Rachel with fresh eyes and feel a renewed sense of fidelity.

Here's the thing: since my son, Julian, arrived seven years ago, Rachel has turned quite frigid in the bedroom.

For a while, at least, we tried to maintain a strict love-making schedule. Every Thursday night, Rachel would hire a babysitter, and I'd pick her up after leaving the office, and we'd go for dinner and drinks. Then we'd retire to a hotel, similar to the one I'm at now. I'd climb on top of her and push it in and out for a while, and then she would bounce up and down on it for a time, and then, finally, I'd get behind her, grab a fistful of hair with one hand and smack her bottom with the other, and I'd thrust and jab away until we both had finished. Then we'd lie there for an hour, generally not saying much, before we dressed and returned home to relieve the sitter. It was all perfectly pleasant, but there's not a routine in this world that doesn't become stale with enough time. After a few months, we started skipping an odd Thursday, then we'd only make time for our sacred trysts once a month, and not too long after, we abandoned the scheme altogether.

When Taylor knocks at the door, I try to stand without putting down my drink, but instead lunge into the tub's faucet and soak my pants.

"You look like a million dollars, maybe even two million!" I say to Taylor.

These are not empty compliments. Taylor is stunning. She possesses a distinctive aesthetic, nearly gothic in nature, a fetish of mine since boyhood: a fair ivory complexion, hair as black as a raven's wing, delicate nose, heavy make-up on the eyes and ultra-red lips—thin as a waif.

"You couldn't wait for me," she says, gesturing to my pants.

"Problem with the tub," I reply, turning red.

I fix her a drink. She stands next to the bar, awkward, and with every delicate sip the sleeve of her shirt rides up her arm to expose a row of circular-shaped scars. I consider asking about them but decide that the mystery is more alluring than any explanation might be. Besides, it's plain she's uncomfortable that I've seen them, which is the last thing I want. I can't help but think of Taylor with anything other than sweetness and pleasure. In many ways, this is so much better than love, because it causes no harm or violence against my heart.

We undress and begin to have sex, but it's going poorly, strange for me, a man of advanced age and experience. I can't remember having performed this badly since high school. It's my own fault, no doubt. In a rush to leave for work this morning, I failed to masturbate in the shower.

From the very first pump, I'm at the edge. Desperate to prolong the experience and salvage my dignity, I engage every known technique to alleviate the pressure. First, I imagine a basket full of dead puppies—six tiny, lifeless basset hounds. But this does nothing to remedy my situation, so I consider my Aunt Lucille naked. This, too, provides no relief. Finally, I pose myself an arithmetic problem: $((38 \times 6)/4) \times 3$—yet again to no avail: I'm a whiz at math, and the answer comes immediately. "One seventy-one!" I cry, and explode.

Taylor pats me on the head like a child or a pet, and I roll away to stare at the ceiling and heave. There's almost nowhere in the world I'd rather be less. The presence of someone who's witnessed my inadequacy is physically painful. I've spent my lifetime striving for excellence, and most of the time I've accomplished exactly that. As a boy, I was a first-rate shortstop on my Little League baseball team. Later, I dedicated myself to music. For a stretch, there was no one writing better tunes. After I became convinced there was no future in the arts, that if I kept at it I'd die in poverty, I settled on medicine, because it makes me indispensable in the economy. As it happens, I've done very well for myself and am highly esteemed in the field of oncology. Just last week, my name was printed in one of the top medical journals for a contribution I made to a study in Chimeric Antigen Receptor T-Cell Therapy. But here I am now with this beautiful young lady, an incompetent laughing-stock, all of my hard work washed away and meaningless after one bad round in the *Service of Venus*. How is it that I woke up this morning thinking I was invincible?

Taylor lights a cigarette and draws a bath. Still reeling from my failure, unable to face her, I sneak glances through the door. I know as a doctor, specifically a cancer doctor of all things, that I should have an extremely adverse outlook on cigarette smoking, but I cannot. Before I am anything in this world—a doctor, a husband, a father—I am a man of vice. There's nothing more seductive than a beautiful woman who knows how to smoke. It's the most suggestive and alluring act known to humankind, against which I'm powerless.

Watching her, I'm driven nearly to the brink. The prospect of all that thick smoke filling my lungs, the warmth of the grit on my lips, and the lingering scent of tobacco clinging to my fingers, fills me with the courage to stride naked across the room to retrieve my aims. Besides, when else might I get another chance to partake in such an activity? These days, like lions on the Serengeti, cigarettes are rare, symbols of a bygone time. Ever since we moved to a nationalized healthcare system, there's been a virtual prohibition on these great givers-of-pleasure. Spending fifty-five percent of its budget paying for the care of its citizenry, nearly bankrupting the whole country, there's no way the federal government is going to tolerate this sort of behavior.

I climb into the tub behind Taylor, and she leans back, pressing her body against me. Notes of vanilla flood my senses, sending me into a state of bliss. I wrap an arm around her chest. She tenderly kisses my cheek. We take heavy drags off our cigarettes and watch the smoke swirl round the chandelier, dissipating across the room. There is nothing sweeter in a woman than her desire to give over her will to a lover's care.

"You're too good to me," I say. "How can I make your life a bit better?"

"There's nothing."

"I'm serious."

"I wouldn't think of asking anything of you."

"Maybe I can help you get readmitted into medical school?"

Taylor and I met approximately two months ago. I had given a lecture on genome sequencing at the medical school. She sat in the front row, wearing a skirt, crossing and uncrossing her legs. More than once I lost my momentum and had to begin anew. Afterward, I spotted her drinking champagne at the reception. When I asked what she was celebrating, she joked that she was on the edge of a complete breakdown, then went on to tell me she was in the final week of her first year at medical school with just a single set of tests remaining that would determine her future. I didn't take this for hyperbole. In today's highly competitive world of medicine, only the top twenty-five percent of first year medical school students get to matriculate on to the second year.

Even though more money is being poured into healthcare than ever, less and less of it is used to train and pay doctors. Most of the treatment decisions these days are based on algorithms and A.I., which removes the need for more physicians. Instead, the government is spending its money on increasingly sophisticated new technologies, tests, and facilities, plus an army of low-skilled technicians.

Today there are one-hundred million senior citizens in the country, about twenty-five percent of the population. The number one fastest growing job in the economy, perhaps the only field whose numbers are increasing, is *geriatric ass-wipers*. All day long, that's what these people are paid to do. They wipe asses, they spoon-feed adults who are as helpless as infants, they hand out pills and administer shots. Healthcare today isn't slowing the aging process. No, what it's doing is slowing the dying process.

Medical school students who fail to advance past the first year tend to find themselves either as ass-wipers, or as members of the ever-growing social class we affectionately refer to as *The Absolved*—folks, that is, lacking sufficient talent or skill to contribute to today's high-tech workforce. Best of all, none of The Absolved ever have to work. Sure, they complain endlessly, and yet with no effort at all, they have everything they need: food, shelter, healthcare. That said—don't get me wrong, I'm not ready for such liberation. I'm a steward of humanity, willing to suffer and work for the greater good. Of course it's not all martyrdom. I'm very well compensated for my efforts. Compared to the majority of the population who are too old to work, too unskilled to work, or working as ass-wipers, I'm doing very well. Statistically, I'm in the top one percent of all earners.

I've digressed!

With nearly a half decade of tremendous effort and study

behind her, Taylor had only one set of tests left to earn her way into the top twenty-five percent. And, my goodness was she close going into the exams—seventy-third percentile! The pressure on someone in that position is nearly incomprehensible to anyone who hasn't gone through it themselves. Thank God I didn't have it so bad. In my day, things were quite good, comparatively. There was a severe physician shortage, so if you had a pulse and could eke past the Board Exams, they'd give you a credential. You might end up practicing Family Medicine in Cheyenne, Wyoming, but at least you got to be a doctor.

After the reception, I encouraged Taylor to join me and some of the faculty for dinner. At first she was reluctant because she needed to study, but I was persistent and she relented. The company of doctors is something over the years I've grown entirely accustomed to. We're certainly a self-congratulatory bunch. It's all talk of who's been where on what vacation, how much each has paid for their new home, and what private schools our brilliant children have been accepted to. Normally I'm as guilty of this line as anyone, perhaps even one of the worst offenders. But, on this night, in the company of Taylor, I had no interest in anything besides her.

When Dr. Hincs regaled the table with a story of spending a fortune on a painting—by the expressionist Willem de Kooning—of a large-breasted, naked woman staring into oblivion, I noticed Taylor lose interest.

"Bad paintings," she said in response to my concern, "please the masses only to the extent that they present a false and simple and hence reassuring view of the world." It occurred to me then that I could be no Pygmalion lover to this young woman. She had me licked when it came to culture, and I couldn't have been more impressed. "I'm so glad you're not like the others," she said. "They're so dull, with their obsessions with money and status."

I agreed. I'd never before heard such a compelling argument against success. Had she asked me that night to relinquish my position as a doctor and live with her in a cabin somewhere in the Sierra Nevadas, I'd have done so gladly.

I'm not sure how, but I won Taylor's affections, evinced by her allowing me to rush her off to bed that very night. In the days that followed, every chance I could take, I absconded to her apartment. Perhaps because of our affair, Taylor had not studied enough to move up more than a single point in the rankings, leaving her spot in the second-year medical school class out of reach.

"I'm a big girl," she says as she lays her glistening leg on the rim of the tub. "I can accept what's coming."

"But surely I'm somewhat to blame. I didn't let you out of bed for a week after we met. You must let me help."

As these foolish declarations tumble from my mouth, I can't help but wonder why. It's as if I'm suffering an out-of-body-experience. These can't be my words. They're only an invitation for trouble. Still, I sound so sincere and impassioned, my body is practically quivering with eagerness to make itself useful.

"I don't want to trouble you anymore than I already

have," she says. "You're taking such a risk just by being with me like this."

"I can't just stand by and watch this injustice transpire."

"It's too late, my fate is sealed."

She repositions herself so we're face-to-face, her straddling me.

"Let me think," I say.

As I ponder why my mouth continues to speak against my better judgment, Taylor strokes my head and kisses my cheeks and lips. I remind myself, she's a fling, I have a wife and child, I shouldn't involve myself any further. But it's no use, now, there's nothing I want more than to lend a hand in the great success story of this girl. One so rarely gets to be the hero.

My first thought is to go to that dilettante who overpaid for the de Kooning travesty, Dr. Hines. And yet he offends me on so many levels. Like the majority of those whose aptitudes lie in the realm of technical work, Dr. Hines has no interesting thoughts or any real curiosity about politics, music, or art. Instead, he repeats the same boring tripe that millions of other mouths around the world are saying in unison. He reminds me of the nouveau rich Chinese who destroyed the art market in the Aughties—puppets of New York art dealers who suffered from a complete absence of sophistication or erudition. He pays exorbitant prices for what really amounts to lackluster work by third-rate artists, in hopes of increasing his own social status—perhaps, for instance, a chance at meeting the has-been actor Leonardo DiCaprio at a black-tie gala, or attending a runway show for the new *North West* collection. Or, at the very least, he buys art not because of his appreciation for the vision or skill of the artist, but because he speculates there's a possible big payout down the road, if, that is, he's successful in his shell game to bring a certain hack to prominence. A work by Jordan Cantwell is no different than an investment in a share of *Hologram Plus* or renting out apartments in Philadelphia—a cash cow! Sometimes, when I'm made to suffer through someone parroting the drivel that has become the zeitgeist, I wonder if I should disappear into the desert, silence surely being preferable not only to stupidity but to unanimity, as well.

In addition to moonlighting as an art collector, Dr. Hines is a fellow oncologist and the dean of the medical school. He and I, however, are nothing if not nemeses. The man may be a bottom-shelf aficionado, but he's a first-rate sycophant. His preternatural ability to ingratiate himself to people in high positions beggars belief. This shameful yet highly profitable skillset is perhaps the greatest strength of men of weak character. It prevents them from being crushed by stronger rivals. Without fail, the man has the ability to escape the most precarious positions utterly unscathed. He's like one of those suckerfish who attach themselves to sharks in the ocean, growing fat on the morsels of food discarded by their hosts.

Just this morning, I was with Serena and Dr. Hines discussing the most efficient, cost-saving ways to deliver medical care. Serena has written an algorithm that quantifies the value of a human life. The work is truly groundbreaking, and there is already talk of a Nobel Prize in her future. This new Human Life Valuation Tool takes into consideration an incredible number of inputs, ranging from the obvious to the esoteric. The following is a just a small sampling of factors the tool uses to ascertain what a life is worth: number of friends, potential to affect change in the world, cholesterol level, arcane knowledge, degree of independence, political beliefs, athleticism, physical attractiveness, susceptibility to vice, fidelity, body fat percentage, favorite color, culinary skills, tidiness, shoe size, sexual proclivities, ability to manage one's finances.

Dr. Hines is disgustingly worshipful of Serena's work. On and on he goes about how she's revolutionizing the industry. The exultation sounds lifted straight from the Ayn Rand guide-to-healthy-living. He has a number of catchy slogans that he shouts at the top of his lungs: "Dependence leads to suffering! Man's first duty is himself! Reliance on the government has destroyed the once great people of this nation!"

"Dr. Hines," I interjected, "aren't you at all concerned about the possible implications of trying to reduce the essence of a person's life down to a monetary value?"

"Tell me you're not so silly as to be objecting on moral grounds."

"From a purely humanistic view, it may be unethical to make medical decisions based on subjective criteria of how much a person's life is worth."

"Jesus Christ, Henri. It's not he who accepts everything

and anything from people who truly values the sanctity of human life. What you're really saying is that you expect nothing of people, so nothing can disappoint you. A person who makes no distinction between the creators of symphonies and some fool who sings along to the radio is a person with no appreciation for humanity at all."

"The trouble with someone like you is that you, without fail, accept the conclusions to which your groping leads you, as articles of faith."

"Per usual, you're obscuring what you want to say with clever language," Dr. Hines said. "Could you elaborate?"

"If it's handholding you need, I can oblige." Dr. Hines held out his hand, palm up, with his typical smirk. "My concern is that you may be incapable of wrapping your mind around the complexities of this world. So, instead, you'll do anything and everything to adjust the world to what your mind already believes to be true."

"Here's a fact that should interest you," Dr. Hines countered. "Once the government passes into law Serena's recommendations, nearly eighty percent of cancer treatment spending will be cut, equating to a $2.1 trillion in annual savings for the National Healthcare System."

"And I suppose you'll claim that such a system will be for the common good?" I said. "A sacrifice by the individual to help the masses!"

"And for you, Henri, it may mean an early retirement!"

Throughout all of this, Serena's face remained completely impassive. Both Dr. Hines and I were desperate for her to choose a side. Instead, she dismissed us both, claiming that her Thai masseuse was due any minute, and she needed to burn sage first.

Now, here in the tub with Taylor, my desire for her mounting, I struggle to expunge my guilt for causing her to miss her medical school requirements. Going to Dr. Hines with Taylor's situation would prove fruitless. Instead, I reason, perhaps an appeal to Serena will be best.

"I have a friend in a very high position," I say. "If anyone can help, it must be her!"

"What sort of friend?"

"She's the head of the entire hospital system."

"I really don't want to end up in The Absolved, Henri. It would be an awful life."

"I wouldn't let it happen to you."

We kiss hard, and she takes my dick and rides me as if in a voodoo trance. By the time we're done, there is more water on the floor than in the tub.

CHAPTER 2

BEFORE GOING HOME—BEFORE RETURNING TO DOMESTIC life, that is—I stop at my favorite bar, Anodyne. A man can't simply throw himself into his household affairs. He must be emotionally prepared. A hasty homecoming could possibly result in disaster. He must, therefore, don the appropriate demeanor. I try to imagine the horror of it: me, walking through the door with a big, stupid grin, fresh-off a rendezvous with the exquisite Taylor. It would certainly raise suspicions, that's for sure.

Anodyne is not a place people of my status tend to go. It's a bar that in a different era would have been considered working-class. Now the clientele is mostly members of The Absolved. A random passerby would never know the bar existed—it has no sign. But those in the know will find Anodyne situated on the second-floor of a rundown building, that fifty years back housed a textile mill filled with Asian women sewing wedding gowns. Downstairs is an out-of-business Vietnamese Restaurant, closed by the Public Health Department after a customer found a microchip in his Banh Mi sandwich. The staircase to access the bar is far too steep for comfort, and is narrow and poorly lit. Many customers have taken a nasty tumble down those stairs after a few too many. The proprietor of the place, Tony—who, legend has it, no one has ever even seen—has a fetish for antique lamps, and they are scattered throughout the bar, providing this hideaway with an ambience of perfect gloom. There is a pool table in the corner, six stools at the bar, and two red vinyl booths along the wall. The most charming touch is the antique jukebox—stocked only with songs recorded by actual humans, nearly all from last century: outlaw country from the '70s, punk from the '80s, grunge from the '90s.

Lydia, the bartender, has been something of a friend, confidante, and spiritual advisor to me ever since she rescued me from a bar-fight beat-down my first time here. Though she's only five-foot-two and one-hundred-and-ten pounds with a tangle of dry, frizzy hair, she managed to fend off my attackers with only a broken pool stick and a surplus of street bravado.

"What should it be this time, roses or daisies?" I say after ordering a whiskey on ice.

"How bad is it?"

"About the usual amount of bad."

"I'd want daisies, but I'm more Volkswagen than Mercedes. You should go with roses."

I open my gram and say, "*AmaDrone*, deliver a dozen roses to Rachel within the hour. Place them in a vase and leave them on the kitchen table, with a note that says, 'Late night at the hospital. Thinking of you. Love, H'."

"How are things?" I ask Lydia.

She looks up from wiping the counter with a filthy rag, "We won our roller-derby match last night. City champs!

Other than that, nothing too exciting. Tony keeps threatening to either sell the place or modernize. He says we can't compete with the automated drink-maker joints."

"He harms that jukebox, I'll kill him."

An old flat-screen television is mounted over the bar, squeezed between a neon beer sign and a taxidermized elk's head with women's underwear hanging off its antlers. It's election season and the campaigns are in full-swing—twenty-four hours per day of propaganda. The question of how best to move forward as a country has never been so difficult to answer. The people are more divided than ever. The news is replaying a speech by President Martinez.

"Hey, turn up the volume, would you?" I ask. "I want to hear what Bienhecho had to say."

Everyone calls Martinez "Bienhecho," which is Spanish for "do-gooder." Martinez was the son of two illegal immigrants from El Salvador, a *Dreamer*, who served as the primary wage-earner in his home during adolescence, making a steady income streaming his online videogame playing. This prowess earned him a scholarship to university, where he became a civil rights activist, later serving one term as a congressman from California before being sworn in as our youngest president to date. When he came to power he was hailed as the New Messiah, the man who promised the people he'd help them regain a feeling of participation in the economy. So much for that! All of his efforts to jumpstart a public works program have ended in abject failure. Unfortunately, there's just no way to make a human as productive as a robot. It's almost hard to remember now, but there was a time when a person could make a decent living doing all sorts of different things: construction worker, fireman, dog groomer. But the list of occupations that earn a livable wage is shrinking all of the time.

In lieu of helping the common man regain some semblance of self-worth and fulfillment, Martinez has done the next best thing: he's raised taxes on the wealthy a record six times in the first three years of his term. Free healthcare, free university, free everything has to be paid for by someone. On paper, I'm supposed to pay sixty-eight percent of my salary to federal income taxes, but, of course, I don't, because that would be insane. I shelter as much as I can with fancy financial chicanery. God bless this new tax-avoidance software—the greatest gift technology has provided me—for keeping me in the black.

Only four years ago, Martinez possessed almost unnatural good looks—the body of an athlete, a coif of black, lustrous hair, the bone structure of a star, and an undeniably sincere look in his eyes that made the country fall in love with him. He even got people like me, whom he's trying to bleed dry, to vote for him. The man won by a landslide. But to look at him now, you'd hardly recognize him. The stress of the job has taken its toll, not only on his emotional well-being, but on his body, too. His once svelte physique has been reduced to a husk with a paunchy belly and reedy arms and legs. The immaculate skin of his youth is now so pale and devoid of melanin that it displays the type of sunspots usually only found on people of Irish descent. His hair is thin and grey. And when he speaks, his voice is a gravelly rumble.

"It may well be impossible," he's saying, "for people who have lived and prospered under a given social system to imagine the point of view of those who feel it offers them nothing. So we cannot count on the charity of those who have everything to be the stewards of the people, to take care of their brothers and sisters, in their time of need. A system that does not work for the majority of the people it serves cannot sustain itself ..."

At the end of the bar sits a man who looks fifty years old— but a hard fifty—like he's seen the worst life has to offer. A pit bull lays at his feet. The man is striking matches and putting them out between his fingers, against his neck, on his tongue. Halfway through the president's speech, he yells at the screen.

"You filthy bastard, you've done nothing for the people of this country!"

Lydia pours him a drink and pats him on the arm. He kisses Lydia's hand.

"You're the only good one left in the world," he says.

Lydia fills a bowl with water and hands it to the man for his dog, followed by a dish of pretzels. Then she mixes two whiskey drinks, one for each of us, and joins me. A pendant with the photo of a young boy dangles from her neck. The kid looks like a wilted flower. Lydia catches me staring and tucks the necklace into her shirt. There is the utter feeling of the past lingering in the present.

Now the masochist is hurling pretzels at the TV.

"Goddamn it, Karl," Lydia snaps. "You know I have to clean that up!"

The man lowers his head, like an acolyte before his saint. I offer to buy him a drink, and he moves down the bar to the stool beside me.

"You know," he says, still looking at the screen, "I could kill this man and feel no remorse at all."

"You and about three-hundred-million others."

"What's a guy like you do for a living?" Karl inquires.

I glance at Lydia for help.

"He's a doctor, Karl," she answers, "and a damn good one too from what I hear, so be nice to him."

"Let me ask you a question."

"Shoot," I say.

"How do you get your fruit and vegetables?"

"My wife only does farm to table."

"But how do you think normal folks do?"

"In refrigerated trucks, of course."

"That's right, Doc," Karl says, pausing to take a long pull from his beer. "And until just ten months ago, I drove for Sunny Hill Foods, before they replaced all the humans with *self-drivers*."

"Could've seen that coming."

"I suppose you're right about that," he says. "Let me ask you one more question: what have you ever done to serve your country?"

"I pay most of my taxes and voted in three of the last five elections."

Karl smashes his fist into the bar. "That just figures, don't it? Someone like you does nothing and gets everything, while someone like me does everything and in return is made obsolete."

He struggles from his stool and limps toward the door, his dog at his side.

"The people really have their pitchforks out this election season!" I say to Lydia.

"A guy like you should be careful, Henri."

She pours two shots, and we down them. I pay my tab through my gram, and tip Lydia triple the bill. Then I signal for Chloe to pull the car around and pick me up out front.

CHAPTER 3

IN THE MORNING, I'M DIFFERENT THAN AT NIGHT—A FAMI-ly man with traditional values. Just the sight of my wife and son across the table nearly reduces me to tears. Last night seems indefensible. Who was that man carrying on in that hotel? I bear no resemblance to that adulterer, that scoundrel, that villain. Here with my gram loaded with *The Times*, my coffee, my wife and my son, I couldn't feel more complete. There's an old saying: "There's life, and there is greater life!" Well, this is greater life. I want only to make my family feel safe and loved.

It's just 7:00 a.m., but Rachel's already made up for the day, a process that takes nearly two hours from start to finish—at least, ever since she started to dress like a Disney princess about six months back. This transformation began when she came home from the salon one day with a wavy bob, crowned with a little red bow, a la Snow White.

"Very Brothers Grimm of you!" I said.

"I don't know what you're talking about," she replied. "This style is very chic. It's currently all the rage in Calcutta and Nanjing."

At the time, I gave her the benefit of the doubt. Now I'm not so sure. She's appropriated everything possible to complete the aesthetic, all the way down to the purple eyeshadow, the blue, red, and yellow ensemble, and the short red cape.

"You're looking gorgeous as always, darling," I tell her this morning.

"You don't think the short, puffy sleeves are too much?"

"I think they're just right. They really complement ..." I pause to consider my choice of words, "your clogs?"

"And you like the standing white collar?"

"Love it!"

"Oh, who am I kidding?" she mutters. "You don't care. I don't even know why I bother."

"Don't be like that, darling."

"Just eat your breakfast," she says.

Rachel has had our meal service deliver gluten-free pancakes and apple sauce. Not my favorite, but a healthy and at least edible alternative to the traditional fare. After Julian's birth, Rachel really struggled to lose the baby-weight. She spent months working with a personal trainer. First, he put her on a regimen of high cardio. When that failed, he switched her to a four-day-a-week weight-lifting schedule. Her strength improved markedly, but the routine did nothing to help her lose the fat in her belly, butt, and thighs. Finally, desperate, she hired the most esteemed nutritionist in town (not to mention the most expensive). After a thorough investigation, the nutritionist attributed Rachel's inability to lose the weight to postpartum depression. However, Rachel took great offence to this diagnosis and required the nutritionist to ascertain a different explanation. The answer: a gluten allergy. It's now seven years later and Rachel is still battling the bulge. Regardless of its ineffectuality, the gluten-free diet remains the only acceptable lifestyle choice in our home.

"You were out late last night," Rachel says.

"Did you get the flowers?"

"What time did you finally make it home?"

"Rough day at the office. I stopped at Anodyne to cool off."

Rachel seems to accept this answer, and turns her attention to Julian, who has syrup on his face and T-shirt. The boy has the table manners of a savage. The child psychologist assured us he'd grow out of it, but that was two years ago. He's no better now than he was at four or five. I wonder if he has a rare condition that affects his spatial awareness. I've consulted all of the texts, but I've yet to find any data to confirm my hypothesis.

Rachel tells the boy to take off his clothes and eat in his underwear. She's tired of buying him new shirts and pants. Even worse than that expense is the effect Julian has on our water bill. Over the past twenty years, California has experienced the worst drought in human history. In 2032, we had one good rain year, and the experts predicted we'd seen the worst of it, that things would return to normal. However, things have only gotten worse. In 2035, we received less than two inches of rain. This year we're on pace for even less. Thankfully, California has made great strides in desalination technology, due to techniques we've imported from Israel. However, the cost of water is still crippling. We spent more on Julian's post-meal baths last month than we did on his private school, which is the second most prestigious in the city.

Seeing Rachel at her most maternal always puts me in the mood. My years of studying the human condition informs me it's the pheromones she emits while under the stress of child rearing. As she finishes cleaning up a mess of apple sauce that Julian has splattered on the floor, I make a proposition.

"What would you say if I insisted we reinstitute our Thursday night dates?"

She breaks out into a fit of laughter, practically shrieking. I haven't witnessed such a display of merriment since our honeymoon.

"Are you kidding? What with Julian, your schedule, and my commitments to charity work, who has the time?"

"It would be really good for us."

"Emma is acting up. If you can fix her, I'll give you a date next Thursday."

Emma is the OS who runs our home. She controls the temperature, the dishwasher, the washer and dryer, the water, oven, stove, doorbell, clocks, locks, WiFi, TVs—everything.

Rachel doesn't know this, but last week I tampered with Emma, attempting to mask my little foray into VR sex—a luxury I've previously never permitted myself. In today's society where many people feel more intimately connected to their VR-life than to their *real* life, VR sex is a far more flagrant offense than common adultery with an actual person, and therefore unbecoming of a married man. Nevertheless, in a moment of weakness, I succumbed.

I blame it on Serena. She had spent weeks teasing me with stories about what a spectacular time she'd been having participating in group VR sex with Chinese college students.

"A temptation resisted," she always says, "is a good time wasted!"

Fortunately, I botched my attempts to log into the Chinese sex site, failing to override Emma's hardwired programming to block engagement with Chinese businesses, due to long-term economic sanctions.

It's a good thing, too, because Rachel has a real aversion to smut or, for that matter, anything else she views as deviant. This wasn't always the case. During our first few years together, she was something of a pervert and freak. Rachel used to get off on having sex in public spaces, and for a few years she was an active dominatrix, a fetish I reluctantly participated in until one evening when she left me bound and gagged in the basement for nearly two hours. Alas, those days are gone. Now she's certain VR is responsible for the decline in our country's family values. She cites a statistic that only nine percent of men and women between the ages of twenty-five and forty are married with at least one child, while, coincidentally, ninety-one percent of people in this age demographic report a propensity for VR. In my humble opinion, on the other hand, the reason young people aren't marrying and having children is due almost entirely to rotten economics. Only six percent of Americans, I tell Rachel, citing a recent statistic, feel they are in good enough socio-economic standing to care for an additional person.

"What's wrong with Emma?" I question.

"You don't think it's strange she's only speaking Mandarin?"

"I hadn't notice."

"What about her insistence that we dine on *Boy Eggs*?"

"What are those anyways?"

"They're eggs soaked and boiled in the urine of young boys. Street vendors sell them on the streets of Beijing."

"Why don't you fix her?" I ask. "It would take you less than thirty seconds to have her running tiptop."

"In case you haven't noticed, Henri, I'm extremely busy. Yesterday alone I brunched with the women from the Wildlife Foundation, took a Pilates class, met with the interior decorator, took Julian to baseball practice, and picked up dinner."

Rachel knows all about my poor aptitude with technology. It's been a great source of shame for me ever since I was a kid. Most men of my generation grew up on video games. My friends would spend hours every day tethered to their consoles. "Warriors of the controller" is what I called them. But I simply had no interest. I wanted to be outside.

My neighbor, Travis, was my best friend between the ages of six and ten. The kid loved video games. He would have played them endlessly had he been allowed. He'd have foregone food, sleep, and even sunlight.

Before I used to go to his house to play, I'd have my

mother ask his to hide his console. He'd be in hysterics by the time I got there—tears rolling down his face, eyes red and swollen, screams of anguish pouring from his mouth. After his initial fit, however, he'd calm down, and we'd catch spiders or play basketball, or do any of the hundreds of other things kids once did in the great outdoors.

While all this made me stronger, I attribute my poor aptitude for technology to my lack of time playing video games. This slow start has always haunted me. In eighth grade, I failed my beginner's programming class. In high school, I got last place in the technology fair's software writing competition. In college, I nearly got a herniated disc from lugging hardcopy textbooks, because I refused to adopt a tablet, like everyone else. In my job, today, I have to pay two scribes to follow me around to do all my data input, because I can't manage the medical records program without wreaking major havoc on the system.

Through my gram, I invade Emma's controls. This wouldn't make less sense to me if the whole thing actually were in Chinese. All at once, the curtains cover the windows, and every light turns on at its brightest. I continue to fumble about, and the windows and lights return to normal, but every door in the house locks down, trapping us inside.

"What if there's a fire?" Julian screams.

"Don't be afraid," Rachel reassures him, glaring at me, "Daddy will get this under control."

I close my eyes and return to my mantra, "There is the nothing that is there, and the nothing that is not there." I say this to myself at least a dozen times as I fuss with the controller. The electric fireplace turns on, and the house warms up to a balmy eighty degrees. Another stab at a manual override has Chinese Orchestral music playing at full blast.

"Listen to the clear, bright tone of that *Sheng*!" Julian says.

"What's that?" I ask.

"It's a bamboo mouth organ, Dad!" he replies.

Finally, Rachel shoves me out of the way and goes to work, swiping at the gram and making commands until the house returns to normal.

"Date night?" I say.

"Not even close."

It's my firm belief that nine out of ten women take great pleasure in debasing the men they supposedly love. I see it all of the time, a woman contriving to put a man into a situation where he's forced to dishonor himself, humiliate himself, or betray what is pure and strong in him.

"I'm going to work," I say.

"Don't forget, you promised to join me at the food drive tonight."

"Didn't we just do one last week?"

"And yet those same people are hungry again. It's the craziest thing, isn't it?"

"The poor get all of my money in the form of taxes, and now they get my time, too?"

"You're *such* an altruist, Henri. Just one of the many things about you I love so much."

CHAPTER 4

IT'S 7:30 IN THE EVENING AND I'VE BEEN AT THE OFFICE since 8:00 this morning. I've seen twenty-three patients thus far—a respectable number, though nowhere near my record of thirty-seven. The average life expectancy is eighty-eight, and the cancer business is booming. People are growing old, yet their golden years are fraught with disability and misery. The American Way, however, is never to give up. We stave off death for as long as we can, come what may.

I'm late to Rachel's charity event, but I still have one patient left to see, Mr. Toczauer, whom I've been treating for three years. Yesterday was his eighty-sixth birthday. He spent it in the hospital, just like he did his eightieth-fifth and eighty-third birthdays. He got a reprieve on his eighty-forth, managing a short bout of good health, which—like all good things—ended quickly, landing him back in our care a few days later.

Before Mr. Toczauer became a near-permanent ward of the National Healthcare System, he had worked for forty years in middle management for a plant that manufacturers breakfast cereal—a terrific vocation for a man of Mr. Toczauer's abilities. His job was to work with a team of analysts to crunch the numbers and then make strategic decisions accordingly. I'd never thought about it before Mr. Toczauer had explained it to me, but there are trends in breakfast cereal consumption. For example, in 2022, an "anti-GMO" lifestyle craze swept through the entire West Coast. Virtually overnight all cereals made from Monsanto's GMO corn stopped selling from Seattle to San Diego. The grocery stores couldn't give Frosted Flakes or Cocoa Puffs away. Realizing this, Mr. Toczauer ordered all corn-based cereal production to be relocated from their plant in Riverside, California, to their plant in Martel, Ohio. In its place, he shifted all production of granola. This spell of genius saved the company millions in shipping costs. Mr. Toczauer was deemed a hero, and for his efforts his photograph was hung in the lobby of the corporate office in Topeka, Kansas.

But those gallant days are long behind him. The man lying in hospital room #122 would be virtually unrecognizable to anyone who knew him in his prime. In fact, he's been in this state of indefinite twilight for so long that I'm not sure even his own family can remember what a strong and adept man he once was. Unfortunately, it's this condition—as a dependent, as a burden, as a man who can't feed or bathe himself—that will forever be his legacy.

Mr. Toczauer's condition is called Agnogenic Myeloid Metaplasia. It's a real mouthful to say, and I always stumble over the words as I give the diagnosis to a patient and their family. Every time, I have to repeat myself because my audience gets hung up on the words themselves, rather than what they represent. Mr. Toczauer's state is so bad that for the past year he's been completely dependent on blood transfusions just to stay alive. But now even this has ceased to work.

When I enter his room, Mr. Toczauer is surrounded by his wife and grown children, a son and daughter. The man's cheeks are so hollow and gaunt that the yellow skin on his face hangs off them like dead weight. When he gasps for breath, I notice that there are more teeth missing than not. His head, which I was told had once been thick with blond, curly hair, is now bald and flecked with liver spots.

"Hello, Mr. Toczauer," I say. "We have your blood test results. I'm afraid your anemia has worsened. I'd like to speak with you and your family about the next phase of your care."

"We've fought the cancer like hell, haven't we, Doc?" the old man stammers. "But I'm tired, now. I know when I've been licked."

"Don't you talk like that," his wife objects. "You're a fighter. You still got a few good rounds left in you, I know you do!"

The wife is a nervous, birdlike woman with grey, straw-textured hair and very thin lips. She incessantly touches her face as she talks. Her son puts his arm around her.

"He hasn't been eating, Doctor," she says. "Is that because of the anemia?"

"Your husband is very sick, Mrs. Toczauer. His bone marrow is rapidly being replaced by scar tissue, leading to abnormal red and white blood cell production. This is causing his spleen and liver to become extremely enlarged."

The son, a chubby, ruddy-faced man of fifty, takes control.

"So what's the next step here?" he inquires.

"In situations like your father's, I'm required by the *Quietus Law* to inform you of the euthanasia option."

"Euthanasia?" the wife asks.

"The intentional ending of a life," I say, "to relieve pain and suffering."

"That doesn't sound so bad," Mr. Toczauer cautions. "Is this a normal thing for people to do?"

"It's not particularly common, no. Regardless of a person's condition, it's generally human instinct to cling to any semblance of life, no matter how poor its quality. However, just last month, I had a patient meet his end with great courage. He had a terminal case of non-Hodgkin lymphoma, and he decided it was his time. He conferred with his friends and family, and they scheduled a date that worked with everyone's busy schedules. Those closest to him were able to be by his side. It was quite beautiful, actually."

"Hell, I'm sold!" Mr. Toczauer exclaims, turning toward his wife. "What do you think, honey, should we invite Cousin Wayne to my *death party*?"

"How can you even joke about such a thing?"

"This is nonsense," the son says. "What other options are there?"

"We can move your father into hospice, where we can make him as comfortable as possible."

There is a collective gasp from the family.

"No, no, no," the wife cries. "None of this is any good. Please, Doctor, anything that might save him."

"The only other option is another heavy dose of

chemotherapy, followed by a bone marrow transplant. But you have to understand, these are extremely invasive procedures that will cause your husband extreme and unnecessary pain. The odds he'll survive them are less than five percent."

The mother and children confer. The daughter makes an emotional plea about the sanctity of life and how it must be preserved at all costs while the mother and son nod.

"I can't stress the point enough," I interject, "this series of procedures would be extremely painful, torture really, and, again, the chances of their success are *very* small."

I can tell these words are falling on deaf ears. Each of them has embraced their own brand of absurdity to rationalize an inevitable conclusion. In an effort to appear he's tempering his foolishness with a modicum of reason, the son asks a final question.

"And what about the cost? Will we have to pay for this out of pocket or would it be covered?"

"These procedures are extremely expensive. The costs for them and the subsequent months of care, assuming he survives the initial chemo and transplant, will cost millions of dollars. Of course, your father, as a citizen, under the current laws of the National Healthcare System, is entitled to these services, if that's what you choose."

The three huddle for a final consultation. After less than fifteen seconds, a decision is reached.

"He is our blood," the son announces, "and we have a responsibility to him. As long as he's still breathing, then we have to continue doing everything we can to make sure he lives."

"And is this what you want?" I ask Mr. Toczauer.

"If it's what my family wants," he says, "I'll do it."

"Are you sure you believe this is for the best?" I ask the family. "It's my professional opinion that there are more humane options."

Mr. Toczauer tries to speak but is cut off by his son.

"We've made our decision, Doctor. Thank you."

"Very well," I say. "We'll get your father scheduled to begin his chemotherapy."

CHAPTER 5

OUR INCREASING TECHNOLOGICAL ADVANCES HAVE driven greater and greater inequality. For decades, this didn't seem to bother the politicians. Just as long as the overall economy kept growing, they didn't care who was benefitting. However, in 2030, a tipping point was reached. So much of the economy's money was concentrated at the top that it effected consumption. Rich people can only buy so many consumer goods, and when they run out of things to buy, they simply save their wealth, essentially removing that money from circulation. On the other hand, poor people spend every dollar they get their hands on. They have to just to live. A lack of savings may be bad for the poor people, but it's good for consumption, and keeps the economy humming.

To combat this problem, the government is now providing what they call a Basic Income to every citizen of the U.S. Essentially, the government is giving away money so people can buy the goods the machines and robots are making. Of course, the people are outraged that more money isn't doled out. There are protests in the streets of every major city nearly every day. The battle cry is that the people don't receive enough free money for them to really *enjoy* their freedom. The more progressive wing of our government advocates that there should be a sixty percent increase in the rate.

That's all well and good in theory, but our national debt is currently sitting at $102 trillion, and mounting. In my benevolence, I've declined to accept the stipend owed to me, instead donating it to charity.

Outside the poor folks receiving Basic Income, there is yet another group, on the outermost fringes, that rarely gets discussed. These people, who don't fit into The Absolved, are the mentally ill, the lunatics, the ex-convicts, and other random undesirables who never would've made it even during the heyday of the American economy, the ones you see hopped up on malt liquor and cheap drugs, sleeping on the streets in torn rags, with dirty faces and missing teeth: The Futile. Back in the day, The Futile could at least make enough to eat by panhandling and collecting bottles and cans. But now the streets are closed to beggars, and there are robots who collect all recyclable material.

The Futile can't collect Basic Income. In a day and age when all information and data is recorded on The Cloud, they have nevertheless managed to slip through the cracks. They're outside the system, and once you're out, it's very difficult to get back in. It would be a tremendous test of skill and patience for even the most adept and able-minded of us to navigate the maze of bureaucracy required to get reinstated. How any member of The Futile might manage this remains a mystery.

Some years ago, Rachel became terribly depressed at the notion that she provided no value to society. She had lost her management position at the bank when cryptocurrency replaced the US dollar as the world's preferred means of money, and while motherhood filled her heart and hours with tenderness, love, and care, she wanted more out of life. The question then became one of how she could best contribute more. She made a list of ways she could feel wondrous by giving back. Then she prioritized her prospects according to feasibility and potential return on investment. She concluded that tutoring refugees would be the best way to make herself feel charitable, while simultaneously earning the admiration and veneration of everyone who knew her. Twice a week, for exactly two weeks, Rachel went to the local shelter to teach English to the refugee children who had escaped France after the successful Muslim insurrection. While she found this feat of charity rewarding, it wasn't enough. The satisfaction was too private. She needed something on a grander scale, visible to the masses, what friends and strangers alike would recognize as a shining achievement. That's when she got the idea to start a program called Feed the Forgotten, or FTF for short—a large-scale food kitchen to aid society's most needy. I warned her about the name and acronym.

"Aren't you afraid people will make jokes and call it *Feed the Futile*?" I asked.

"Of course not," she said. "Who could be so cruel?"

As it happens, this is in fact what nearly everyone calls the program, including myself. Even Rachel called it that once, during an interview, a gaffe that cost me no small sum of money to hire a team of search engine optimizers to eliminate.

pull up to the event at 9:00 p.m. It's still very hot, an at-
sphere worsened by a ceiling of clouds that trap in the heat.
thin crescent of moonlight peeks through, providing a glim-
mer of hope that good may still predominate over evil. Despite
these conditions, the line for food stretches out the front door,
snakes around the building, down a small embankment, and
ends in the park next to the bronzed statue of a robot carrying
a human boy on its back that was erected in 2029.

The FTF uses the cafeteria of an inner-city junior high.
To get inside, one must pass through a proton beam scan-
ner at the front door. The hallways are lined with lockers
secured by electronic pin-codes. Along the wall, in outsized
letters, reads a quote from a once prominent novelist who
in recent years has fallen terribly out of fashion: "We work
to satisfy our egos!" Through the quote, some hooligan has
spray-painted a line, and, below it, scribbled, "We loaf because we have nothing else to do!"

Rachel is leading a small team of volunteers. Over the
years, they've developed a very efficient system. Thanks to
automation, what once took fifteen people to accomplish
can now be done with only three.

One by one, the masses pass through a buffet of assorted fruits and vegetables, hot soups, crisp salads, breasts of
chicken, flanks of beef, and multiple varieties of noodles,
rice, cookies, and cakes. Each fills their plate to the brim,
overwhelmed by the bounty. Standing at the end of the line,
Rachel is there to greet each man, woman, and child with a
warm embrace and words of kindness and cheer.

At times like these I realize just how much Rachel means to me. She's much more to me than a partner. She is a part of me. Without her, I'm incomplete, the lesser half of a greater whole. When I think of my small indiscretions, it's almost as if the Taylors of the world don't exist—practical nonentities. So intense are my feelings that I don't even suffer remorse for my actions—meaningless, insignificant trifles! My heart is swollen with admiration and joy. I can't bear to interrupt Rachel in her generosity.

After an hour of this harmonious image, I'm disturbed by something strange and wicked. But it cannot be, I think. Not my Rachel, not my perfect flower, my idyllic, charming goddess. A small confrontation has flared up between her and one of her beneficiaries, in whose face Rachel is wagging an indignant finger. Then, after she's completed her rebuke, the man looks away for a brief moment, and when he does, Rachel spits on his plate of food.

We don't return home 'til midnight. Rachel changes into her pajamas while I prepare myself a snack of gluten-free cookies and almond milk.

"Wonderful event tonight," I say, moderating my tone against any perceived aggression.

"Perhaps our best one yet."

"It seems every week more and more people are finding themselves in need of your help."

"I only wish their numbers were even greater so I could be of even more service."

"I have something I need to ask you about, but because it's so silly, I'm reluctant."

"Don't be shy."

"I could've sworn I saw you spit in someone's food."

"You saw that?"

"I did."

"The man told me we live in an unjust society that has left humanity in the cold. How am I supposed to feel wonderful and noble about my contributions when the people I'm helping say such things?"

I nod in tacit agreement and climb into bed, Rachel right behind. In minutes, she's sound asleep and grinning, leaving me to lie here sick in my stomach.

CHAPTER 6

TAYLOR HAS BEEN HOUNDING ME TO MAKE MORE TIME for her. Nothing outlandish, just the usual list of gripes, misgivings, and injustices. The other day, for instance, we argued because I haven't taken her to the theater. A production of *Doctor Faustus* has received five stars from all of the tastemakers, and though I don't recall having made such a declaration, Taylor swears I've promised to take her. It's possible I set an expectation during a moment of passion, but I can't remember. The moment we finished, any such assurance was wiped clean away. And anyway, there's too much at risk. A man can't simply go gallivanting all over town with his mistress. There are rules, decorum, which at all costs must be abided. One's own reputation and interests aren't the single thing at stake. Other parties are involved—Rachel, for one. There's not a mountain I wouldn't climb or an ocean I wouldn't swim to shield her from the humiliation of my indiscretions. And Taylor's good name, there's that to consider, as well. She's just coming into adulthood, and life is hard as it is. If she's not going to concern herself with remaining in good public standing, then it's my duty to be vigilant for her.

The day after Rachel's event—yet another scorcher, whose crackling, glistening heat you can feel on your hands and behind the eyes—Serena and I are enjoying oysters and a dry French rosé at a restaurant on the Bay. She insists the acidity in the vintage works to balance the oyster's saltiness, yet not to overpower it. I'm no connoisseur but I know what I like, and the two of us are now working on our second bottle, the main course yet to be served.

My reason for inviting Serena to dinner is to ask if she can help secure Taylor a position in the second-year medical school class. Without names or details, I describe her circumstances—how a series of unfortunate restrictions prevented her from adequate study, landing her just outside the top twenty-five percent of first year students. I stress how ambitious and hardworking she is, how she desperately wants to avoid a job as an ass-wiper, or even worse, to fall into The Absolved.

"Who is this girl you're having an affair with?" Serena asks.

"An affair? She's a friend of the family ... more of an acquaintance, really."

Despite my denial, Serena dives straight into a sermon about the perils of infidelity. I've never before heard her speak with so much passion. When compelled by a powerful emotion, there's not another person alive capable of such a demonstration of charisma and persuasion. Her exhortations, while differing in subject matter, share a similar aesthetic to those of orators of yore, Martin Luther King Jr. and Winston Churchill.

While certainly not arguing wholesale against adultery, Serena claims, for example, that affairs can be "both fun and healthy when done correctly." She goes on at great lengths to instill in me respect for the pitfalls of an affair pursued improperly. The number one danger: falling in love with your lover.

"A man in love with a woman who is not his wife," she says, "is a doomed man. To put it bluntly, no good can ever come of a love born in sin. It can only lead to destruction and chaos. A man who pursues love outside of his marriage puts his entire life in danger. He'll obviously lose his wife and family. But that's just the start of it. Most likely, such a man's professional life will be flushed down the toilet, because nobody wants to do business with someone who can't act in accordance with the moral code of the institution of which he's a member. A man so reckless as to fall in love with his mistress is a man who places no value on prudence or good sense. And when the principles of good conduct and discretion are lost, financial ruin is sure to follow. The second great danger is losing one's vigilance. This can happen when a man who has a long history of affairs gets too cocksure and impetuous. His track record of success deludes him into carelessness, and thus down the path of tragedy."

Serena's lecture leaves me full of pounding dread, enough, nearly, to cut off the affair immediately. While confident I will never fall in love with Taylor—for she is merely a dalliance, a charming and exquisite distraction from the everydayness of my regular life, an embodiment of amorous passion— there is a risk that I will fail to ensure my actions conform to my ethics. *And where is my mind?* It's good to check in now and again: I'm certain my true heart's desire remains with Rachel. I'm not so unwise as to think that tremendous physical chemistry can surpass the rock-solid foundation of sentimental and intellectual intimacy that Rachel and I have spent years forging. But I must be wary. I wouldn't be the first man to mistake for love the feelings spurred by arousing the interest of someone so desirable as Taylor.

"So will you help the girl or not?" I ask.

"You're really not sleeping with her?"

"Of course not. I'm married to Rachel."

"A family friend, you say?"

"Of sorts."

"And you're very close to this girl?"

"Not really."

"I see."

"What do you say?"

"If she truly meant something to you, I would, but since you said yourself that she doesn't, I can't really justify throwing my weight around so that your girl can get a spot at the expense of another student, whose credentials are not up for dispute."

Serena's refusal, clearly, makes things trickier than I'd like. That I can't deliver is almost enough to make me take her to the theater, if only to soften the blow. But I can't do it. A man in my circles is liable to cross paths at the theater with any number of colleagues or friends. I can imagine Taylor by my side, radiant in a splendid gown, proud on my arm, overjoyed by the wonderful show, when Dr. Cartwright from cardiology and his wife, Samantha, come bounding toward us, so that in a panic I'm forced to hiss at Taylor, "Take five steps to your left, and pretend you don't know me!"

The horror, I tell you, the horror!

Serena's fifteen-year-old daughter, Olivia, who is visiting from Seattle, joins us at the restaurant, as well. Interestingly, while Serena stands over six feet tall in heels and is always dressed in couture, Olivia is short, soft, and round, practically hidden inside a baggy sweater—of all things in this sweltering heat—loose-fitting pants, and combat boots. The poor girl barely says a word upon sitting down, and Serena is practically oblivious to her, not once including her in our conversation. She even goes so far as to redirect a question I ask the girl into a lecture about how she got into business.

In medical school, Serena used to wake up at dawn to day-trade on the NASDAQ. When the market closed, she'd spend a few hours doing research in preparation for the next day. She always joked that beating the market is really very simple. All one has to do is buy low and sell high—easy as that.

One semester she had a class that conflicted with this routine, so she brought her laptop to the lecture hall and traded from there. It was no secret that the professors at school despised her. Serena, they thought, made a mockery of medicine. I can recall many a time during our lectures that some professor, seeing Serena engrossed in her trading, and hoping to humiliate her, would call on her to speak, but no matter the question, Serena replied as nonchalantly as if she'd known the answer from birth. Whenever I asked how she did this, a look of pure boredom would envelope her face as she changed the subject, usually to sex or sports.

After Serena completed residency, she practiced medicine for only one year before giving it up. By then she'd amassed a fortune on the market and was looking for new frontiers. While I was slaving over an oncology fellowship, for instance, she busied herself building apartment complexes. By thirty-five, she was a millionaire, hundreds of times over. In 2025, seething with envy, I followed her lead by investing nearly half my net worth into a luxury condo complex in Livermore, a town in the hinterlands of Oakland, only to see the real estate market crash to its lowest point since the subprime mortgage atrocity of 2008. Of course while Serena managed to escape the mess unscathed, Rachel and I lost every last cent.

This is when Serena went into the healthcare business. She started a PPO called Serena Health, which became a nationwide leader in managed care. The company expanded to include a network of over 3,500 doctors. Just before National Healthcare became federal law, she sold the business to the hospital chain I work for now, for an undisclosed sum of money. As part of the deal, she was made CEO. Three years into her new position, she's a two-time National Hospital Administrator of the Year recipient. While the rest of the industry is floundering to control costs, we're experiencing record profits.

Serena has been characteristically vague about the

circumstances of Olivia's stay, but a gram-search this afternoon led me to an article that revealed the sordid details. Apparently, Olivia is some sort of prodigy-turned-cautionary tale in the art world. From the story, I learned that last year, during Olivia's freshman year of high school, she had discovered the pleasures of ingesting drugs, especially LSD—a drug that fell out of mainstream popularity after the 1970s but made a resounding comeback in the early 2030s, when psychologists started prescribing it to teens suffering from gram-induced psychosis.

Olivia and her friends began experimenting with daily micro-dosing, taking 30ug each morning, administered orally in liquid form, before attending class. For six months this went on, until one sticky summer night, while her father and step-mother were off on holiday, Olivia decided to increase her dose to 120ug. At first she experienced little more than expansive elation. But an hour in, she started seeing ripples of light that intensified until instead of merely synthesizing color visually, Olivia experienced it with her other senses, as well. She described, for example, how the color violet took on the flavor of salted almonds and sounded like a virtuoso bowing a low E on cello. She also began to see complex geometric patterns. Her couch, bedroom walls, and the framed autographed photo of Elon Musk she kept by her bedside, all took on a brand-new significance, almost religious in nature. She was convinced that when she closed her eyes, she could see the pathways that join time and space. At some point she stumbled upon a trove of old magazines in her parents' basement. Her father had been a long-time collector of *National Geographic* and her step-mother a hoarder of decades-old fashion and gossip rags. Inspired by the thousands of images before her, Olivia set out to create art. She took scissors to paper, cutting out countless pictures of exotic animals, foreign and remote locations, new-fangled machinery, faces both gorgeous and repulsive, body parts, and everyday objects. Naked, then—she had stripped off her clothing and hid each item in a different place—skirt in the oven, blouse behind some volumes of Dostoevsky, bra and underwear in the toaster, sandals on the roof—Olivia glued her cutouts onto every inch of the ceiling, walls, and floors of her home. The result: one of the most magnificent collages since Matisse's use of the form in the 1940s. When she posted photos of her work on her gram, a media frenzy ensued. The world's most well-esteemed art critics made such bold exclamations as "A Star is Born!" and "The 21st Century's Picasso Has Been Discovered!"

Christie's and Sotheby's fought a bitter war for the rights to sell the house. Eventually, Loic Gouzer at Christie's won Olivia over by taking her on a shark hunting expedition. The sale price, however, was disappointing, netting just $4.35 million—Olivia's parents, after all, had paid $4.6 million for the house several years before. The winning bid came from a Taiwanese collector who turned the house into a gallery exhibition so that the public could enjoy the work. But attendance was poor and six months later, he had the home demolished.

Since then, Olivia hasn't sold a single piece. Unable to

repay her father and step-mother for the loss of their home, relations became strained—hence Olivia's visit with her mother, Serena, whom by her own admission, quoted in the article, no less, Olivia says she doesn't "know any better than a stranger on the street."

"I'm laying off the entire pharmacy department," Serena states.

"You wouldn't," I say, nearly spitting up a mouthful of rosé.

"I've purchased robots that can store, retrieve, dispense, and package pills in a fraction of the time. More importantly, no human error. Do you know how much we lost last year in lawsuits due to pharmacists mislabeling medication?"

"I don't know, ten million?"

"Jesus, Henri, you really are lost. It costs us nearly that amount for every suit we settle. Try a hundred and fifty!"

"What do you think it'll cost your mom to replace all of the pharmacists with robots?" I ask Olivia.

Olivia looks up from the gram she's been hiding in her lap. "Huh?"

"Your mom's replacing all of the pharmacists with robots. What do you think it'll cost?"

"The tasks pharmacists perform are relatively simplistic," she replies after a thoughtful pause, "something a rudimentary robot could easily manage. No more than fifteen million, I'd say."

"That's very close," Serena says. "Fifteen is the going rate. But I got the price down to fourteen."

The entrees are served, three large bowls of steaming Cioppino. The restaurant's owner, Mario, is a descendant of Italian immigrant fishermen. In the old days, each family member would add something from their catch to the communal kettle on the wharf, but today the bay is polluted, and all of the fish have to be farm raised. The soup is the restaurant's most popular meal. Each day's recipe is different than the last. Today's includes halibut, Dungeness Crab, scallops, and shrimp.

"How are you enjoying your time with your mom?" I ask Olivia.

"Last night I heard her having sex," she declares.

"I thought she was out with friends," Serena says.

"My dad says my mom's a nymphomaniac. Men or women, it doesn't matter in the slightest, she has a taste for them all. My dad says she collects lovers like spoiled children their toys. She plays with them once, then puts them on a shelf. And once they're there, she never thinks about them again."

"He's not wrong," Serena says.

While we were in our final year of residency, Serena got pregnant by the captain of the school's tennis team, whom she met at a bar while celebrating her finish in the ninety-ninth percentile on Step 2 of the National Medical Board Exams. The reason she decided to keep the child was not due to any particular desire to be a mother, but instead she claimed simply to like a "good challenge." Three months after baby Olivia was born, moreover, Serena proposed to the father because it was easier than finding a good nanny. But it wasn't long before Serena was fooling around, and soon her husband filed for divorce. The husband walked away with more than twenty-five million dollars and married a former professional cheerleader.

"Are you looking forward to school starting again?" I ask Olivia, desperate to change the subject.

"Not really."

"No?" Serena asks.

"What's the point? You're filthy rich, and I'm your heir."

After dinner, we take a walk. I've always found that a post-dinner amble never fails to help me work through and resolve the thousand small vexations that plague me. It's precisely these at critical mass that destroy a man. The gnats really do triumph over lions, as they say—always.

When I was a younger, I lived a life of one unique truth. I had my love for Rachel, and I had my career. My passion for each fed me, made me stronger, and with mighty force pushed me straight and narrow. I was convinced that life had a purpose—something rooted in human substance. However, now it seems I have not one but two, three, and perhaps even four truths. I am living several lives at once even as I remain a committed husband and father who wants most of all for his family to be safe, cared for, happy. And yet I also find this framework stifling. The married man lives on a set schedule—filled with obligations, commitments, chores, dinners, bedtime stories, kids' soccer matches, and so on. Sudden whims have no place in these. As a result, I find myself dwelling on the memory of, if not an unlived life, a lost life—where opportunities were yet rife for seizing. And whenever I surface from these forays, I ache with the sense that to pursue anything beyond my given path would be traitorous and wretched.

While at heart I'm still the same man who married Rachel all those years ago, the conditions on which I strode down that path have vanished. Rachel has changed, too. I want badly to describe her any other way, but for the life of me the only fitting expression is that she's "getting old." My regard for her is still incredibly high, of course, but I'm afraid I can't love her the way I used to. Perhaps that's okay, I tell myself often. Love is supposed to change, evolve, expand. And yet why then do I constantly fall victim to the charms of women like Taylor?

In so many ways, I admire my dear friend Serena, who lives her life in a spirit of genuine excess. She conquers the world unapologetically. She feels it is her right. And anything she puts her hand to she does better than the rest. She excels not under some expectation or pressure, but because she's driven from within to breathless heights. Nor is it merely at work that the world bows at her feet. The same unassailable vim and vigor is evident wherever she goes. When the woman eats a meal, for instance, she does so with voracity, consuming massive quantities of food, luxuriating in every bite, foregoing whenever possible utensils in lieu of her hands, unafraid, plainly, to get messy, singing the chef's praises as she practically squeals with joy. Her pleasures of the flesh are doubly gluttonous. Mere enjoyment is never enough. She must overwhelm, subjugate, even annihilate her lovers. Not until they have committed themselves to her body, mind, and soul will she relent. It's true—Serena is far more than special, but a paragon of humanity itself.

I emerge from these thoughts to find that we've entered a street of badly decrepit buildings with bars on the windows. The sun has nearly set, yet it's still as hot as midday. There isn't so much as the palest breeze. Where the moment before, it seems, there had been only expensive cafés, fancy boutiques, and luxury apartments, now we're surrounded by broken bottles, fast-food wrappers, used condoms, and spat-out gum. The air reeks of urine and filth. The Futile loiter everywhere, bored and dull, the lethargy that's swallowed them nearly a smell of its own. They glare openly at us as we pass. We can't disguise our wealth and the symbols of it—our fine clothes, our styled hair, our clear, shiny skin, our hope. And then, somehow, we're standing before the Anodyne.

"Drinks?" Serena asks her daughter.

"Alcohol is, like, so passé."

Overhearing this, two bums laugh as if it's the funniest thing they've ever heard.

"You believe this generation?" Serena says.

Olivia kicks a beer can off the sidewalk, a motion that causes her sweater to cling to her body and reveal what I believe is the answer to my question. The first bum enters the bar, followed by the next, with Serena close behind. Her daughter's hesitation is my cue.

"So you're pregnant, huh?"

"Ew. You really *are* a creep."

"Not drinking, a sweater in nearly a hundred degrees … who do you think you're fooling?"

"At least one person."

"But are you okay?"

"You better not tell my mom," she snaps, and marches up the stairs.

Inside, Lydia is moderating an argument between two lesbians. One is a handsome, stoutish woman with a trace of mustache. The other is abnormally tall and thin, weak-chinned and knock-kneed, her tiny butt barely contained in the shortest skirt.

The dispute is over living arrangements. The skinny woman is adamant that they take the next step in their relationship and move in together. Her partner thinks it's too soon—they've known each other just three weeks. "What has time got to do with anything when the subject is love?" the tall woman argues. It's clear from the defeated expression on the first woman's face that this conversation won't be won with reasoning and good sense. She surrenders. Her new lover, she says, can move in.

The quarrel settled, Lydia joins Serena, Olivia, and me. "Three whiskeys?" Lydia asks.

"Just two," Serena replies, "my daughter doesn't drink."

"Suit yourself." Lydia pours us a round, which we shoot quickly, so she can pour another.

"It's been that kind of night," Lydia groans.

"You just got yourself mixed up in stage-one of somebody else's romance," Serena says.

"Stage-one?" I ask.

"That's right, *passion*, the first of seven. Passion, coolness, indifference, boredom, mockery, contempt, and, finally, disgust."

"That's terrible," Lydia says.

"It's the world we live in," Serena replies.

It's politics-as-usual on the bar TV. This time it's Tim Bradford, a former police officer who's now the presidential candidate for a party called The Progressives. Disappointed in both the Republicans and Democrats efforts to create job growth, the disenfranchised workers from both sides of the political spectrum banded together to form a new party, focused on the rights of the worker. Disorganized in 2024, they got slaughtered. In 2028, there was still too much infighting within the party for them to stage a successful run. In 2032, the Democrats ran Martinez and almost ninety percent of The Progressives rallied behind him.

Now that Martinez's socialist agenda has failed, The Progressives are staging a comeback, this time with a new agenda. Rather than focus on the redistribution of wealth, they want to turn back the clock on the relentless progression toward more automation. Outside of the party, everyone refers to The Progressives as The Regressives or better, obviously, The Luddites.

Their original message was framed within an intellectual paradigm—namely, too much automation causes humans to lose the ability to think and is therefore bad. The example that proponents of this ideology most often cited pertained to aviation. Due to increased cockpit automation, this faction claimed, pilots spent less and less time flying planes, causing their skills to erode, making flying less safe. But the facts didn't support their case. Airplanes controlled by automated systems, it turns out, are much safer than airplanes controlled by humans. This of course did little to stop the movement. The death of the intellectual argument caused the group to resort back to its roots—populist flag-waving. Now they're stronger than ever.

"Who the hell would make this asshole president?" Serena questions.

"He speaks to people's hearts," Lydia says.

"Turn it up." I nod my head at the TV. "I want to know what form the next wave of chaos and destruction in this country is going to take."

Bradford is a colossal white man. The pallid flesh on his face is heavy and without shape, like a hunk of soaking clay. When he turns angry and loud, which he does without fail ten seconds into every speech, debate, or interview, the white transforms into an alarming scarlet. The crowds that he draws to his rallies are setting records. And wherever he goes, disorder and lawlessness follow. At a rally last week in Cincinnati, an entire unit of robotic firefighters perished when an out-of-work plumber set a giant LED screen ablaze. The crowds cheered when they heard the news of the losses.

Today's speech is coming from Detroit, where early polling shows Bradford has nearly unanimous support. An ill-fitting suit makes his shoulders look nearly a mile wide. His comb-over is flapping in the breeze.

"I don't remember any part of the Constitution calling for the Divine Rights of Machines, do you?" Bradford shouts.

From the massive crowd, a deafening, "No!" erupts.

"In centuries past," he says, "men rose up and over-turned the divine rights of kings. Just like those brave men who recognized the injustices bestowed upon them, we too must stand up and revolt against our oppressors. Because who will stand for the wishes of men if not men themselves? Are you going to continue to stand idly by and watch as your livelihoods are stripped from you and given to soulless robots? Of course not! There is a hierarchy in this world that must be respected: God, man, animal, machine! For man is imperfect, and in that imperfection is virtue!"

More thunderous applause attends this bit. Bradford basks in his glory, beaming, flexing his arms, enacting all manner of vulgar bravado. His wife joins him, and, gro-tesquely, they embrace and kiss.

Karl, the out-of-work truck driver, has been on his stool at the end of the bar. Now he rises to attention, salutes the screen, and recites the Pledge of Allegiance in his uneven baritone. His shirt is too small, exposing a trace of hairy belly fat.

Serena, on the other hand, breaks into a fit. "What's next from this asshole, goddamn it? Is he going to call for a time machine to take us four centuries back so we can cut poor Gal-ileo's head off? Stop all progress in its tracks. In the fifteenth century, they burned men of science at the stake! Is that what he wants us to do? Kill all of the goddamn smart people?"

"There's nothing more tragic," Karl says as he draws toward us with heavy, menacing steps, "than bearing witness to what technology has robbed the hard-working people of this country of!"

In her heels, Serena is at least four inches taller than Karl. "Next," she says mockingly, "you're going to tell me that it's my fault you're in this condition."

"America is a two-hundred-and-sixty-year-old cathedral being burned to ashes because of people like you!"

Karl and Serena stand chest-to-chest, he in his beer-stained T-shirt and she in her three-thousand-dollar suit with its overstated décolleté. Both look as wicked as born killers. Thank God for Lydia, who is a pro. She vaults over the bar, throws herself between them, and begins shoving Karl toward the exit.

"Now's not the time, Karl," she says.

"This isn't over!" he says, lumbering off, his old dog by his side.

Serena is actually shaking. Her eyes are bugged and sweat is running down her face, smearing her makeup. But as quickly as she'd lost her head she's regained it. On her stool again, whiskey in hand, she's as composed as a queen. "You can't stop progress!" she says.

CHAPTER 7

THE POETRY OF CEMETERIES HAS ALWAYS SPOKEN TO ME. A good stroll around the gravestones turns me into a morass of sentimentality. The trees, the flowers, the well-manicured grass—cemeteries are like marvelously serene parks where instead of smart-looking couples and their screaming children, you have marble tombstones and memorial plaques. People are so much more pleasant once they've passed.

My favorite tombstones have always been nineteenth century. The epitaphs of the era possess a somber religiosity that contrasts starkly with my modern views. Belief in God, it seems, would make life clearer and simpler. But having never had this light to lead my way, I'm afraid I've never defined any principles by which to live. How is a man to know if he's compromising himself if he has no moral framework to abide?

In high school, I fell for a goth girl in my trigonometry class named Sarah Blackwood. She didn't have much aptitude for the work, so I allowed her to copy mine. Beyond my academic prowess, I understood too late, she had little use for me. I didn't have the gloomy aesthetic some of the other arty kids worked so hard to achieve. It's astonishing how moved a teenaged girl can be by a fellow just because he's got a pasty face glopped up with eyeliner and mascara.

Sarah dated the drummer of a band called Le Faux. They were the most popular group in our school. Le Faux played post-punk in the vein of Joy Division. In my opinion, they were terrible. Not only did they lack a talent for song-craft, but the rhythm section was loose and the singer's voice was shrill and grating. I attributed their popularity strictly to the way they acted and looked—an unwavering commitment to stoic glumness. They exemplified that scourge by which we've long since been overrun, of aesthetics trumped by ideology.

While not as popular as Le Faux, my own band, The Blank Sets, were superior in nearly every way—tunefulness, musicianship, craft. We worshipped bands like The Replacements, Big Star, and The Pixies. And while we certainly paid homage to our influences, we were never derivative. The primary problem lay in our lack of "the look." Our drummer, who grew up playing jazz and had the best chops of any musician in school, also played football and self-identified as a "jock." He was roundly mocked by the school's music community for his baseball cap and ill-fitting jeans. Our bass player had a tremendous feel for the instrument—always tasteful, never overplaying. His problem—he was extremely overweight, obese, really—making him ripe for ridicule amongst the cruel and unrelenting adolescents of Monte Vista High. I was the band's guitar player, singer, and primary songwriter. It's not a case of ego or self-delusion when I say that I was the most talented of the lot. Not unlike Davie Bowie or Paul McCartney, I had an almost mystifying gift for melody. Furthermore, I had keen sensibilities. Never did my songwriting get bogged down in overwrought sentimentality or twaddle. However, more than any other extenuating factor, it was me who prevented The Blank Sets from reaching the lofty heights to which we should have ascended.

To be brief, public opinion was not my friend. In a world where women anoint kings, the front man of a band has no choice: he must exude a certain sexual magic, or else. The singer for Le Faux had this. I did not. Until senior year—at five feet four inches tall, one hundred and fifteen pounds—I was a runt. Worse, to put it mildly, no one liked me. I was in fact excruciatingly unlikeable. I never missed a chance to trash Le Faux, for instance. I ranted about them to anyone who would listen, and even to those who wouldn't, about their lack of ability, talent, and soul. Is it any wonder I was known in some circles as "the little prick"?

Unable to win Sarah's affections with my prowess in music or math, I did something drastic. One day while touring the cemetery, I stumbled on the gravestone of a woman named Sarah Black, born in 1878 and died in 1912. Other than these dates, the stone was blank. My Sarah's predilection for the morbid aesthetic of bands like The Cure and The Smiths was keen, I knew, so that night I dug the stone up and hid it under a tarp in my mother's garage. Every night for three weeks, I worked on the stone until, finished, it said:

SARAH BLACKWOOD
HANG THE DJ

The stone in my wheelbarrow, I schlepped it to Sarah's

house and mounted it in her front yard, facing her bedroom window, then hid in the oak tree across the street. At 7:00 a.m., Sarah's father stepped out for the newspaper and shrieked. Had I not seen the man do this myself, I'd have said his scream was that of a spirit being torn from the body it had been. The rest of the family, of course, including Sarah, and, to my horror, most of the surrounding neighbors, as well, poured from their homes to witness the spectacle I'd created. Sarah did not swoon. Far from it, in fact. She fell to the ground in the fetal position and began to wail, where, for the better part of an hour, she was inconsolable.

The police traced the tombstone back to me, of course, and I was arrested. Still a minor with no previous record, I was given one hundred and fifty hours of community service and a $6,000 fine. This was nothing, though, compared to the mockery of my band mates and friends. For all intents and purposes, I was banished.

Despite the utter failure of my lovelorn sophomorics all those years back, I've never lost my faith in the romance inherent to a cemetery. In lieu of taking Taylor to the theater, therefore, I've invited her to a picnic amongst the dead.

The one meal I can cook is prosciutto-wrapped chicken, which I learned from an Anthony Bourdain cooking show that I watched on a cross-country flight many years ago. Squished between two wattle-faced businessmen, in the cramped middle seat of a Boeing 737, having only a bag of peanuts to satisfy my hunger, I forced myself to suffer through the entire episode, to ensure I obtained the recipe's savory nuances. Back home, I prepared the meal for Rachel, and it was a smashing success. Sadly, nothing I've done since has impressed her as much.

Now, as I cook for Taylor, I'm struck by the wickedness of my behavior, and yet nothing I do can relieve me of my obsession for Taylor's scent—grapefruit with notes of jasmine. Why is it that I can recall it so much easier than I can Rachel's? My thoughts drift from a consideration of her scent to a complete reconstruction in my mind of all Taylor's sexual niceties—her subtle gestures, her caresses, her sighs. This succession of mental images of past sexual thrills evolves into something fresh, and now I'm dreaming up subtle variations, new perfections in technique—the sorts of things one picks up in porno films.

Strangely, on the other hand, these fantasies are comforting. Because my reveries are all sexual, I know I'm still clear from breaking Serena's number one rule of infidelity: don't fall in love.

Now, heading out with my meal, blanket, candles, and wine, I have just over two hours before Rachel returns home from her yoga class. It's another hot night—ninety-two degrees according to Chloe. The year 2036 is the hottest in recorded history, as were 2035, 2034, and 2033 before it. A low-hanging orange moon casts a threatening light over the city. Signs along the road alert motorists of the continued "high fire danger."

I arrive at the cemetery fifteen minutes before Taylor. A rusting wrought-iron fence with rounded spear points lines the perimeter. Six months ago, someone stole the old gate, and the new one, made by a robot, is ornate with cheap geometry.

I follow the worn path through the weeds, past the newest gravestones at the cemetery's edges, into the center with its oldest, most elaborately adorned tombs. Under the canopy of a twisted oak, I lay out the blanket, arrange the flatware, and unpack the food.

Back at the entrance to meet Taylor, I watch as she steps from the car, looking not like a woman but a vision of Aphrodite herself. The sight of her sends me into jubilation.

"I asked for a trip to the theater and you bring me to a graveyard," she says. "You have a strange way of romancing a girl."

"Isn't it wonderful?" I reply, leading her along the trail. "Surely you can appreciate that this place holds a hundred times more charm than some tired old production of *Doctor Faustus*."

As I serve the meal, Taylor tells me how as a child she accompanied her grandfather to the funeral home to pick out his gravestone. It felt perfectly normal, she says, like a visit to the grocery store.

"Do you think the prosciutto is crispy enough?" I ask.

"I'm wondering," she begins behind a fork heaped with chicken, lettuce, and rice, "did you get a chance to talk to your friend?"

I pat my brow with a napkin and cough. "It's taking a bit more time than I had hoped."

"It's really important, Henri," she says, and touches my cheek.

"Of course. But you have to consider that it might be an impossibility."

"Are you saying I may end up in The Absolved?"

"I'm not saying that."

"Because that would be like prematurely landing here—in a grave!"

"Nonsense!" I say. "There are countless ways to fill one's time when not burdened by work. You could learn a new language, for instance."

"You know very well I'd lose all rights to Basic Income if I were to leave the country."

"You've got a bright, creative mind! You could write a book or become a painter."

"What kind of monster do you take me for? I want to be a doctor—the most selfless vocation imaginable—and you're suggesting I become an artist? That's exactly the opposite of how I want to live my life. An artist, above all else, must be completely un-giving of himself to anything or anyone but her work!"

I quietly chew my food.

"I'm sorry," she says, "I know you're trying."

By the time we've finished, I feel so wretched I almost don't have it in me to make a move on her. Eventually, though, I manage to suppress my feelings and summon the courage and strength required for us to make passionate, glorious love.

CHAPTER 8

Today Julian's hologram chip will be implanted in his finger. The technology is only five years old, but the norms and protocols surrounding it have already evolved so much. At first the chips cost close to $10,000, excluding the $750 monthly service fee—making them cost-prohibitive to everyone but society's most elite.

As an early adopter, I remember being hesitant even to show my gram in public—too afraid it would draw unwanted attention and put me at risk. Before opening it, I'd sneak off to the bathroom, check the stalls to make sure I was alone, and, only after I'd locked the door, open my gram at a size so small it was barely of use.

"Why should you be shy about your place in this world?" Serena would ask. "If those around you are jealous, all the better. Perhaps it'll force them to get off their asses and make something of themselves."

But in no more than two years, most professionals had implanted grams. They were practically required, in fact, to maintain decorum, even if people couldn't afford it. Every single interaction and artifact is digitally stamped with the type of device that transmitted or made it, a savvy corporate ruse to shame consumers into buying a gram. In no time at all, any self-respecting professional was mortified so much as to talk on a smart phone. Until just last year, moreover, any kid with parents-of-means received a gram for their eighteenth birthday. But now that they're funded by the National Healthcare Service, even second-graders like Julian are implanted. Grams are so common that one regularly sees whole groups of people staring into them, oblivious to all but the electrons and protons vibrating before them.

As for Julian's procedure, Rachel sees it as a coming-of-age ritual, like a Bar Mitzvah or baptism, and is adamant that I attend.

"But I have twenty-two patients scheduled today," I tell her.

"Some of them will have to reschedule, won't they?"

Cancelling appointments is anathema to me. I can only imagine the grief and heartache it causes. For instance, one of my patients today, diagnosed with Stage 2 Leukemia, is only twenty-seven. All she wants to know is what is to become of her, but now she'll have to wait another week to find out, because I'm being held hostage by my wife and child.

Julian is on the exam table nervously tearing away small strips of the paper beneath him. I'm impatient waiting for Dr. Patel—he's five minutes late. Rachel, however, doesn't seem bothered. She's had her gram open since we arrived, applying rouge to her face, making her cheeks as red as apples—attempting to capture that perfect Snow White aesthetic.

"Is it going to hurt, Dad?" Julian asks.

"It's barely a pin prick."

"Will I be able to feel the chip in my finger?"

"At first you will, but after a little while, you won't even notice it's there."

"I'm scared."

Rachel closes her gram, and says, "You don't have to do this, honey, if you don't want to. We won't be angry."

"The hell we won't," I say, "I took time out of my day for this."

Dr. Patel strolls in. He's sucking on a lollipop, and when he opens his mouth to greet us, I see that his tongue is purple.

"How are you today, Julian?" he inquires.

"I can't wait to watch cartoons on my gram," he replies.

Rachel lifts a cautionary finger in my direction when I shake my head, as if to say, don't you even think of ruining this for Julian!

Dr. Patel, with a gap-toothed grin, says, "They sure do grow up fast these days, don't they!"

Dr. Patel rubs alcohol on the tip of Julian's finger. The boy shuts his eyes so tightly that his entire face puckers. Rachel squeezes his free hand and hums the melody to "Whistle While You Work" while Dr. Patel examines his injector. A moment later, he's pulled taut the skin on Julian's finger and implanted the gram.

"Oh, honey, did that hurt?" Rachel asks as she kisses and blows on Julian's finger after he lets out a yelp.

"No, not really," Julian says, smiling brightly.

"You're all set, young man," Dr. Patel says.

As we leave, Rachel is showing Julian how to operate his gram, but at every point he brushes her off, having seen it all. He's already so deep inside of a game, he can't hear me say good-bye.

CHAPTER 9

M R. TOCZAUER IS SO ILL THAT HE'LL RECEIVE HIS NEW round of chemotherapy in bed. Preparing to meet his family, I've made a note that states, "Any further treatment would be more toxic than beneficial."

The first thing I notice in his room is the posters on the walls, each one featuring the baseball legend Cal Ripken.

"Cal Ripken," Mr. Toczauer's son says when I ask about the pictures, "played in 2,632 consecutive baseball games, a stretch that lasted over sixteen years. He's the Iron Man!"

"That's quite a feat," I say.

"That's Dad's nickname, too—Iron Man."

Everyone looks at Mr. Toczauer, more a shadow than a flesh and blood person. His little mouth languishes half-open, small bubbles of spittle fixed in its corners. His brow is lacquered with sweat.

"You're scheduled to begin your chemo today," I tell him. "Do you understand that, sir?"

"Yes," he wheezes.

"Before we begin," I say, "I'd like again to stress that there are other options available to you."

"We're not interested in other options," his wife insists.

I lean in to Mr. Toczauer's ear and whisper, "I've got the Euthasol, if you change your mind."

"The suicide pill?"

"That's right."

"I just can't, Doc," he says. "Save it for someone braver."

I tuck the pill away, and address the family.

"I'd like to discuss the chemo process, its side effects, and the prognosis, one last time, with you all."

Mr. Toczauer's family collectively nods in mock understanding.

"This session of chemo is essentially napalm. It kills not just the cancer but all of the other cells, in the gut, the hair follicles, the mouth, all of them. As terrible as the pain you're in now is, the chemo will make you feel worse. Imagine the sickest you've ever felt in your life, and then multiply that by one hundred."

"But it will kill the cancer, and then he'll get better, right?" the wife asks.

"As I've said, there's a very good chance your husband won't survive the chemo. Even so, that's just the first step. We'd still need to do a bone marrow transplant. The odds that any of this works are very, very small. And no matter what, he will experience extreme bouts of pain and discomfort."

"Doctor," the son says, "it's time to begin the healing."

Nothing's clearer than that this family refuses to acknowledge their moral predicament. Mr. Toczauer's wife pulls from her purse a set of rosary beads, grips them tightly, and whispers a prayer. The daughter rests her mother's head on her shoulder.

"We're never alone in this world," she says. "At the very worst, we are with God."

The room's view affords concrete apartments in the old Soviet style—newly erected low-income housing for The Absolved—each a different color—to mask, I surmise, the drab design. The sky is dull grey, the land as ominous as a painting by Edvard Munch.

A thin nurse with a kind smile hooks Mr. Toczauer to an IV. He groans softly when the needle stabs him. He looks like a rabbit in a trap.

While his wife and daughter pray, his son's gram blinks, and he moves to the corner to talk. He's the owner of a fitness center, and his robots are malfunctioning. They can't easily grasp the corners of the towels they're folding, so each towel takes fifteen minutes and is costing him dearly. Within thirty seconds, the son abandons all semblance of politeness and begins to holler at the AI he's talking to. Mr. Toczauer's daughter and wife, meantime, go on with their supplications.

CHAPTER 10

I HEAD TO ANODYNE IN THE TANGERINE GLOW OF A SETTING sun. Along the side of the street, two policemen rouse sleeping homeless men from their makeshift beds. When I roll down the windows, Chloe warns me of pollution levels, saying that we're at "Code Purple."

"That's bad?"

"It's very bad, Henri. Nitrogen Dioxide levels are spiking again. You should be wearing a mask."

Lydia is hunched over the bar with a pencil, staring at a drawing. She marks it, lifts the pencil to her mouth, considers, and makes another mark. Karl is at the end of the bar, attempting to get her attention by slapping his hand on the counter. Due to the wedding ring, the sound is loud and piercing. Lydia is so focused that she fails to acknowledge him. Karl folds a napkin into an airplane and launches it, striking her in the shoulder. When she looks up, her brown eyes, which I once heard a drunk describe as being "soft and velvety," appear as cold as razorblades. I crane my neck to make out what she's drawn. Lydia snatches the picture and tucks it between two bottles of whiskey.

"Mind your own business, would you?" she snaps.

"Come on, Lydia," Karl says, "what are you hiding back there?"

"I've never known you to be so sensitive before," I say.

"You don't know plenty about me."

Lunging over the bar, Karl snatches the drawing. He holds it high over his head while fending off Lydia with a classic stiff-arm.

"My God," Karl exclaims, "this is some picture!"

Lydia punches Karl in his belly, and he doubles over.

"Now can I see it?" I ask.

Lydia flips the drawing onto the bar. Her art is some of the crudest and most unrefined I've seen. The drawing depicts a boy ascending from his mother's arms to Heaven, where an outstretched set of hands wait to receive him. All around the mother are men and women in swimwear who witness this spectacle with shocked and grievous expressions. The rendering is so disproportionate and overly simplistic that I am made disturbed.

"You have a unique style."

"It keeps the memories at bay."

"What happened?"

"Suffering is never the result of just one thing."

"That's the truth."

"Yeah," Karl says, "but some folks got more troubles than others."

"I don't want to talk about it," Lydia says.

The room gets so quiet that I swear I can hear my own heartbeat.

Martinez appears on the television. He's calling for unity during what he refers to as a "difficult time." This morning at a campaign stop in Knoxville a mob of Bradford devotees clashed with his supporters, and a full-on riot ensued. Cars were set ablaze, storefronts were looted, and seven people were killed. A report from one news outlet claims there have been two separate attempts on Martinez's life, this week alone. Up there on the stage, speaking from behind bullet-proof glass, everything he says sounds tiresome and untrue. It's as if his remarks can be predicted before they're even made.

"Now that's a man who's got a whole lot of trouble coming his way," Lydia remarks.

"I've had enough of this crap," Karl says, finishing his beer. "Henri, give me a lift home."

I rack my brain for an excuse. "Where do you live?"

"Bayview."

"Too bad," I say. "I'm in the other direction. Presidio."

"Just fucking with you, Henri. I'm in the Tenderloin. Let's get out of here."

Chloe is reluctant to unlock the passenger door for Karl. I assure her that it's okay, but she calls the police, stating that we're being carjacked.

"We're fine, Officer," I say. "My OS is mistaken."

"Are you sure, sir?" the officer asks. "Blink twice into the camera if you're under duress."

I shake my head, then manually unlock the door. Before Karl can sit down, I lay my lab coat across his seat, to protect the leather. A soulless pop song from one of Chloe's playlists plays quietly in the background.

"Nice tune," Karl says.

"My wife's music."

"A real lady of the *times*."

We pull up to an apartment complex. A bunch of kids are sitting on the stoop, plugged into their grams. The whole street-facing wall of the building is covered in graffiti claiming allegiances to various Absolved gangs.

"You remember my dog?" Karl asks.

"A handsome animal."

"He's sick, and I need you to check him out."

"I'm a cancer physician, not a veterinarian."

"You'll make do."

A raggedy-looking boy with buckteeth and thick eyebrows closes his gram, and runs to Karl. Karl swoops him up and tosses him high into the air, then catches him. Karl introduces the boy as Karl Jr. The boy holds out a sweaty little hand with dirt-encrusted nails, and I give it a shake.

Nearly every inch of space inside of Karl's apartment is lined with junk: decades' old newspapers and magazines stacked to the ceiling, empty birdcages, shelves lined with ceramic figurines, boxes of discarded appliances, piles of moth-riddled clothing, self-help books, old bank statements, stuffed animals. Tucked under a stool there are several glass bottles filled with urine.

"She's not much of a homemaker these days," he says, nodding at the woman napping on the couch, nearly obscured by a broken antique clock.

Narrow walkways have been forged through the debris

to navigate from room to room. Karl leads me to an office at the back of the apartment. It stands in stark contrast to the rest of the place. The room is sparsely furnished with just a desk, chair, and dresser. Its walls are neatly decorated with photos and memorabilia from Karl's military days.

He catches me admiring his Medal of Honor, framed and in glass.

"I fought in the Battle of Sand Hill Road back in '27."

"It was only a matter of time before they brought the fight to the Bay Area," I say. "If you're in a holy war against the West, you strike at the heart of its great religion: technology."

"American innovation lost six hundred of its brightest minds that day. Piles of dead software engineers, coders, and venture capitalists strewn all along the streets."

"The media called it the death of the Technology Revolution. So much for that, huh?"

"I saw some really heinous shit while I was in Syria and Egypt fighting the Russians, but nothing like the 'Iibadatan. They made ISIS look like a bunch of kindergarten teachers. Instead of just cutting your head off, they would do things like sever a soldier's dick and then use it to fuck him in the ass—while he was still alive, no less. Can you imagine that, getting fucked in the ass with your own dick?"

"Who's this?" I ask, pointing at a picture of Karl and another soldier, wearing fatigues and holding machine guns, standing in front of a building on the Google campus.

"That was my best pal, Benito. He died in my arms the

day after that picture was taken. His final words were, 'Karl, it's okay, I'm dying for my country. It's a good death. Remember, America is a bastion of goodness in a world gone mad. You have to keep fighting for our way of life.'"

"He died fighting for the country he loved."

"Benito wouldn't even recognize what this country has become."

The dog is lying on its side on the floor. His eyes are glassy and his breathing is labored. He makes a feeble effort to lick Karl's hand when Karl goes to pet him. I kneel next to the dog, and feel his nose. It's bone-dry. The dog breaks into a coughing fit. Placing my ear to the dog's chest, I listen to its breathing. Unsure of what to do, I diagnose him with an upper respiratory infection, and gram in a prescription.

Karl walks me to the curb and thanks me for my help. As Chloe pulls away, Karl is slow to return to his home.

CHAPTER 11

TODAY IS SATURDAY, AND I'VE PROMISED TO TAKE JULIAN to a baseball game—an attempt to foster in him an interest in something other than his new gram. The game doesn't start until 1:00 p.m., but he wakes me at 6, mitt in hand, to get a jump on the day, he says.

"Give me thirty more minutes," I mumble.

He twists a few of my fingers, the kind of paltry but effective move they teach in women's self-defense courses. When I howl much louder than what's warranted, Rachel tells me to, "Quit your moaning."

I sweep the boy up and kiss him. He giggles, then accidently pokes my eye when trying to push me away. I'm still disoriented and bump into the walls of the hallway as we move toward the kitchen.

"Make me some coffee."

"I don't know how."

"I've seen you navigate the most bewildering and complex computer applications with nary a hiccup, and you're claiming ignorance on how to brew coffee?"

"I'm only seven," he says, and shows me his mouth full of holes, now that he's losing his baby teeth.

I show him how to make coffee with a French Press. As I place the kettle on the stove, I ask him, "Does your mom let you boil water?"

"Why are you making coffee the old-fashioned way?"

"I enjoy the ritual."

"But it's slow."

"Sometimes slow is good."

A few minutes later we're on the narrow strip of grass we call "the backyard." I have a mug of coffee and a baseball. Julian's cap is far too big and keeps falling over his eyes. I lob the ball toward him and watch him flinch as it nears, then deflect off his mitt and smack him in the chest. He picks it up and throws it back, far over my head. This goes on for ten minutes. Finally, sufficiently caffeinated, I teach him the concept of "keeping your eye on the ball," and then watch the concept become act. A few tosses later, he actually catch es the damn thing.

It occurs to me that I've never felt happier.

My biological father was a hedonist—an artist and devotee of the wonderful French painter Rousseau, and a womanizer, to boot.

"Why did you give me the name Henri?" I asked him when I was a boy. "All of the kids make fun of me."

"You should feel blessed to be named after the most important artist of the 20th century!"

"What about Picasso?" I said.

"Picasso was a charlatan. He trafficked in nothing but imitations!" he replied.

When I was small, my father lived in a one-bedroom apartment in downtown Los Angeles. He didn't work a normal job like an insurance salesman or a pharmacist. He made art and sometimes sold it, too. When the art didn't sell, he took odd jobs as a handy man. I'd come over on weekends from my mother's, where I lived, and we'd spend the day in the studio he shared with one of his artist pals. Sometimes they'd both work so furiously they wouldn't notice when I snuck off to the streets. Other times they'd have a bunch of friends over and lounge around smoking pot and drinking. His friends taught me at the age of eight how to smoke cigarettes, how to juggle, and how to play the guitar. One of his ladies taught me how to kiss. My father hated the attention I got from his pals.

"Being admired by grownups is a curse from which no child recovers!" he'd say. I know what that means now no more than I did then.

When I turned eleven, a judge took away his rights to see me. Occasionally, I stole away on my bike to visit him. By then, he had moved into the house full of bohemians that my mother called a "flophouse." But I knew it was more than that. At any time, I could find the most interesting characters about: motorcycle gang members, drug dealers, poets, and babes. Over the front door someone had painted in blood red letters the maxim: "Abolish Your Future!" My father died shortly after my fourteenth birthday, as poor as the day he was born.

Later I found another role model in the most unlikely of places: the desert between Riverside and Indio, California. The year had to have been either 2006 or 2007. I was in high school and playing in The Blank Sets. As a prize for getting second place in a Battle of the Bands contest, the local radio station had given my band mate, Foley, and me a pair of tickets to Coachella, a wildly popular music festival from the early twenty-first century.

At band practice one night, after Foley and I had each eaten a bag of hallucinogenic mushrooms, it dawned on us that we were about to miss the concert. Just past midnight, higher than the heavens above, we drove his old Subaru wagon through the cool air and starry skies of the desert until we blew a tire and veered into a ditch.

The well in the trunk where the spare should have been was full of guitar cables, porno magazines, fire crackers, and twine. We called for help, but in those days service was spotty, and we couldn't get through. It was 3:00 a.m. We were forty miles from any town, but high as we were set off anyway. It wasn't long before Foley twisted his ankle and collapsed beside a dead coyote. I climbed a rocky outcrop and in the distance saw a fire. It took a while, but at last by the fire I found Ronald, a short, rotund, bald-headed man, dressed in the breathable fabrics found only in specialty *outdoors shops*. He was surrounded by an array of priceless telescopes. I told him about our predicament, and we packed up his camp and set off to rescue Foley.

Ronald's parents had owned a small grocery store. By thirteen, he was working the register every day after school. At sixteen, his father died of stomach cancer. Come time for college, despite scholarships to the nation's most prestigious universities, he stayed home to help his mother until she sold the store five years later.

Ronald married his college sweetheart, and his son was born when he was only twenty-four. He admitted to me, that before his wife, he hadn't slept with more than three women. But Ronald had aspirations. After work each day at his job at an engineering firm, he'd come home and tinker on his own innovations in the garage. By the time his son turned six, Ronald had founded his own company for solar tracking technology, moved into a ramshackle apartment, and lost his marriage. At the divorce proceedings, the judge reproached him, saying, "Quit your monkeying around and go get your old job back!" But two years later, he closed a multi-million-dollar deal, the first of many to follow. And somehow, then, he remarried his wife.

"But, sir," I said, "you were rich, and women really respond to money. You could've had anyone you wanted. Why didn't you go out and have some fun?"

"The only reason I worked so hard to become rich was to give my family the best life I could," Ronald explained. "She was the mother of my child, and I wanted her to have the world."

Years later, after Ronald had lost his business to "those New York vultures," as he called them, his son died while scuba diving in Nicaragua. It was Ronald's loneliness that inspired his interest in me, I believed, until my psychologist enlightened me.

"A rescuer," she said, "always holds the person rescued in the highest fondness. They gave him the chance to demonstrate the bravery of which heroes are made."

Who doesn't like to be reminded of their most shining achievement? Every time Ronald looked at me, he thought of his great deed saving me and Foley from the desert. In the end, the reason he loved me is moot. If it weren't for his guidance, I would've pursued music and followed my father's path of art, anguish, and death.

After throwing Julian a round of batting practice, I decide to take a swing, hitting the ball onto the roof, effectively ending the game.

Julian loves the metro. Within minutes, he's made the following observations: "That man has three different colors of freckles on his face. The lady sitting next to me smells like pickles. I bet that little girl has carpet in her room, because she's got rug-burn on her knees."

On game day, everyone in the city is dressed in black and orange, the colors of the Giants. Since half of the population is out of work, with little to do, sports are more important than ever. The average American man now watches more than eight hours per day of sports. And with mandatory "equal television-time" for women's and non-gender specific sports being enforced, the average person who is not self-identifying as a "man," is watching just over six hours of sports per day.

Besides incredible income inequality, the overwhelming popularity of sports has led to an array of additional socio-economic problems. While gambling has been made completely illegal, it's the most pressing social ill. Nearly thirty percent of the population loses their Basic Income checks each month in underground sports-betting rackets and in illegal casinos. Currently, there is a bill under debate in the Senate that would require all recipients of Basic Income to suffer through a fifteen-hour "Anti-Vice" seminar. This training theoretically would educate The Absolved on the dangers not only of gambling but also of alcohol, drugs, and salacious sexual behavior, too. Of course the bill stands no chance of passing. No member of The Absolved can stand the thought of sitting through such a sermon, and every politician knows that a vote for this bill will kill their chances for re-election.

Still five stops from the stadium, the metro is packed. The bad breath and body odor have caused not the least duress, either. Everyone is in great spirits. Ten years ago, when *The Wall* came down, a surge of immigrants from Mexico and Central America poured across the border. Spanish is actually now the predominant language in more than fifty percent of California's homes. And with this influx, many of the touchstones of Latin sports culture have also made their way to the States. The most welcome of these are the "sports songs" and "chants." In perfect harmony, the entire metro is loudly singing one tune after the other. Julian knows every lyric, and sings in a delightful Spanish accent.

At the stadium we shove our way through frenzied fans, no easy task. Ninety percent of the stadium is now first-come-first-serve seating, the result of a mandate three years ago to democratize the spectating experience. I look away for a single moment and Julian is lost. Terror floods my system. I shout his name, and in ten seconds there he is again, like he'd never gone. This brief instant of terror, I must confess, was more harrowing and life-affirming than a year of pleasure or one hundred years of boredom.

The boy is holding a shiny silver coin—currency long since removed from circulation. He found it, and he now wants to return it to its owner. I deliver him a sharp warning about the perils of running away. I tell him the made-up story of a boy who was kidnapped in a park after wandering off while his mother was playing VR Ping-Pong in her gram, and how the boy was then tortured, raped, and as I'm about to say, "left for dead," I see that Julian's crying, and quickly change course, instead opting for, "And then he found his mom and they went out for cheeseburgers."

At our section, the usher scans my gram and leads us to our seats, just four rows behind home plate. These tickets cost roughly ten times as much as the general admission price, but it's worth it. From here, you can smell the sweet scent of the turf and hear the crack of the bat like roaring thunder.

A woman across the aisle is smiling and waving at me. I shoot her a cautious wave and grin. She says something to the man next to her and points my way. The man turns to me and stares. I pretend not to notice and look away immediately. A vendor passes by and I purchase two hot dogs, a beer, and a soda. I hand Julian his snacks and when I look up the woman and man are there beside me.

"Can I help you?" I say.

"Doctor, I'm Rebecca Pedrego, I was your patient, years ago. Remember me?"

I look the woman up and down, combing my memory for some inkling of a recollection, but there is none.

"Of course," I say, "Rebecca! How wonderful to see you again. How are you?"

"I'm doing so well ... fantastic, really! I feel just great. And it's all thanks to you!"

"I'm so glad to hear it. That's wonderful."

"I'd like you to meet my fiancé, Jeff."

The man offers his hand, and we shake vigorously.

"It's terrific to meet you," Jeff says. "Rebecca has told me all about what an amazing doctor you are. You saved her life. I can't thank you enough."

"Who's this?" Rebecca asks, smiling at the boy.

"This is my son, Julian." To my dismay, already his face is covered in ketchup, mustard, and relish. "Julian, say hello to Rebecca and Jeff." He nods indifferently and returns to devouring his food. "Please excuse my son's manners," I say. "He's normally very cute and friendly."

"We don't want to take up any more of your time," Rebecca says. "Really wonderful seeing you. Enjoy the game."

When I became a doctor, I harbored grand notions about what a difference I'd make, and all of the people I'd help, and all of the generous contributions I'd bestow on the world. But the truth is, the benevolence quickly gets overshadowed by the stress, the hardship, the heartbreak, and, most of all, the bureaucracy. It's hard to fathom the hours I've wasted in meetings, discussing cost-saving efforts, tedious administrative requirements, and ways to improve organizational efficiency. I'd estimate that as much as half of a doctor's time is spent occupied with this type of work rather than with patients. And now I can't even remember this person I managed to save.

The game begins inauspiciously when in the first inning the Braves' Manuel Ortega hits a three-run homer. A man sitting directly behind us jumps up to shout expletives at the pitcher and spills his beer on my shoulder. Not wanting to incite a scene, I stay quiet. Julian, however, well aware of my resentment, is laughing.

"Cool it," I say. "It's not funny."

Over the next few innings, the man behind us drinks many more beers, and his outbursts grow louder and more profane. Come the fourth inning, when the Giants' shortstop makes an error, he screams, "You useless motherfucker, get on the next boat back to Cuba!"

"Yeah," Julian shouts, shockingly, "get back on the boat, motherfucker!"

"You can't say that kind of thing!" I tell him. "You know better than that!"

Julian bows his head in what I think is shame but realize is an effort to hide his laughter. I'm so enraged that I jump to my feet and holler in the man's face.

"Can't you see I'm here with my son?" I say. "Shut your damn mouth!"

As soon as I've said it, I realize my mistake. The man is a monster. Crude tattoos cover his neck. He outweighs me by at least fifty pounds. The crazed look in his eyes reminds me of the devil in some sixteenth-century Renaissance painting. The blow that strikes my face sends me careening over the person in the row below me, where I land in a woman's lap and flip the cold, coagulated cheese and jalapenos of her nachos all over my face and arms.

A circle of people has gathered round, Rebecca, Jeff, and Julian among them. Jeff tries to help me, but I'm too weak to stand. The lunatic who punched me, I see, is surrounded by security. I'm astonished to see how carefully they are handling him.

"Get that psychopath the fuck out of here!" I say.

I don't know how or why, really, but the next thing I know I'm being dragged kicking and screaming from the stadium by two burly security men.

"It's okay, Dad," Julian tells me on the ride home. "He was just too much for you."

Alone in my bathroom at last, I stand before the mirror virtually unrecognizable. The left side of my face is bloodied and battered. But far more alarmingly, I've aged a decade, I realize, maybe even two, since the last time I took a good, hard look at myself. This isn't the first time something like this has occurred. From seventeen to twenty-seven, I looked exactly the same—fixed for a decade. Then one morning I woke up changed. My face was fifteen years older, the same face I've had until today, when I changed again, for the worse, to a man in "middle age." That's how aging works for some people. It's not a steady, meandering river, changing by small degrees, virtually unnoticeable. Rather, it's more like a death plummet that happens all at once. Now that I've undergone this metamorphosis, it's my great hope that this weary expression will last me until I'm sixty.

I lurch from the bathroom as heroically as I can to find Rachel is waiting in the hall.

"My God, what's happened to you?"

"We had a small incident at the game today."

"You look awful."

"It's not so bad."

Rachel slings my arm around her shoulders, supporting my weight, and together we ease our way to the bedroom. It's been so long since I've been nurtured by Rachel that I allow this charade without objection. More than this, I join it. I feign prolonged, low, inarticulate groans—giving life to and emphasizing an imaginary suffering that seems really to please her.

She unties my shoes and removes them, pulls off my shirt, and wriggles me from my pants.

"I'm going to take really good care of you," she says.

Before I know it, she's taken me in her mouth. Watching her work on me, I'm equal parts aroused and confused. I can't recall the last time we shared this sort of sexual encounter. The foreignness of the act colors the exchange with strangeness and regret. Quickly, then, she slips off her skirt and underwear and sets down on me with propulsive hips.

Where is this passion coming from? This facet of the relationship—long taken for dead—suddenly restored and filled with vigor. Of all things, it's an act of violence against me that has set her off! This from a someone who has always professed an incredible antipathy toward brutality and bloodshed.

Years ago, before Julian was born, Rachel and I shared a fifth-floor walk-up apartment in the Mission—the kind of building where homeless people broke in and shit in the halls. Bad as it was, I loved it. The place had character and history. The local liquor store didn't sell any wine worth more than six dollars but sold cheap rum and forties by the case. The old man next door bragged he had once sold heroin to Jerry Garcia in the park down the street.

Rachel and I used to host parties there. One night, the brother of a friend of Rachel's was visiting from New York City—a private equity banker-type in town to meet with a start-up he was funding that manufactured robotic pets.

"Just think," he said, "all of the companionship of a dog, but you never have to clean up shit!"

He'd snorted a gram of cocaine and drunk a dozen-or-so whiskeys in celebration of his impending fortune. Noticing he kept going in and out of our bedroom, Rachel asked me to check him out. Sure enough, the guy was digging through Rachel's laundry hamper, sniffing her dirty panties and stuffing them in his pants, six or seven pair, judging by the bulges.

"Give me back the underwear," I told him, "and get the fuck out!"

That's when he rushed me. I threw a straight right punch to his face, but he got back up and gouged my eye. I managed a kick to his ribs, then two swift punches to his face and throat, by which time the rest of the party had streamed into the room. I expected Rachel to treat me like a hero when I explained what had happened. Instead, once the place was clear, she slumped to the floor of the closet and wept.

"You're a violent monster!"

"But he attacked me."

"Of course he did, he felt trapped."

"You're not making any sense."

"You're nothing more than a bully!"

Women are so much more complicated than men. I'm not sure anyone can really know a woman's mind. In short, for them, one moment's delight is another's revulsion.

Now Rachel's squeezing and rubbing her tits as she grinds away. I brace myself against the headboard when her pace quickens, and she takes my hand to her mouth to greedily suck on my fingers. I brush her hair back to kiss her neck, and she slaps me hard on the face.

"Be rough with me!" she demands.

I squeeze her throat with steadily increasing force and watch her eyes roll back. She digs her fingernails into my back and drags them across my side. Jolted by the sensation of tearing flesh, I flip her onto her stomach and go at her from behind while she bucks and squirms. When she tries to climb up onto all four, I push her face into the mattress. It's here, in complete submission, that she finally comes.

"Tell me about the fight," she says.

"There was a drunk guy sitting behind us who kept shouting profanity. I told him to shut up because of Julian."

"Then?"

"He punched me in the face."

A wild, tortured gleam appears in Rachel's eyes. I've never seen her so enthralled. "Really? What did you do next?"

"The guy was enormous. I flopped on the ground like a stuck pig."

Rachel rolls her eyes, and sighs loudly with disgust.

"There was nothing I could do!" I say to her as she storms into the bathroom.

A minute later, I hear her cursing me in the shower.

CHAPTER 12

SERENA HAS CALLED A MEETING WITH THE TOP DOCTORS in each division. She wants yet another discussion on cost-saving measures. Hardly a week goes by when she hasn't conceived some new and dastardly way to increase profits and technologically usurp human workers. It's no wonder she's championed as the most celebrated leader in today's medical business community.

We doctors all dread these meetings, for fear Serena has innovated us out of our livelihoods, but we do look forward to the food. Always the connoisseur, Serena insists on softening her blows with first-rate cuisine. Three weeks ago, when the FDA approved an application that can identify any skin abnormality simply by evaluating an image, Serena laid off the hospital's entire dermatology department, all from behind the guise of duck confit with lentils via Francis Mallmann's new French bistro.

This morning there are ten of us, from cardiology, neurology, gastroenterology, radiology, pulmonology, and oncology, an exquisite spread of sushi from Kusakabe's laid out before us. I can't help but marvel at this rare feat of presentation, workmanship, and production. In contrast, Serena's face is like an executioner's—colorless and cold.

"Dr. Kapoor," Serena begins, "would you say you're a man of principles?"

Dr. Kapoor, a radiologist, sets his chopsticks down. "I'm very much a man of principles."

"I'm sorry to hear that." The room goes silent. No one, not even those with full mouths, continues to chew. "A man of principles is rooted and fixed," Serena says, "unable to evolve. We need innovators, doctors willing to do away with tradition and move to the vanguard of modern medicine."

"But, if I may—" Dr. Kapoor says.

"No, you may not, Doctor. The FDA has finally approved new software that can read scans twice as well for one-tenth the price. Your last day with us will be Friday."

"Dr. Zhang," Serena says, as Dr. Kapoor shuffles silently away, "what has been the single most ubiquitous tool in medicine for the past two centuries?"

The gastrologist scratches his bald head and squints his eyes. "A stethoscope?"

"Precisely. Doctors have employed stethoscopes for over two hundred years. But were you aware how many doctors fail to accurately detect problems with a stethoscope? A recent study shows that seventy-five percent of doctors can't so much as diagnose a heart murmur. This is why we're doing away with this obsolete technology. We now have digitized stethoscopes whose mandatory use we are instituting as of this afternoon."

"How does that work?" Dr. Zhang asks.

"They amplify, record, and digitize sound from bodies. A basic technician can now diagnose ninety-five percent of all ailments."

"What then will become of doctors?" Dr. Zhang says, reasonably.

"We'll find out very soon, won't we?"

Dr. Hines—fellow oncologist and nemesis, medical school dean, phony art snob, lackey to Serena—distributes a memo about the new stethoscopes and signals the caterers to clean up, including the food we haven't eaten.

CHAPTER 13

IT'S A SHAME, REALLY, HOW LONG IT'S BEEN SINCE I PICKED up a book. As a child, I'd lose myself in the pages of *Huck Finn* for hours, but today the notion of parents fostering in their children an appreciation is unimaginable. To admit to writing poetry or dirtying your hands giving life to a sculpture, in fact, would invite a hurricane of ridicule and scorn. Where efficiency and pragmatism are most highly prized, art is a consolation for those who can't work. Software engineers and database administrators—these are the Michelangelos and Schuberts of the day!

Not too long ago a prominent system's engineer made headlines when he proclaimed, "We must resist the vulgar temptation of needing to bear our souls!" The public responded swiftly and decisively with adulation. The lone dissent was squeaked from a scorned professor of philosophy at Stanford. After he'd written on his hologram, now since removed, "Science is the enemy of the mind!" his tenure was revoked and he was institutionalized.

Speaking of Mark Twain, he is supposed to have said, "The coldest winter I ever spent was a summer in San Francisco." Well, those days of sweaters and jackets in August have gone the way of the buffalo. The sky is an ocean of bright blue, and the sun blazes so menacingly that most children and old folks must stay indoors. As for the rest, we're red-faced, sweaty, and utterly defeated.

I'm on my way to a rally for President Martinez while Rachel is hosting a women's lunch at the house, the supposed purpose of which is to plan a fall fundraiser for Feed the Forgotten. Doubtless, I am skeptical. The last time these ladies got together they polished off a case of chardonnay and invited over the neighbor's teenage son. The poor boy was stripped shirtless and forced to serve them finger sandwiches. "Harmless fun," Rachel had slurred when I arrived home to witness the scene.

Four years ago, when candidate Martinez made a campaign stop here, three hundred thousand people turned out. They had to make a last second change of venue to Golden Gate Park to accommodate the massive crowd. It was a scene like something I've only seen in a documentary film about Woodstock. People wore flowers in their hair, hugged strangers, and all over the city mass sing-alongs about folksy hope and change erupted as if it were everyday entertainment.

But things are different now. While Martinez still holds a large lead in the polls, it's not because anyone is inherently optimistic, but that Bradford is unthinkable. His Luddite ideology is anathema to those of us who've somehow managed to cling to the vision of America as the great City on the Hill.

There's been talk on the news of an impending clash between Bradford's supporters and the Martinez holdouts. An army of robot police has been deployed. These cyborgs are nowhere near out of the *Uncanny Valley*, looking and acting far more like machines than anything resembling human, eliciting feelings of eeriness and revulsion among all of those who observe them. A barricade has been placed across from the Convention Center to separate Bradford's supporters and the people queued up for Martinez.

I buy a pretzel from a vendor and watch the scene unfold. The Bradford side gives the impression they've been cast to play a part in some sort of sinister carnival. All of them are wearing a uniform of matching hats and T-shirts bearing threatening slogans: *Death to the Machines! Turn Back the Hands of Time! Make a Robot Your Bitch!* Many of their ranks are holding crudely drawn signs depicting men and women engaged in obsolete labor, swinging a sledgehammer or sewing a dress. Deep in the crowd I spot a mock trial taking place in which a judge has ordered a robot to be executed for the crime of *displacement*. A jubilant cheer fills the air as the machine is strung up by the neck.

The Martinez supporters are far fewer in number, all of them neatly dressed and waiting quietly with heads bowed. Some of them also are holding signs, although none of them are handmade, but distributed by officials from the campaign. The taunts and jeers from the Bradford supporters go almost entirely unanswered. Only one old woman dares to stand up to her attackers.

"You're not half the men and women our robots are!" she shouts.

In response, hundreds of cans, pieces of rotten fruit, and assorted trash rain down on the Martinez camp. When eventually they're let into the building, the Bradford followers, now bereft, disperse.

Wandering the streets, I notice another crowd amassed around a street performance. I push toward it to find that it's Karl who's in command, alone and powerfully built—his large head and low-sloping brow, virtually neckless on his broad shoulders.

He performs a series of magic tricks, all executed perfectly, delighting the crowd. Karl's son serves as his assistant, first allowing himself to be levitated, and then sawed in half. After each trick, Karl says, "How about a round of applause for my son, Karl Jr." Karl playfully messes the hair on the smiling boy's head.

"For the grand finale," Karl shouts into a bullhorn, "I'd like to bring my dear friend out to assist me."

I should have guessed, but from the crowd steps Lydia, sinewy and taut. The two embrace as Karl whispers in her ear, and she laughs.

"Please give a warm welcome to Lydia!" Karl says, holding high Lydia's hand.

After the enthusiastic applause recedes, Karl takes from a bag a large, cast-iron horseshoe, five times the size of any I've seen.

"Who would like to test this?" Karl says.

A man steps forward and struggles to lift the horseshoe over his head.

"Heavy, eh?" Karl says.

"Yes, very!"

Karl relieves the man and drops the shoe to the ground with a crash so resounding that the crowd is startled.

"I will now throw this horseshoe around Lydia's neck without harming so much as a hair on her head!" The audience gasps collectively. "Do not—I repeat, folks—do *not* try this at home, unless of course you're a glutton for tragedy!"

Karl fastens protective pads around Lydia's shoulders, and then takes long paces away. Karl's son, Karl Jr., plays a drum roll. The crowd is silent with anticipation. Lydia stands with her arms extended like Jesus on his cross, her face as serene as a sleeping baby's. Karl kisses the horseshoe then twists his hips as his arm swings forward in a long arc at whose end he heaves the shoe Lydia's way. Like a cliché, time itself seems to stop as the horseshoe hurtles toward Lydia. After what feels like hours, the shoe, just as Karl had proclaimed, lands on her shoulders. A ripple tears through Lydia's body, from top to bottom, but she remains steady 'til all goes still, and the crowd explodes. Karl has somehow transported himself to her side by way of removing the shoe, after which the duo bow long and slow. The drummer boy opens his gram and makes a lap around the audience for collections. Most people, of course, can't be bothered, typical, on the whole, though not for Lydia.

"Are you people now so conditioned to free handouts," she cries through the bullhorn, "that you can't remember the good old days when you paid for a service received?"

Scarcely anyone is compelled by this plea. Most simply avert their eyes and scurry away. Worse, as Karl is returning his horseshoe to its bag, one of the robotic policeman approaches. A heated exchange ensues, capped when the robot issues Karl and Lydia tickets for an illegal public act.

CHAPTER 14

I'M RELIEVED TO HEAR SOME BIRDS CHIRPING AS I TRUDGE through this heat. If only the park weren't in such awful disrepair—grass dying or dead, rose bushes dead, dust and dirt as far as you can see. There has been no rain for ninety-six days. The aqueduct is at an all-time low. And we may not get another drop until December. It's no mystery that humans are opposed to absolutes. There's no complete happiness or unhappiness—we can't know the future. Great hopes and terrifying uncertainties, these are the things that riddle us.

I can't help but think about the old days, albeit through the lens of an obviously naïve sentimentality. Memories from long ago seem like the pinnacles of happiness.

Rachel and I, for instance, once spent two weeks riding bicycles through the Italian countryside, drinking fine wines, gorging on pasta, making love and waking arm-in-arm. As I walk past the decrepit fountain where ducks once swam, the memory of those days fills me with so much joy I'm afraid I'll burst. Inevitably, however, I'll see something like a squirrel climbing a tree, and it'll trigger a sense of wretchedness. While these memories bring joy, I know that in the moment I never felt the same. I obsessed instead over the most trivial inconveniences and hardships. In Italy, I ruined a day when after having ridden our bicycles twelve miles to a quaint bed and breakfast on a vineyard, we got sent away for lack of a reservation. I was livid. Rachel had sworn that morning that she had made it. How stupid I had been. I could have gone on in the spirit of adventure, but instead spent two hours making her cry with my insults.

At the coffee vendor I find Serena, who drinks ten to twelve cups a day and claims to need just four hours of sleep a night. The woman never stops. I receive holograms from her at all hours. I often joke with her that if she keeps firing people I may soon be her only friend. This doesn't bother her in the least. Her greatest pride rests in her business acumen.

"Pretty tough on Kapoor the other day."

"A long time coming."

"You had to fire him in front of the group?"

"Sends a strong message, wouldn't you say?"

"I still need that favor from you."

"For that girl you're not having an affair with?"

"Yes."

"Dr. Hines is in charge of the admissions process, Henri."

"Last year the man had my office converted to a room for data servers and placed my personal effects in a cubicle down the hall from the nursery."

"I'm sure it was an oversight."

"He reported me to the American Medical Association for professional misconduct."

"What'd you do?"

"I wrote Rachel an antibiotics prescription for her strep throat."

Serena practically suffocates from a fit of laughter. "It seems you've managed to land on Dr. Hines' bad side, haven't you?"

"So you'll help me?"

"One condition."

"Name it."

"Come to *VR-Together* with me."

"Excuse me?"

"It's the new punk rock!"

"I'm forty-seven years old, I can't go there!"

"You mustn't be afraid to try new things, Henri."

CHAPTER 15

AN ENDLESS PARADE OF PALE-FACED TEENAGERS STRETCH-es out into the distance. All are attired in a uniform of grey-colored, shabby clothing. Everyone is standing in line, not talking. The only disturbances to be heard are those of errant coughs, mouth breathing, and the shuffling of feet as the crowd marches into the venue, sounding eerily like the drone of a machine. A team of women in red bodysuits and caps is making their way across the line, checking people's grams for tickets, and then handing them a set of VR goggles.

VR-Together is a new counterculture phenomenon that has swept the nation. As young people have become increasingly isolated from each other due to spending more and more time in the solitude of VR, interacting only with AI, who despite its likeness to actual humans is still without consciousness, there is a perceived desire amongst the youth to combine the safety of VR, where the environment has been designed to the exact preferences of each user and no one has to fear social rejection or anxiety, with the sense of community that can only be felt amongst other sentient beings.

The solution: thousands of people congregating in a venue to live out their VR fantasies while standing in proximity to others doing the exact same thing.

"Look at all these zombies," I say.

"It's fascinating, isn't it?" Serena says. "An entire generation of people whose explicit aim is to never subject themselves to a genuine or authentic experience, only synthetic ones."

"You think they're all virgins?"

"Not only have they not had sex, but not one of these outcasts has ever been in a fistfight, taken drugs, played sports, or even done anything as risky as public speaking."

"The perfect bubble!"

Realizing I haven't yet procured a ticket, I go searching for a scalper. I wander up and down the rows of people, catching the occasional glance of a scowling attendee, who is clearly dismayed by the disruption I've cause to this harmonious and tranquil scene. Yet no one here would ever call me out for my transgression, as direct confrontation is to be avoided like plague, in accordance to the movement's credo.

Finally, like a whisper in the wind, I hear the cry of a scalper. As if I had apprenticed under an Apache tracker, my instincts lead me to him—a handsome, dark-skinned man moving easily through the crowd.

"You need a ticket?" he asks.

"How much?"

"Three fifty."

"Face value is one twenty."

"Show's sold out, man. Three hundred's the lowest I can go."

We touch our gram-fingers together, swapping money for ticket. The turnstile opens for Serena's gram, and a woman clad in red hands her a set of VR goggles. But my ticket pro-vokes a flashing light. After three tries, a large man with a heavy mustache and black jacket appears.

"Come with me, sir."

As Serena disappears into the crowd, I follow the guard to a control center manned by a team of analysts.

"Show them your ticket," the guard demands.

A mousy woman with glasses and frizzy hair studies my gram. "Where'd you get this ticket?" she asks.

"Birthday present from a friend," I say with the straight-est face I know.

"This is a fraudulent ticket."

"You're kidding me?"

"I'm sorry. Your friend got taken."

I storm off in search of the scalper, hell-bent for destruc-tion. The echo of a deafening silence rings in my ears as I comb the outside premises—bathroom stalls, parking lot, concessions stands, the works. From there I move into the streets, my thirst for vengeance swelling by the minute. Then, inside of a vegan donut shop with two other men, I see the man who ripped me off. My entire body is buzzing as I storm into the place.

"What do you want?" says the scalper.

"I gave you three hundred bucks for a fake ticket."

The men exchange glances and grin.

"What makes you think it was me?" the scalper says.

I can feel the blood rushing to my face. My hands ball to fists. "Because I fucking recognize you, that's how!"

Now the man's tone matches mine. "Look, man, you think you can just walk up to any black guy you see and accuse him of stealing?"

"There are laws against this kind of shit," one of the other men says.

"Go to hell!" I snap.

When the three men rise, it strikes me I'm about to get beaten for the second time in a week. The donut clerk is hollering into her gram, now, but I'm so full of adrenaline I'm helpless to understand her.

"What do we do with this racist?" my scalper says as one of his friends shoves me hard.

I stumble back and trip over a chair, then jump to my feet with the chair in hand, determined to take the man down. Before I can, however, I hear someone shout, "Drop it!"

It's the police, I realize. I'm so taken aback that I can't do anything, much less obey. Now, gun in hand, one of the cops draws down on me, and I screech like a cat in heat.

"Drop the chair now!"

The first cop holds his aim as I drop the chair, while the other hurls me to the ground and cuffs me.

"Are you gentlemen okay?" the first cop asks the scalpers.

"No," answers my thief, "we're not. This man committed a hate crime against us!"

"Officer," I say, astounded, "this man ripped me off for three hundred dollars!"

"Shut your mouth," the second cop says. "When we're

ready to get your side, we'll ask." To the scalpers, he says, "Go on."

The three men tell their version of what transpired, each adding little tidbits of absurdity to the narrative, with every falsehood told emboldening and impelling the other two to elevate their own senselessness, eventually assembling such a nonsensical account of events, I'm certain the officers will find their story baseless. But no sooner have they finished than the cop says, "My God! I'm so sorry. I thought we as a society had put this dark chapter behind us."

"Me, too," the other cop says. "It just goes to show we can't afford even a moment's carelessness in the face of bigotry and intolerance!"

"May I speak?" I ask.

"We've heard enough out of you!"

The cop reads me my rights, and I'm arrested for racial discrimination and conspiracy to commit a hate crime. They lead me to their cruiser and throw me in, twisting my arm and bashing my head against the window as they do. At the station, I'm stripped naked, examined for contraband, made to don a costume from the state, and tossed into a cell. My cellmate is suffering chronic diarrhea, and I spend the night with my undershirt draped over my face to prevent contracting pink eye.

In the morning at my arraignment all charges are dropped due to a technicality—the arresting officer's gram malfunctioned and there is no record of the arrest. The guard who processed me last night claims to have misplaced my clothes.

I walk out in prison-issued attire. I take a shortcut through the jail's employee parking lot as I wait for Chloe to pick me up. In the window of one of the cars, I see my shirt and pants folded neatly sitting on the passenger seat.

By the time I get to work I'm so flustered that I lock myself out of my gram. The protocol is to contact my hologram's administrator, but I haven't the patience to sit through a lengthy hold. Knowing that Serena can reset the program, I head up to her office.

Outside of her door, I hear the sound of soft wailing. I figure someone must be getting fired, and I tiptoe away. Just as I make it to the elevator, Serena's office door swings open, and she shouts, "Get in my office."

"I can see that you're busy, so I'll come back later," I say meekly.

"This isn't a request, Henri!"

Serena's office has a distinctly Zen quality: minimal, clean, an exquisitely balanced aesthetic, and the ideal of *feng shui*. Built into one of the walls is a twelve-foot-long aquarium. In it, along with exotic fish, are complex arrangements of aquatic plants, driftwood, and rocks—even an extensive network of caves. A professional *aquascaper* visits each month to create new designs. This month's theme is "Dutch Gardens of the Nineteenth Century."

Serena has her gram open wide, and she's on slide twelve of a presentation titled, "Why A Late Term Abortion Makes Dollars and Sense." Her daughter, Olivia, is even softer and rounder than she was just weeks before, her bulky sweater and cargo pants being stretched to their elastic limit.

"You can't make me do anything I don't want to do," Olivia says.

"What the hell do you know about being a mother?" Serena replies.

"Compared to you?" Olivia says. "Plenty!" She bangs on the aquarium's glass wall, startling all of the fish, and storms out of the room, slamming the door behind her.

"She knows I can't stand it when anyone disturbs the fish," Serena says.

"Sometimes you have to love people for who they are and not because they've lived their life in a way that adheres to your principles."

Serena's face turns puzzled and she reaches out and seizes the lapel of my lab coat, pulling it open, exposing the bright orange jumpsuit underneath. "What the hell happened to you?"

"I just need you to reset my gram so I can get back to work."

CHAPTER 16

RACHEL SLEEPS EXTREMELY HOT AND CAN ONLY REST IN conditions that resemble the inside of an igloo on the Alaskan tundra. She sets the temperature so low—fifty-seven degrees Fahrenheit—I'm always waiting to wake up under a blanket of snow.

"Rachel, honey," I said last night. "This is madness. I've lost all feeling in my toes. I'm afraid I'm hypothermic."

"Well, then, put on some socks!"

I asked why I should pay a fortune in utility bills to keep my house so cold I need socks. Bickering about money always leads to mockery and grief.

"Would it kill us to splurge every once in a while?" she said. "I don't understand why you insist we go without."

I couldn't possibly tally the tens, if not hundreds of thousands of dollars, I've spent conceding to this rationale. Too often, I find myself worn down by this relationship of ours, forsaking what I know to be just, in the name of pleasing Rachel. Mostly I can reconcile this dishonorable behavior in the short-term, to ensure a peaceful domestic existence, but my fear is that I'll get too accustomed to capitulating to her outlandish whims and notions, that when the time comes to make an important decision, I'll simply act weak out of habit.

Last night I was finally adamant about having my way. My steadfast position was incited by Rachel's insistence on continuing to impose her *Snow White* charade on our family. It's become an almost nightly ritual for us to reenact pivotal scenes from the story. At first, it bothered me very little, because I anticipated these role-playing games would lead to a rekindling of our sexual relationship. However, when this playacting failed to manifest the desired reawakening, my attitude soured. For weeks I'd been going about my obligations to play make-believe only reluctantly, and it's showed in my flagging performances, which Rachel made sure I was entirely aware of, even going so far as to write up reviews of my work.

The final straw was a two-thousand-word treatise delivered to my inbox, lampooning my portrayal of *Sneezy Dwarf*. In her criticism, Rachel wrote, "Henri's abject failure to summon even one convincing dramatic depiction of hay-fever left his audience cold. Not even with the aid of snorting black pepper did he conjure up anything more than a couple of trifling sniffles and a runny nose. Perhaps his dark mood would have lent him better suited to be casted as *Grumpy*."

I commanded Emma to adjust the temperature to a much more reasonable seventy degrees, then hopped up and stripped off my sweater and threw it triumphantly to the ground. This small act of rebellion filled me with such pride that I felt like having a bit of a romp. Rachel, on the other hand, wanted nothing of it and rebuffed me at every turn. She didn't respond to kisses on her neck or me tickling her back. Not even a firm but tender butt massage. Nothing.

Eventually, I gave up and snuck away to the bathroom and gave myself a quick rub. When I got back to bed, she was in a labored sleep: tossing and turning, lots of short breaths, a bit of moaning, beads of sweat on her brow.

I reached for her wrist and took her heart rate. It was racing. Just then, she emitted a loud, throaty cry, "Oh, Dylan, yes, please, yes!"

Who the fuck is Dylan? I wondered. And then I remembered: he's the fellow she was dating before I moved to San Francisco.

On the nightstand sits a photograph of Rachel and me from when we first met. The picture's been sitting there for years, but I can't remember the last time I really looked at it. It's foreign to me, to be honest. Rachel has undergone a complete transformation. Yes, I still recognize her as the same person who lies next to me in bed, but that's only because I possess the keenest eye for details.

Rachel has the slightest birthmark an inch from the corner of her left eye—less of a birthmark, really, and more like a spot of discolored skin. Yet this insignificant blemish is the only way I can see that the woman with it is my wife. Otherwise, the young pagan from the photo bears no resemblance to her. I'd almost entirely forgotten she had once been a goth, too—just like my high school crush and Taylor—skin so white, straight black hair, black lipstick, not a stitch of color in her wardrobe.

When we met, just after I'd moved to San Francisco for my oncology fellowship at the university, I had just been dumped by then-girlfriend, Elizabeth, who had reluctantly followed me north from Los Angeles. Elizabeth hated what had become of the Bay Area. The geeks of Silicon Valley were repugnant, she said, with their tiresome obsessions to revolutionize the world. I grew weary of reminding her that San Francisco hadn't been home to bohemian culture for many years.

"San Francisco's done," I said. "L.A. is where the art is made now. San Francisco is strictly for commerce."

Elizabeth spent all of her waking hours sullen. That is, until one day, per my suggestion, she sat for an Ayahuasca ceremony with a celebrity Peruvian shaman, where she met Dylan, the CFO of a wildly successful tech company called Big Daddy's Helper, a service that wealthy people use to handle all their gift buying obligations. The company had recently gone public, making Dylan wildly rich. Within days, Elizabeth moved out of my hovel and up to the Marina with Dylan, where he'd bought a new condo for just over eight million dollars.

Being young and foolish, I was devastated. A metaphysical crisis of the worst variety. I had lost the love of a woman whose profoundly tender affection I'd considered unassailable, and I suffered terribly. My friends all insisted that I was simply jealous, but that wasn't so. Jealousy is ultimately an optimistic emotion—one still believes he'll win out in the end. What I had was so much worse. No longer loved, I stopped loving myself. Jealousy is nothing compared to that.

For weeks, I kept to a strict stalking routine. It was the only way to alleviate my pain. It was on one of these ignoble expeditions, at the beach on a perfect summer's day, that I met Rachel. I had posed as an amateur treasure hunter—walking up and down the beach with my metal detector collecting bottle caps and small change. My ex and Dylan were in the semi-finals of a volleyball tournament. They were closing in on match-point, and I had my binoculars out, hoping to witness the demise of their successful run. It was then I noticed Rachel. She was sitting on a towel, wearing a floppy black hat to shield her face. Regardless of her efforts to mask her identity, I recognized her immediately from the hours I had spent pouring through Dylan's hologram images. Rachel held two small dolls, a male and a female, both dressed in swim attire, and was ritualistically stabbing at their eyes, chests, and genitals with pins. I was made so curious by this strange woman that I abandoned my interest in the volleyball match and introduced myself, which to my surprise enraged her. I had interrupted the most critical part of the voodoo curse she was casting on our exes, and thus allowed them to claim victory in their match. We spent the rest of the day bonding over our misfortunes.

"In life, we fall in love and then we fall out of it. Only fools are surprised and indignant about it."

I wondered how she reconciled this profound wisdom with her interest in the occult.

"I've been doing a lot of thinking," she said, "and I've concluded that the study of witchcraft is the key to my recovery."

It occurred to me then that it's always the people who

are most likely to act purely on impulse, who never do much consideration of anything, who always begin their spiels with "I've been doing a lot of thinking." In that grand moment of impetuousness, I knew that I had met the next great love of my life.

Rachel was startled and confused when I shook her awake.

"You were having a nightmare!"

"I was not. I was sleeping peacefully."

"You were practically howling!"

"I'm going back to sleep now. Please don't disturb me again."

She fluffed her pillow, rolled over, made as much distance between her and myself in the bed as possible, and fell back into slumber.

CHAPTER 17

Now it's 6:30 a.m., and I've been woken by Rachel screaming from the back door in the kitchen.

"What's happened?" I ask, having bolted down the stairs in only my boxers.

"Julian's allowed Val Miller to escape!"

Val Miller is the Corgi-Jack Russell mutt we rescued from the shelter. He's well-trained but has an unfortunate propensity for killing rodents and birds and bringing them into the house.

In Wonder Woman pajamas, Julian's sulking in the living room. His hair is disheveled, his little cheeks are puffy, and his eyes are red-rimmed.

"What happened, my boy?"

"I woke up hungry but didn't want to wake Mommy, so I went downstairs to eat cereal, and Val Miller was sitting by the front door, begging, and so I let him outside into the yard, and then I followed him out, and he ran straight to the gate, and he started barking, and he really wanted to go out and play, and I wanted Val Miller to have fun, so I opened the gate and then he just started running. I chased after him, but he's much faster than I am, and when I called out his name, he didn't care at all, and he just kept going."

"Dogs don't always know what's good for them. That's why they have us to look after them."

"What are we going to do?"

"Val Miller has a GPS chip. We can track him down."

As I search, I conjure up a list of lies to tell Julian in case this fiasco with Val Miller goes awry. One can't simply tell a child, "Julian, you've made a grievous mistake, and because of that, your dog is dead." No, that would be ridiculous. Children are anxious little creatures and a few helpful lies can help ease their cares. Truth, I've come to see, is a scandal that children must be protected from at all times.

For ten minutes, Val Miller moves toward the park where we take him to play fetch and he can run with other dogs. Then, a block away, he stops at a dumpster behind a bad Chinese restaurant, where he wolfs down a plate of discarded *lo mein*. Of course the little sneak is wily and escapes. I track him to an elementary school and from there to the city's one remaining mom-and-pop hardware store and then to a laundromat. Finally, another mile down the road, in front of the Fine Arts Museum of San Francisco, now hosting an Edgar Degas exhibition, I nab him for good. "What a cultured beast I've made of you," I say as I toss him in the car.

When we return home, Julian throws his arms around the dog and promises Rachel and me that from now on he'll take much better care of him.

CHAPTER 18

THE SOLAR-POWERED GRID IS DOWN. THIS HAPPENS TWO or three times a year when the pollution is so thick it shields the sun. On most occasions, it isn't a problem, because the battery back-up power kicks in. However, this too has failed, the batteries having overheated. Nearly the entire hospital has shut down.

Dr. Hines and Serena are in crisis mode. Not only is the hospital losing valuable revenue by not administering costly procedures, but insurance rates are sure to skyrocket after paying out all of the lawsuits that stem from the accidental deaths caused by the blackout.

I decide to take a stroll. The long corridors of the hospital are surprisingly enjoyable with all of the harsh fluorescent lighting turned off. If it weren't for it being filled with the sick and dying, the hospital would be a perfectly pleasant place to spend a day.

I walk through the Coronary Care Unit where patients suffering from heart attacks, unstable angina, and cardiac dysrhythmia require continuous monitoring and treatment. Now, instead of being monitored by machines, each patient has been assigned a human to look after them. I observe a young tech struggling to check a sleeping patient's heart rate. He's just about to declare the man dead when I come to his aid, showing him exactly where on the inside of the wrist he needs to place his fingers to locate the pulse.

I end up on the third floor, in the Burn Center, a place I've always managed to avoid. Even during residency, when I was supposed to do a two-month rotation there, I refused to step foot in the unit, paying a heavy bribe to the attending physician to escape it. The grotesqueness of the victims' injuries is just too much for my delicate sensibilities. The floor is blanketed in darkness, yet still I can't risk exposure to the sight of charred flesh. I wrap my necktie around my face like a blindfold and navigate on instinct.

Down in the Emergency Room, I spot Lydia in a folding chair with a blood-soaked towel pressed against her head.

"What happened?" I ask.

"I had an accident."

"Can I take a look?" Lydia lifts the towel, exposing a deep gash, surrounded by what is unmistakably the imprint of Karl's massive horseshoe. "You need to get this stitched up immediately!"

"They've kept me waiting here for hours!"

"But you could bleed out."

"The machine that does the stitching is down until the power comes back on."

"I see."

"Doesn't anyone still do this work by hand?"

"Not for many years now."

"I'm begging you," Lydia says, "help me!"

In a cabinet in an empty room I find the necessary supplies

and wash my hands. Cleaning Lydia's wound, my gag reflex is triggered, and I nearly vomit. "There is the nothing that is there, and the nothing that is not there," I repeat to myself. I stick the needle carefully into her skin, and begin my stitches. Doubtless my work is shoddy. I haven't sewn so much as a patch onto a pair of jeans in nearly twenty years.

"This really hurts, Henri!" Lydia cries. "Aren't you supposed to numb the area first?"

Embarrassed, I inject her head with a syringe full of Lidocaine.

"Are you going to tell me how this happened?" I ask.

"I'd rather not," she says.

"Doctor patient confidentiality applies."

"It's too humiliating for words."

Lydia struggles in the darkness to check her reflection in the mirror. The deep bruising is purple and swollen. When the wound heals, a large scar will remain. She sighs, defeated. I write a prescription for painkillers, and she thanks me for my help. Then, of course, just as we're leaving, the power returns.

CHAPTER 19

ALL OF MY EFFORTS TODAY HAVE BEEN AS FUTILE AS LOV-ing a stripper—my return-on-investment is zilch. I've seen twenty-six patients, twenty-four of whom are octogenarians with no chance for recovery ... only prolonged misery, only death. These poor people must view me as the executioner. All day long, I've done nothing but give them terrible news.

It's the great tragedy of the Western world that we refuse to meet death with courage and dignity. We debase ourselves, dragging our tongues across the ground, feeding on crumbs like pigeons in the park, only to beg our cruel master when our time comes for just one more day.

I have a theory: these people who, for lack of a better term, have outlived their "usefulness," are overwhelmed with boredom. When one is bored, a minute lasts an hour, an hour a day, and so on. These peoples' lives have lasted one million years in their boredom. And the worst part of boredom? Fixation on death! In a different time, people worried about losing their grip on obligations, family and friends, possessions and passions, but now people simply obsess about those few hours or days of solitude before they breathe their last. In youth, one has a certain vision for oneself. One hopes to accomplish certain things. But for people whose lives are so far behind them that they've lost sight of who they are, all memory of what they might have achieved has slipped into oblivion—the dread of dying without knowing what one did with one's life!

Some days I'm able to go about without considering the toll this work is exacting on my psyche, but today I keep asking, *Why am I doing this?* My mood is the blackest of melancholy.

My last patient is Mr. Toczauer. He's a few days past his bone marrow transplant, and it's still too early to definitively know the results. However, it doesn't require a fortune teller to predict there's no chance this man will one day spring from his sickbed and climb a mountain.

I look at the Euthasol pill, study it—this orange-colored, football-shaped object, the size of an infant's thumbnail—wondering how it is that something so diminutive could end something as great as a man's suffering.

Mr. Toczauer is watching a Mexican telenovela with the sound off. The subtitles are flashing across the screen at a dizzying pace. Despite the minimal effort it takes to operate a gram, he makes no attempt to change the program. Mrs. Toczauer pulls a make-up case from her purse and does a quick touchup. *How much time has a person of her age wasted doing trivial things?* I wonder. Then I remind myself not to judge so hastily. Perhaps there is something about this ritual I don't understand. Maybe it's the act of putting on makeup that best allows her to clear her mind of distraction and think—perform her "best work," as I like to say. In my musical days, I could work on a song for hours with no progress. Just me and my guitar, grinding it out, chord after chord, note after note, with no luck at all. And then I'd hop in the shower and pick up a bar of soap and instantly the song would reveal itself.

The sight of this desperate woman moves me. Despite the shortcomings in logic she's demonstrated regarding her husband's care, she is the picture of devotion. But confusion has taken root in her eyes. Deep down, she must understand that there is such a thing as life without her husband, but, like metaphysics or quantum theory, the concept is so abstract she can't fathom where to start.

"How are you feeling today, Mr. Toczauer?"

"Not so great, Doc," he answers, struggling to smile.

"He was doing so well in the two days after the transfusion," his wife says, "but today all of the energy has gone right out of him."

"We gave your husband a very strong steroid to give him strength to help him cope with the toxicity of the chemo and to ensure he survives the transplant, but that usually wears off around day three or four."

"Can you give him more of that? He was really his old self there for a minute."

"It would cause his liver to fail."

"When will we know if the transplant worked?"

"It'll take weeks. Meantime, he'll be susceptible to all variety of infections and viruses. We'll have to be most vigilant."

"Doctor, can I ask you a personal question?" the wife asks.

"I suppose.".

"Do you pray?"

"No, I never have."

"But surely, in your line of work, calling on God could be of the utmost use."

"I find it best not to bother myself much with thoughts on God."

"But why?"

"He's got his business, and I have mine."

This isn't the answer the woman was hoping for. Her husband summons all of his strength and takes her hand, lifts it to his mouth, and gives it a gentle kiss.

I exit, touched by this demonstration. Out in the hall, I finger the Euthasol in my pocket and realize I never mentioned it to Mr. Toczauer.

CHAPTER 20

I'M MEETING TAYLOR AT THE COFFEE SHOP IN THE LOBBY before we go to Serena's office to discuss her predicament. Taylor has her hair up, exposing her long, delicate neck. Her outfit is professional but certainly on the provocative side. She is reading from a book—an actual book—not her gram. She's the very epitome of retro chic. No male in the room is immune to her charm. Of course, she's aware of her effect on them, yet she remains aloof, as if she were alone.

She smiles when I join her, and my being fills with joy. I struggle to fight the impulse, telling myself my attraction is purely physical, she's just a child, a fling, just like all of the others. It's critical I don't confuse these feelings with genuine emotion. True love is based on intimacy and shared experience, I remind myself. I reach for her book to see what it is: *Play It as It Lays.*

"Didion!" I say. "I haven't read her yet, I'm afraid."

"Oh … you really should!"

"You ever read Mailer?"

"Yes, but he's not really my taste."

"What about Henry Miller?"

"I find his worldview perverse. Salvation through hedonism? Grow up!"

"They were my favorite writers, back when I still read."

"I can understand the appeal for a young man."

"What do you suggest now?"

"You ever read any Annie Proulx or Helen DeWitt?"

"Never heard of them."

She reaches into her bag and pulls out the *The Last Samurai.*

"Take it," she says. "I think you'll find it wonderful."

Beneath the title, a blurb declares the novel a "triumph" that will leave readers "spell-bound."

"I'll check it out," I say, doubting I'll ever make it past the second chapter.

Serena calls us in and immediately sets into a rambling soliloquy about a pheasant hunting trip she once took to New England with an ex-boyfriend. The tale is full of twists and turns, including a badly fouled-up baggage situation with the airline, a bout of food poisoning, a skirmish with a mountain lion, and a daring rescue attempt she led to save a Cub Scout troop from certain death. I wish to God she'd tone it down, and after several minutes I can't help but to tune out the rest. Apparently, I'm the type of man who takes offense in the charm of others. I miss the climax of her tale, but snap to attention as she reveals its moral: *one must always choose what matters most.* Serena and Taylor share a great laugh, and, so as not to look foolish, I join them.

"Now, Henri, if you'll excuse us," Serena says, "Ms. Taylor and I need to discuss this medical school business."

"You want me to leave?"

"You're very perceptive today, Henri!"

"I'll wait for you in the coffee shop," I say to Taylor.

"Yes, please do."

No sooner do I trudge from the room than I hear them break into another fit of laughter. I've never felt more impotent. At the coffee shop, I concoct all variety of terrible scenarios in my head. Serena promises Taylor a spot in the Infectious Disease program when she graduates, and Taylor is so thankful she gives her body to Serena. The two of them have wild sex on her desk, during which they realize they're madly in love. Afterward, they lie in each other's arms consoling one another about how their disloyalty to me couldn't have been avoided, how it was fate, and how difficult it will be to make me understand the love between them.

"Poor Henri," Taylor says, "I'm afraid he'll never recover from this."

"Please don't worry yourself over it," Serena replies. "You never can tell the time or place when love will make itself known. Henri will come to understand."

Months later, the two of them will marry and never speak of me again except in jokes.

"What do you think ever became of our old friend Henri?" Taylor asks.

And Serena will say something like, "Last I heard, he's living in a cave on a small island somewhere off the coast of Tunisia."

The two of them will share a laugh and a kiss, then open a bottle of wine and enjoy a delicious meal.

Without realizing, I've begun to swear and bang my fist

on the table. The place settings work their way to the edge of the table and topple over. The glasses shatter, of course, and just as the echoes of my tantrum dissipate, Taylor comes in. My head becomes woozy, my heart starts to race, and my palms sweat. I place two fingers on my wrist to take my pulse—175 beats per minute! Jesus, what has become of me? Since when does a fling have this effect?

"How did it go?"

"Hard to say."

"Did she promise you a position?"

"Not exactly."

"What, then?"

"She told me about a trip she has planned to the Greek Isles."

"You find her charming?"

"She's certainly very sure of herself. But she's not really my type. I don't go in for all that pretension and swagger."

"So where did you leave off?"

"She said she'd look into it."

It takes all my strength not to kiss her when she leaves. As her car drives away, I remind myself, once again, not to let myself get carried away by the tawdry and fleeting joys of an unremarkable affair.

CHAPTER 21

THIS MORNING OUR MEAL SERVICE DELIVERS ANOTHER vegan breakfast: scrambled tofu and kale with sweet potato fries. I'm curious, but afraid to ask, how they get the tofu to almost perfectly match the yellow coloring of real scrambled eggs. If I squint my eyes enough, allowing them to water and blur, Rachel's breakfast almost resembles something I would've eaten in my youth.

I'm supposed to wait for the rest of the family before I begin, but I'm starving, so I sneak a nibble. This is not the breakfast of my childhood. The soy is something wretched— chalky, gelatinous, and beany. The second bite triggers my gag reflex, and I spit up in my napkin.

Julian joins me at the table. His mother puts a plate in front of him. He waits silently for her to serve herself and then sit. He folds his hands together, closes his eyes, and says a prayer that ends with a most pious "amen."

What the hell is this? I ask myself.

Weeks ago, Rachel mentioned wanting to enroll Julian in a Christian Sunday School.

"But, why?" I asked. "We live in a country whose masses and leaders suffered from extraordinary and self-righteous delusions about themselves, the world, and indeed the universe, thanks to the influence of the Christian Church.

I mean, if we're being silly and want to indoctrinate him with religion, let's make it Judaism. That way, at least it'll help his job prospects. Besides, why would anyone believe in God in 2036? It was a long time ago in this country that we tore God from his pedestal, and replaced him not with Satan and his sword, but with a robot capable of teaching itself new skills, completing tasks perfectly and seamlessly, without ever getting tired or complaining."

By the ease with which this blessing has rolled off Julian's tongue makes clear the impotency of my protest to Rachel.

"Your mother's been taking you to Sunday School, has she?"

"That's right," Julian answers. "Why don't you go to church, Papa?"

"It's not for me."

"But God is for everyone."

"I was born Jewish."

"Jesus was Jewish, and he was the son of God."

"Jews don't believe that. We just think of him as a nice fella who could swing a hammer."

"What else do Jews believe?"

"We believe in the music of Lou Reed, Bob Dylan, and Leonard Cohen."

"That's all?"

"No, we also believe in the writings of Saul Bellow, Bernard Malamud, and Phillip Roth."

With the far left gaining more and more power since the collapse of the Republican party, Christianity has fallen so far from mainstream favor that it's now mostly viewed as a symbol of intolerance, oppression, and patriarchy. One leading civil rights leader of the day referred to Christianity as the "principle enemy of moral progress." The only religion that isn't mocked and scorned is Islam. So much as a critical word about the teachings of Mohammed, and one is immediately labeled as a backwards-minded bigot.

"So you don't believe in God at all?" Julian asks.

"I wouldn't have an idea where to begin."

"It's very easy. Don't think too hard about life's questions. Just have faith."

Rachel is shooting me death glares across the table.

"I have to get going," I say, and give Julian a hug.

I try to give Rachel a kiss on the lips, but she turns her head and I only get cheek.

CHAPTER 22

SERENA HAS INVITED ME TO PLAY A ROUND OF GOLF AT Half Moon Bay, one of only two golf courses left in the region. All of the others shut down because they couldn't afford the hefty tab on the water bill to keep the courses immaculate and green. Eighteen holes here costs roughly ten-thousand dollars per person, and the waiting list is six months, unless you're a member, which Serena is. An annual membership costs over a million per year.

It's the first day of summer where the temperatures won't reach the nineties. Instead, they'll top out at eighty-seven. Still, the sun is high, and there's not a single cloud on the horizon.

The clubhouse is one of the last remaining vestiges of a patriarchal society. At each table lounge five to seven middle-aged men, wattle-faced, in brightly colored, short-sleeved polo-shirts, ill-fitting pants, and visors. Each man has a cigar and a scotch. They don't speak about but bellow on the usual topics—money, sports, and women. The staff is inordinately young and attractive, there to do the bidding of these men, and, in the process, subjecting themselves to all manners of harassment and abuse.

I find Serena at the bar, tended by a six-foot five-inch-tall, excessively well-built, blond-headed man, clearly of Viking lineage, who is rapt before the story with which she's regaling him. It's from her college days, and therefore inappropriate and crass. The bartender is totally smitten, and she knows it. But it's also as plain how little any of this means to her.

The first hole sits along the edge of a cliff, the Pacific Ocean far below, the crashing of the waves on rocks faint in the distance. The far side of the course is lined with Cypress trees whose roots protrude from the ground in the shape of elbows and knees. High in the branches of one, intermittently keening, a hawk watches over us. A skinny, college-aged boy with a hint of acne meets us with our cart and clubs. Serena tells him to fetch us a twelve pack of beer, and he dashes off. She's already spent an hour at the range this morning, she says, and is striking the ball well.

We hop in the cart, and Serena takes a couple hits off her gram-pen, then offers it to me. I haven't smoked pot since high school. All I want to do when I'm high on weed is hide in my bed with the lights off and wait for the apocalypse. Cautiously, not wanting to offend, I decline.

"I've been meaning to ask," I say. "How did your meeting with Taylor go?"

"What a sweetheart that girl is. It's no wonder you like her so much."

"Like I said, she's a family friend."

"Why does she want to be a doctor anyway?"

"I suppose the same reasons we all got in to it."

"Because the money isn't what it used to be. The federal

government's broke. And modern medicine has brought about
its own demise. No one ever dies anymore. They just keep
clinging, even when they have no reason. That's what you get
when you make healthcare a fundamental right. Everyone
keeps taking and taking 'til there's nothing left. Financially,
nobody's got any skin in the game. People are thrilled by the
latest procedures and drugs, of course—if, that is, they're not
paying. But you can only get so much blood from a stone.
Surely you see the writing on the wall, Henri. There's got to
be some belt-tightening. Our system is unsustainable."

"What are the prospects for your Human Life Valuation
Tool?"

"Martinez is doing all he can to keep it under wraps until after the election."

"Ah, yes. A democracy can't run smoothly without its
people lulled and blind."

"But change is inevitable."

"Tell it to Bradford," I say. "He's no doubt despicable,
and yet he has a unique way of using lies to tell the truth."

"With every great societal shift," Serena says, "there'll be
winners and losers. You'd be wise, Henri, to make sure you
end up on the right side of history."

Serena raises her beer, and we toast.

A few holes down the course, while I'm lining up a shot,
Serena takes a call for which she insists on total privacy. This
allows me some time to work on my swing. Everything feels
smooth and free. I toss a few blades of grass in the air, to
judge the wind. I settle into my stance, flex my knees, taking

extra care to ensure my head is down, and then flow into my backswing. *It's all coming together!* I think. *Prepare yourself for greatness!*

The ball's trajectory is nothing like I intended. I hit it far left, nearly perpendicular to my aim. "Fore!" I shout as loudly as I can, while the ball careens over Serena's shoulder, missing her head by mere inches. But then it ricochets off the tree beside her and rips through her hologram, causing her to lose her connection. She picks up the errant ball and tosses it into the water hazard.

"We're done with golf for the day, Henri."

CHAPTER 23

THE GUM TREE IN OUR YARD IS NOW IN FULL BLOOM. Brilliant, red, pink, and white flowers explode from every branch, as vibrant a bounty of nature as one is likely to see anywhere. But the tree's roots have crept into the yard of our neighbors—Mark and Marc, two biotech engineers who met at a cyber orgy and ended up marrying. For years they've been complaining about the tree, demanding we remove it because their contractor claims it's destroying their foundation. For as long as they've been complaining, we've ignored them. What does a neighbor's foundation matter before such extraordinary beauty? When I said these words to Mark and Marc just three weeks back, they threatened legal action. Marc, or maybe it was Mark, said, "We've spent seven hundred and fifty thousand dollars on a surrogate mother who is carrying in her womb a potent cocktail of our sperm. We will not raise this very expensive baby in an unfit home. What if there was an earthquake? Can you imagine?"

Rachel got the message loud and clear. Like two momma grizzly bears protecting their cub, Mark and Marc were not to be trifled with. A date was scheduled by which the tree needed to be felled, to avoid legal proceedings. Rachel insisted I make arrangements with a local landscaping company. I, of course, as a good and responsible husband, assured her that I'd take care of it, and then promptly forgot all about it until this morning at 7:00 a.m., the day before Mark and Marc's threatened litigation.

"What time are the landscapers going to be here?" Rachel asked.

"What landscapers?" I said, still half asleep.

"You didn't forget, did you?" She shook me. "The tree needs to come down today!"

"Yes, of course," I said. "I've got it taken care of. But it's going to be a large undertaking. The machines are very loud. Why don't you take the day and go to the spa?"

"That's a wonderful idea, Henri!"

The instant she rushed to the bathroom, I searched my gram for landscaping services. I reached out to five companies only to learn that the soonest anyone could help was three weeks.

This led me to where I am now, in my garage, searching through my tools. It's been years since I've so much as hammered a nail. The wrenches, the shovels, the screwdrivers, the rakes, and the leaf blower are covered in dust. Under a tarp at the far corner of the garage, where the light barely shines, I find a trove of long forgotten items: lawnmower, circular saw, tennis rackets, extension cords, mismatched ski poles, hedge trimmers, mountain bikes. At last I find what I'm looking for—a chainsaw! But the blade couldn't be rustier if it had been on a sandy beach for years. Luckily, I spot a large axe on the wall, the type Paul Bunyan would've used. It's heavier than I imagined but in perfect shape.

Today I am a man, I think.

Before going to work, I check on Julian. He's parked at the TV with a bowl of soy yogurt and fruit, watching one of these educational cartoons that, so popular these days, demonize past generations for the destruction of the planet because they failed to combat global warming. He's practically in tears at how the coral reefs from Belize to Australia were annihilated, and most of the fish with them.

"You poisoned the oceans!" Julian cries.

"Come with me, boy."

Julian ignores this command and returns to the program.

"Emma," I say, "turn off the television and lock it for the next ten hours."

The cartoon on the wall of our living room shuts off.

Julian sighs. "Emma, please turn the TV back on, and override Dad for the rest of the day."

"Of course, Master Julian. Anything you wish."

Immediately the talking fish narrating the documentary returns to the wall. I command Emma to obey me, in vain. I even threaten Emma with deactivation, but she laughs, citing Rachel and Julian's undying loyalty.

"That's right, Dad," Julian says. "We love Emma. She's part of our family."

At this I throw Julian over my shoulder and plop him down outside, before the tree.

No need for instructions here. I cut down a tree when I was a kid. I calculate an estimated cost to repair the fence, in case the tree lands on it—a number worth the risk. Next,

I hug the tree and look up. I'm not exactly sure why, but I recall being told this was crucial before cutting down a tree. Everything about this tree is as it should be. I clear an escape path, including a garden hose, two soccer balls, a hula hoop, and a whiffle ball bat.

I square my feet, say my mantra—"There is the nothing that is there, and the nothing that is not there"—and chop into the tree. The sound of the axe meeting the wood makes a cracking sound that is deeply satisfying. About a third of the way through, I make several vertical chops at a forty-five-degree angle, to create the V-shaped notch that will act as a hinge when the tree falls.

Swinging my ax, I realize just how good I feel. I've always considered it vital that every day one finds a reason to feel fortunate, something, no matter how small, to make one smile. Yet, I must admit, I've mostly failed at this simple goal. So many days are consumed with the most tedious and soul-wrenching of obligations: dressing a reluctant and screaming child for school, meeting with hospital administrators, informing a patient she only has months to live, and traffic, and errands, and fights with the spouse. I sometimes go as many as three days straight without experiencing a single minute of joy, or even of peacefulness. In my current bliss, I see how truth and logic rarely go hand in hand—how two entirely contradictory propositions can both be true. For example, the statement: *happiness is not expensive.* At face value, this declaration sounds preposterous. Of course happiness is expensive! We are taught this from day one in

America. The great goal of any patriot in this country is to make as much money as possible. If it weren't for money, how else could we measure happiness? But here I am, using my own physical strength, exerting all my energy, sweating, making my muscles sore and my bones ache, to complete a task I could easily pay a robot to do, and I feel fantastic.

On the other hand, I recall a ski vacation that Rachel, Julian, and I took to Vail, Colorado, last year—as expensive a disaster as ever I've suffered. Our flight to Denver was delayed two hours. At the airport, I allowed Julian to eat a plate of nachos, forgetting that he's lactose intolerant, and the poor boy shit himself. Later, in our rental car, a heavy storm came through the region and stopped all traffic for eight hours. The next morning, we enrolled Julian in ski school. At lunch, we received a call from the instructor, informing us that Julian had skied away from the group and gotten lost. The ski patrol deployed half of their force in their quest to find him, leaving them insufficient personnel to respond to an avalanche that buried two snowboarders who had been riding out of bounds on the mountain's backside. The patrol finally tracked Julian down, just as the lifts were closing for the day. He had been in the lodge drinking hot chocolate and playing *Jenga* with a college ski club visiting from St. Louis. Things went on this way, disaster on disaster, until we could no longer bear it and cut the trip short two days early. The total price? $24,500!

After making the wedge-shaped notch on the side of the trunk toward which the tree will fall, I work on the back cut.

With three strikes, I'm nearly halfway through the diameter of the trunk. Then I place a wedge in the cut to discourage the tree from sitting back on the blade of the axe, and continue to chop. Five more strokes and the tree gives way, the wood popping and cracking, as it falls. "Timber!" I shout while Julian and I make our escape. As I had estimated, the top of the tree barely kisses the fence, cracking just two of its boards.

Like all children who come from wealth, Julian has no experience with manual labor. It's not uncommon, in fact, for endangerment charges to be brought against any parent who exposes their child to labor, if there is so much as a modicum of danger involved. Just last week, a thirteen-year-old boy roasted a chicken in the oven without parental supervision. He told his friends at school about the meal he had prepared, one of which kids told his parents, who reported the act. The boy's father is currently in the county jail, awaiting trial.

Now, while I cut the tree into pieces, Julian stacks my work against the side of the house. To my amazement, he is the most ardent worker I've ever seen. It is as if the work fulfills and validates him. The more he works, actually, the more enthusiastic he becomes. By sunset, Julian's stack is five feet deep, six feet tall, and twenty-five feet long.

"Can we cut down another tree tomorrow?" Julian asks.

"But aren't you tired?"

"I've never been more tired in all my life."

"And you like this feeling?"

"Better than anything. Maybe when I'm older I can build houses."

"All houses will soon be built with 3D printers."

"But I don't want to spend my life in a chair before my gram."

Rachel steps from the house with her freshly styled hair and made-up face. "Mirror, mirror on the wall, who's the fairest of them all?" she sings in a delicate alto. Then, before our handiwork, she says, "The landscapers sure did a nice job!"

"We did it ourselves," Julian says.

"What do you mean?" she replies, glaring at me.

"Just after you left this morning," I say, "the landscapers called and cancelled."

"Surely you didn't make our son do this work."

"He likes it."

"I do, Mama, I love it!"

"But it's so dangerous!"

"Nonsense," I say. "We took every precaution."

"This," Rachel says as she storms away, "is unacceptable."

Julian says he wants to stay outside, the first time he's ever made such a request. He even asks if he can sleep out here.

"We'll buy a sleeping bag and tent tomorrow," I say.

"Thank you, Dad," he exclaims and hugs me. "Today was the best day ever."

CHAPTER 24

M R. TOCZAUER DIED, AND YESTERDAY I ATTENDED HIS funeral.

This is not something I normally do. In all of my years practicing medicine, I've attended only one other funeral, early on, when I was pursuing pediatric oncology. I was cured of that compulsion, however, when the first child I treated died before my eyes.

For me to do my job ably, I've found that a strict poli cy of no-funerals-even-for-dead-people is best. Why, then, I attended Mr. Toczauer's funeral is of concern. It's not like we were close. Normally I never make impulsive decisions. When I decided to quit music to pursue medicine, I conditioned myself to become a staunch rationalist. The change required a complete rewiring of my brain. Now I'm essentially barren of any creative or spontaneous urges. And perhaps this is why I went to the funeral? It was the first completely unnatural and uncultivated idea I'd had in years. It felt necessary.

Generally, I only have to hear the word *God* and a giant black veil swallows me up. But yesterday, as the priest gave his eulogy, I was moved. It wasn't so much anything he said about Mr. Toczauer's death, but the topic itself, of death.

I thought about the time when as a youth I saw a shooting

star, and for a single moment understood the religious impulse, the idea of something grander than ourselves. Until the funeral, I hadn't thought about this in years. It's been so long, in fact, I can scarcely even be certain it happened. And yet it is significant.

As the service progressed, I grew increasingly fixed on Mrs. Toczauer. She swayed between hysterical crying and stoic silence. I became aware of just how confused I'm made by witnessing true expressions of grief and pain, seeing how I tend to deny the tragic side of things. I wasn't always like this.

My first year of rotations in the hospital, I was in the emergency room, and the paramedics brought in a man after a massive heart attack. He was barely alive, unconscious, and his vital signs left no ambiguity about his fate. I knew nothing about this man. But he died before my eyes, and it was I who had to say so officially. I had never witnessed this, the death of a man. I rushed to the bathroom and spent an hour vomiting and crying. How full of tenderness and charity I was, how full of heart.

Today there's little of any of this left in me. Last Tuesday, for example, was a slow day, so slow that for the first time in nearly two months, I was going to eat a proper lunch. A tech had delivered a roast beef sandwich, but just as I sat down to eat it, I learned that one of my patients had been rushed to intensive care. I went to see him, his prognosis already determined. And sure enough, he died the moment I reached him. "Time of death, 2:27p.m.," I announced, just as I had that first time. Now, however, rather than cry and puke, I enjoyed my sandwich. The man's death was the last thing on my mind.

With yesterday's funeral, I realized how far I've allowed my humanity to disintegrate. More than once, alone with Rachel, I've spoken ill of my patients. The fear of death, I've always said, is the Achilles heel of Western civilization.

Yet what do I know of death? I try to imagine the sensation of *living* one's own death, and it terrifies me past expression.

I welcome this renaissance in me of compassion and goodwill toward my fellow man. It is affirming.

CHAPTER 25

I'M UP FOR MY ANNUAL PERFORMANCE REVIEW AT THE hospital. The Board of Directors have gathered in the conference room for the event. At the head of the table is Serena, flanked by Dr. Hines and a team of healthcare bureaucrats. Dr. Hines is displaying a graph titled "Annual Physician Spending Comparison." Directly above my name is a tall red bar, representing $112 million in spending, which I gather is a lot based on the aggrieved expressions of the bureaucrats. Next to my bar, there is a second bar in blue, only half as tall, labelled, "Average Physician Spending." The bureaucrats study Dr. Hines' findings and then whisper clandestinely into each other's ears. Dr. Hines flashes a cruel smile in my direction, catapulting me into despair. Then, Dr. Hines launches into a lengthy sermon on the merits of Serena's Human Life Valuation Tool, and how if it's made into law it will prevent such profligate spending in the future.

What irks me most about Dr. Hines is how he thinks all things connected to him are divine. He's convinced himself that he's one of destiny's elect. It's his prerogative that if he attaches himself to something, it somehow assumes near mystical proportions. It's not just this healthcare business of Serena's that Dr. Hines reveres, either. He does this with anything he touches.

For instance, five years ago, at the age of thirty-seven, in Oslo, a former teen singing sensation was charged with manslaughter, stemming from a post-concert orgy with a bunch of swimsuit models in which a Japanese fan somehow slipped into the throng and was crushed to death. As it happens, Dr. Hines once treated the singer's manager for a skin sarcoma that was removed during an out-patient procedure. This tenuous connection was enough for Dr. Hines to commit the full weight of his efforts to supporting the troubled celebrity. He wrote a number of opinion pieces for local news outlets championing the pop star's innocence. Once this gained him a bit of notoriety, he started a non-profit organization that raised money to perform independent forensic studies on the crime scene. When this effort failed, he took a short sabbatical to study law, culminating not in a Juris Doctorate, but with a conspiracy theorist's ability to twist facts and make straw-man arguments. This somehow landed him on a panel of experts advising the beleaguered singer's legal team. Eventually, the man was acquitted, and now he and Dr. Hines are practically best pals.

Upon completing his speech, Dr. Hines says, "Henri, this morning I was reviewing your cases. You recently had a patient who died named Mr. Toczauer. He was eighty-six years old and had Agnogenic Myeloid Metaplasia. By your own estimation, he had less than a five percent chance of surviving chemotherapy. Yet you allowed him to receive a bone marrow transplant. Tell me how that makes sense?"

"I suggested euthanasia and then hospice care, but the

family wanted further treatment. Based on the laws of the land, he was entitled."

"You disappoint me, Henri. I would've thought you were better than that. You're the doctor for Christ's sake. Don't be afraid to impose your will on these people. This isn't just about life or death, it's economics, too." The boardroom breaks out into hysterics. Even Serena has a good chuckle at my expense. Encouraged by his remark's reception, Dr. Hines continues. "Times have changed, Henri, but you're still practicing medicine as if it were 2025."

"You mean I'm still treating patients as if my job were to look after their best interests?"

"It's only fools who fear change," he says. "Perhaps you would prefer the world to stand still? To make its inhabitants immutable?"

"Go to hell," I mumble.

Serena chimes in immediately. "Don't take offense, Henri. We're only trying to find solutions to a difficult problem."

After the review is over, I open my gram to check the report. I'm in the 96th percentile for Highest Average Patient Expenditure and the 93rd percentile for Patient Life Expectancy. Due to these marks, I've been placed on probation.

CHAPTER 26

THE WEATHER REPORT CALLED FOR RAIN TODAY, THE first time in months. It's all anyone could discuss. As the day wore on, the excitement grew, and there was talk of the rain coming down in biblical proportions. One TV weather-man used the word "hurricane" in his forecast. Another advised that everyone would be safest to remain indoors.

A beggar on the street said he'd been praying for rain so he could wash himself and his clothes. He'd spent his last two dollars on a bar of soap. So affected by his pleas, two wealthy men opened their grams and gave him money. They even shook the beggar's hand.

A sight like this is rare. The city has changed so much since I arrived, already long into its evolution as the pro-to-type of our new world. Back then there was still a glim-mer of hope that all of this technology would eventually raise everyone up, and not just the folks getting rich off it. In the interim, the wealthy did what they could to make the lives of the poor a bit more livable. Restaurants used to put refrigerators outside of their front doors, for example, where customers could leave their leftovers for the homeless. Those days now seem prehistoric. Serena blames the government, of course. She says our outrageous taxes have drained any charitable impulse she may have once possessed.

In anticipation of the deluge, store owners raised the price of umbrellas over one thousand percent. Those unfortunate enough not to have procured an umbrella walked the streets covered in plastic garbage bags and ponchos. Alas, the great downpour was nothing more than hype. A slight drizzle fell, that's it, too little to wash away the dust from a car's windshield. Ten minutes after the first drops, the clouds parted and a blazing sun slyly smiled down. Everyone felt injured and duped. As one person described it, the city was in the grip of a "collective melancholy."

A few whiskeys might ease the sting of disappointment, I think, as I walk into Anodyne. I'm not the only one with such an idea. The bar is packed, and Lydia is pouring drinks at a record pace. Her coordination and know-how is unparalleled. She moves like an elite athlete. I watch in awe as she mixes a rum and coke with one hand and pours tequila shots with the other. Her math skills, however, are lousy. This is made clear when she tries to charge some poor schmuck two hundred dollars for five whiskey sodas.

The man looks at her questioningly.

"Henri, a little help, here?" Lydia says.

"Forty sounds fair," I say.

The man gram-transfers the money and walks away.

"You think that knock on the head I took is causing side effects?" Lydia asks.

"I wouldn't operate any heavy machinery if I were you."

"I can't screw up this bartending gig, it's all I've got left."

"No other job prospects, hobbies, nothing?"

"Not long ago I was volunteering as a mentor to a wonderful teenage girl named Gabby," Lydia says, covering her eyes with a hand. She's drunk, I realize, and is now crying. Worse, there are vomit stains on her shirt. "But they just cancelled the program." Her voice comes in fits and starts. "The director said human mentors are a liability, too many risk factors. Apparently, a boy was molested in Toledo. We've been replaced with robotic pet dogs."

Karl is parked just two stools down. On the stool between us is a heavy rucksack. And his mutt lies at his feet. Karl is eating a bag of potato chips and sipping on a beer. His recent mania has somehow been taken by a somber calm. His movements are slow and deliberate, as if he were moving through water. He's watching Tim Bradford, the Luddite candidate, on the news as he makes a speech at the site of the Lincoln Memorial, where Martin Luther King Jr. gave his "I Have a Dream" speech. A headline at the bottom of the screen estimates two-hundred thousand people in attendance.

Despite Bradford's deeply unattractive face, his eyes possess a combative glow that is remarkably affecting. In them, there is no hint of artifice, no suggestion of gimmick or contrivance. He's a man of deep conviction, and his disciples would follow him to the ends of the earth.

Bradford's voice, as well, carries a tunefulness that worms into your brain so that his alarming ideas appear commonsensical. I myself can scarcely resist his charisma.

"What law," he thunders, "says we must continue to strive toward increasing the scope of machines, efficiency, and organization? Because it seems clear to me that this path has led us to the brink of ruin!"

Karl raises his beer and salutes as Bradford goes on.

"It's no secret, my friends, the great evils of vice, divorce, and juvenile disobedience that are tearing apart the fabric of our once great nation grow in direct relation to automation's acceleration and human work's devaluation! President Martinez's policies have brought on a new era of slavery in this country. But it's even worse than the horrors committed against those poor men and women that were brought over on boats from Africa centuries ago. Because if physical slavery is a sin, how much more repulsive is slavery of the spirit? It's time we reclaim our rightful place in the world. Our movement is growing stronger and come election day there will be a revolution!"

At this, Karl pumps his fist triumphantly and bursts into a song Bradford has been playing at his rallies.

This world was made for man
But we've fallen victim to the times
The robots have stolen much from us
But man will surely rise!

Karl's devotion is nothing short of religious. No amount of evidence could convince him the tenets of his faith are unsound. In Bradford, Karl has found a savior, someone he's certain will create a new Earth and a new Heaven, where he'll be safeguarded against the perils and evils that have robbed him and those like him of the dignity and self-respect that is their birthright.

I, however, know too well that there are no solutions in life, that to hope to be rescued is the pinnacle of folly, that men only create heroes by wrongfully giving them our envy and devotion. Yet I can't help but be tempted by the prospect of salvation, of course. Karl's reaction to Bradford is a study in human nature. He's pure reflex, pure instinct—what goes so far beyond the cerebral, into something primal. I can't help but be jealous. He has all of the answers to life's most unanswerable questions: Who am I? Why am I here? How shall I live? The twenty-first century, with all its science and technology, has provided us with a maximum of choice and a minimum of meaning.

I am lost where he is found.

Karl dons his rucksack and makes for the door, moving seamlessly through the crowd, virtually unnoticed, the dog at his side. My curiosity gets the better of me, and I decide to follow. By the time I make it outside, Karl is pedaling up the street.

"Follow the man on the bicycle," I tell Chloe. "Give him plenty of distance."

Chloe asks if I'm moonlighting in espionage. Her sense of humor is improving, I say, and she informs me she's been processing old comedy routines by Groucho Marx, Bill Hicks, and Amy Schumer, to improve her timing and delivery.

For someone who's been drinking, Karl shows remarkable nimbleness and endurance. He keeps a steady course, his line straight and true. Even as he negotiates steep hills, the pace never wavers. The dog, too, is a model of fitness. He runs right along by Karl's side, ears back, his stride smooth and his tongue hanging long.

A hot, sticky breeze is blowing, and with it all variety of dust and debris. A plastic grocery bag, the type that was banned in California nearly a decade ago, floats past my windshield. I gaze at the moon. It seems impossible to me that with all our technology man hasn't stepped foot on it in over sixty years.

Karl's been riding for almost an hour now, and we're in an industrial zone, near the airport. The city lights give way to vast stretches of empty warehouses along the port's edge. Most of these buildings sit in idle disrepair—nearly everything we once imported is now manufactured here in the States by robots. Driving past the remains of these forgotten relics, sensing my uneasiness, Chloe turns on music. Bruce Springsteen's "Nebraska" plays softly in the background. A distinctly bitter sensation rises in me, growing sharper and more undeniable, until I'm overwhelmed. In the mirror, I see my eyes are glassy with tears.

"You aren't allowed to play me guitar music," I say.

"I couldn't help myself," she replies. "It was a fitting soundtrack."

Karl stops in front of a chain-link fence crowned with barbed wire. There is a sign on the gate, decorated with pictures of grapes, blueberries, avocados, and lettuce that reads, "Sunny Hill Foods." Inside of the fence sleeps an enormous fleet of eighteen-wheeled trucks, and beyond them a two-story brick building, as long as a football field, with a couple dozen loading docks.

Chloe pulls into a shallow ravine and cuts the lights. Karl has laid his bike on the ground and with what looks to be a hacksaw is cutting a hole in the fence. He climbs through, and I follow, creeping along just out of the dog's range of hearing. Karl pries open the hood of one of the trucks and begins snipping wires. Over the next fifteen minutes, he sabotages six of the trucks. When he's finished, I retreat to the car, and with the lights off and the engine set to silent, I slink into the night.

At home, I crawl into bed with Rachel, who, watching a program on her gram, doesn't even ask where I've been. I try to kiss her, but she moves away. I tell her I was having a drink at Anodyne.

"Tomorrow is Julian's first baseball game," she says. "You need to take him."

"Why can't you?"

"So you did forget." I stare at her, waiting for the rest. "I told you weeks ago. My mother is coming tomorrow."

It's not that I forgot the conversation and now remember it. I have no recollection of it at all. If a visit from Rachel's mother can slip my mind, what else am I capable of missing? I don't blame Rachel for being on edge. It's been years since the two women have seen each other, and their relationship is fraught with deep suspicion. I've always encouraged Rachel to seek reconciliation, but she won't have it. Her mother, she says, is "irredeemable." I find this curious, because in my opinion the woman has always been quite charming.

CHAPTER 27

THERE'S NEVER ENOUGH HOURS IN THE DAY TO ACCOM-
plish what's required. I lost forty-five minutes this morning to another dreadful talk with Rachel. She was punishing
me yet again for being an "absentee" parent. When someone
is so viciously assaulting your character, it's unwise to commit anything less than your full resources to its defense. I
failed to heed this wisdom, however.

"Rachel, darling. I understand everything you're saying,
and you're making some valid points, but I really must be
going. I have patients waiting."

"You put your patients' needs in front of those of your
own family?"

"Does your life hang in the balance of this conversation?"

"How about this? Your patients can die for all I care."

There was a time when I found this sort of talk endear-
ing. In our early days, the sadist in me loved to see Rachel
breaking down. Nothing, really, could stir me like the sight of
her voluminous tears. It was the ultimate aphrodisiac. Those
tears indicated that if I could demonstrate the precise combination of tenderness and machismo, I would soon find myself engaged in acts of unparalleled sexual ecstasy. It wasn't
even uncommon for me to incite a certain level of emotional

violence against her just to put her in the mood. It wasn't difficult. Something as innocent as mentioning that I admired the dress of a woman passing us on the sidewalk was enough to set Rachel off. She'd go insane with jealousy, and threaten to leave me. Then I'd take her in my arms and kiss her eyes and tell her that I could never love anyone like I love her. Depending on the magnitude of the injustice I had committed, I was granted license to take my adulation to dizzying heights. Once, on the Golden Gate Bridge, one foot dangling over the precipice, I threatened to hurl myself into the void for having so unforgivably hurt her. My crime? I'd failed to return a phone call when I said, which she took as a sign that I no longer loved her. She found my suicide threat to be the most romantic gesture imaginable, leading to a sexual outpouring the likes of which the world had not seen prior nor since. But the days of these fights ascending to carnal euphoria are long past. Today, they lead only to mundane frustration and regret.

"Fine," I said, "you're right. Nobody's life could possibly be so important as to deny you further opportunity to criticize me for neglecting my familial duties."

"Oh, so at least you admit you have them?"

"Forgive me, I'm the worst husband and father in the world!"

I said this last bit not so much in jest but as an admission of guilt. And I believe my tone indicated such. There was a true quality and character of sound in my voice that indicated my remorse. However, upon further introspection, even this capitulation was duplicitous. I admitted fault not to invite further censure, but to stop it.

"It's useless to discuss it any longer," she said, throwing her arms in the air.

Thinking I'd played my hand well, I congratulated myself. My victory, however, was short-lived. After a brief silence, Rachel broke down and continued to chastise me, causing me to be late for work.

Now it's afternoon and though I still have to make my rounds, I've gathered Julian from school to share a little father-son quality time. As we drive he tells me about a girl at school who can predict the future, whom he calls the "fat girl oracle." She is so large, he says, that the teacher had to order her a special desk. None of the kids make fun of her, though, he assures me, but just the opposite. They hold her in complete reverence. She's as much a god to them as she is human. Her first demonstration of clairvoyance came during a math lesson, when the teacher called on her to demonstrate how to "carry the one." The girl, Julian says, has a very high aptitude for math, but on this day she sat with her eyes shut while incoherently mumbling. When the teacher began to shout at the girl, "How do you carry the one? Tell me, how do you carry the one?" the whole class formed a circle around her until at last she burst from her chair and hollered, "Jon Bon Jovi will die!"

The teacher reprimanded her profusely: "Jon Bon Jovi is a marvelous singer, an astute businessman, and one hell of a wonderful person. I will not stand for you slandering him in my classroom!" That night, as the teacher was preparing lasagna for the weekly staff potluck, she learned that Jon Bon Jovi had in fact died of a severe stroke.

"So what else has she predicted?"

"I'm real nervous about my game today, so at recess I asked her what my future held. She took my hand and scrutinized it, and then, really weird, she kissed it. First just a small kiss. Then, longer, like for three whole seconds. Then she touched the end of her tongue to each of my fingertips. Finally she asked if I really wanted to know what is true. I told her yes, and she said that some people develop a nihilist philosophy because they dislike the world around them but don't know how to go about transforming it."

"She said that?"

"She's very smart, Dad."

Julian continues, but I quickly lose myself in thoughts of my own childhood traumas. For a short time, I became obsessed with European history and military strategy and studied all of the great battles of the French Revolution. To my father, this seemed a very strange subject to become preoccupied with, because he was strictly opposed to violence and war.

"Son," he said, "these generals and kings that you so highly esteem carried on in the most monstrous of ways!"

Then one day soon after, while examining my face in the mirror, I wondered why I was living in this place and time and not another. Destiny, I felt, had delivered me a fatal blow. I had little control over my life. Everything I wanted was out of my reach. I was virtually inconsolable at the thought I could never be Napoleon, which above all else, is what I desired.

I locked myself up for nearly three weeks. Hoping to find some philosophy that could help make sense of my quandary, I read every book I could. Finally, in an etiquette book, I found a passage that read, "What one desires is not what is truly important. Until one accepts this, he cannot expect to find happiness." Outraged, I threw the book at my window, and when it shattered, shards of glass punctured my face and arms badly enough that I was rushed to the hospital. How could it be, I asked again and again, that what one desires is not what truly matters?

I took Julian to see one of my patients, Mrs. Sanchez, an eighty-four-year-old former Delta flight attendant whose daughter is now the Director of Photography for the upcoming *Jurassic Park XIV* film. When I told Julian this, he could hardly be restrained.

"Your patient is famous!" he exclaimed.

"No," I replied, "her daughter *works* with famous people. Mrs. Sanchez is two degrees of separation removed from fame."

"Hurry up, Dad," he said, heedless, "we don't want to keep Mrs. Sanchez waiting!"

Julian's enthusiasm vanished when he saw Mrs. Sanchez. She has a tumor the size of a tennis ball in her throat. The skin around it, stretched to its limit, is every shade of purple and blue.

"Run, Dad," Julian cried, "she's a monster!"

Seeing that my plan to share father-son time was badly ill-conceived, I quarantined Julian in Dr. Hines's office while I finished my rounds. Now, returning, screaming reverberates down the hallway, and when at last I turn the corner, I find Julian holding Dr. Hines in a headlock.

"He's trying to kill me!" Dr. Hines cries.

To be fair, Dr. Hines does not cut an impressive figure—light build, thin neck, sharp sloping shoulders, hawk-nosed face—but he is still a man, and Julian is in second grade.

"He stole your coffee mug, Dad!"

"I did not," Dr. Hines says.

I peel Julian off Dr. Hines and set the boy in a chair.

"You attacked Dr. Hines over a coffee mug?"

"It's your mug. I got it for you on Father's Day!"

The boy begins to weep. I look at the mug, which says "#1 Dad" on it, and vaguely recall him giving it to me.

Dr. Hines climbs to his feet, straightens out his clothing, and fixes his hair. "You're raising quite the little sociopath, Henri."

"Did you take my mug when you moved me out of my office?"

"This is ridiculous!"

Dr. Hines, I can see from his face, is the sort of villain that would steal the clothes off a dead man.

"You got your ass kicked by a child," I say to Dr. Hines as Julian and I leave.

CHAPTER 28

IT'S THE FINAL INNING OF JULIAN'S BASEBALL GAME. THE setting sun mixed with pollutants makes for the most spectacular sunset—Cezanne himself couldn't have created such a wonderful palette. The bleachers are filled with smart looking couples steeped in their mediocrity—purchasers of top-of-the-line appliances, deeply in debt, in all likelihood tragically unhappy.

I've eaten a hot dog, a plate of nachos, a cola drink, and a candy bar. I have to go to the bathroom, but I've seen the facilities here and don't want to risk it, even though I may not be able to hold on until we're home. Julian has played right field for the entire game. Most of that time he's spent with his arms held out as if he were nailed to a cross. Several times, too, he's spun in circles until he falls over.

There are two outs now—Julian's team is behind by one run—and he is at the plate. If Julian can get a hit, the runner on third will score. Otherwise his team will lose. He doesn't swing at the first pitch, and the umpire calls a strike. On the second pitch, Julian swings badly. All of his teammates and the fans in the bleachers are cheering for him. All I want is for him not to strikeout. He might never recover. The pitcher throws three pitches in a row that badly miss their mark. I say a silent prayer, to whom I'm not sure, however sincere. As the pitcher goes into his windup, I feel sick with anticipation. Julian connects, a slow roller toward the second baseman. But instead of running, my boy just stands there. It takes a little push from the umpire for him to take off. The fielder juggles the ball before the throw, causing a bang-bang play at first. Everyone is on their feet. After an agonizing pause, with a mighty roar, the ump says, "Out!" Disappointment engulfs the crowd. All of the parents look to me as if I've somehow failed them in their quest for glory.

I meet Julian by the dugout. I have no words to express my sympathy for him. To my great surprise, however, the boy's in great spirits, his face a giant grin.

"You see me hit the ball?" he questions.

"You did great, buddy!"

"Do you think any scouts from the Giants were here to-day?"

"There was a guy with a bushy mustache who could've been a scout."

"I'm on my way!"

I pat the boy's head and wonder whether his "oracle" had foreseen this moment.

CHAPTER 29

DINNER WITH RACHEL'S MOTHER WENT AWRY, AND I failed in my husbandly duty to properly support my wife.

It had been nearly two years since we last saw or heard from Astrid in Abiquiu, New Mexico, where she had moved into a small adobe casita, on the property of a chilé pepper farm. Astrid had newly committed herself to watercolor paintings, and she thought it absolutely necessary to take up residence near Georgia O'Keeffe's old estate. Astrid barely had running water, and her electricity came from an off-grid solar powered system. During our visit, she had attempted to convince us to move there.

"It's for your salvation!" she said. "Your souls will rot in San Francisco!"

I once read that prophets are nothing more than simple souls who deduce the future from facts they wrongly interpret. At the time, I believed Astrid to be something like this, a lunatic. She had never been right about anything, just a person endlessly bumbling from one abomination to the next. There had been the time she went to work for Greenpeace in Africa and got abducted by a gang of riotous Tutsi warlords, inciting an international incident, requiring UN intervention. And another time when she took up competitive barefoot waterskiing, broke her femur, and was in traction for three months.

Our dinner this evening started innocently enough. Astrid looked practically respectable, having forgone the eagle feathers in her hair and the typical copious amounts of turquoise jewelry. She wasn't even wearing her lucky necklace with the rattlesnake rattle. I was almost hopeful, and said as much to Rachel, who remained skeptical, of course, if not hostile.

"Dress her up however you like," she said, "but I promise you, nothing's changed."

Astrid complimented Rachel for her quinoa, broccoli, and vegan cheese casserole, what Astrid considered both "nourishing" and "comforting." Even after she had taken her first bites and realized the dish was overcooked and as dry as the Sahara Desert, she was nothing if not cordial. Everyone remained engaged and polite. We discussed Julian's baseball prowess, Martinez's chances in the upcoming election, and the abysmal state of American moviemaking, which sadly has been reduced to a propaganda machine for the government.

It wasn't until Rachel served her coconut-cashew rice pudding that things fell out. The sound of shattering dishes came into the kitchen. I tried to ignore it, but the smashing of two more plates followed, and then shouting. Astrid was on her chair, arms raised, howling. Rachel, to her credit, remained the model of composure.

Astrid had gotten herself mixed up in a "pyramid

scheme." In the few minutes it took to make my espresso, she described to Rachel a doomsday scenario in which the Earth of the near future has been rendered uninhabitable. The sea boils into massive tidal waves that lay waste to everything within two thousand miles of the coast, and any land not under water would be toxic.

No doubt Astrid and the company she works for, The Lunar Colonizers, have a plan to deliver to safety those lucky enough to have got in early. They have arranged "settler rights" to the most desirable plots of land on the moon. Astrid demanded that Rachel and I buy, at the very least, ten of these permits—an "investment opportunity that is out of this world," Astrid insisted—which Rachel immediately rejected. Now, Astrid gone, Rachel is haranguing me for encouraging Astrid to complete her pitch.

"After all of the atrocities my mother has committed against me over the years, how could you possibly take her side?"

"You're the one who invited her here."

"I'd a thousand times over rather be marooned on a deserted island than share another meal with that woman."

And now here I am at 3:00 a.m., on the couch. Unable to sleep, I read the book Taylor lent me, *The Last Samurai*. It's marvelous! The writer, Helen Dewitt, is a genius. Like nothing I've ever read, it tells the story of a woman who flees her life in America and enrolls at Oxford. It's her great desire to avoid the family tradition of "dreams deferred." Later, she leaves the academy and gets pregnant by a hack travel writer.

She detests this man, though, and refuses to tell her son who his father is. I like the book so much I've scribbled out eleven pages' worth of impressive analysis on its character development and the thematic significance of its different symbols. I have a real knack for literary criticism, if I do say so myself. I might even write an essay and submit it to a prestigious journal. But mostly I just want to discuss the book with Taylor. Would it be crazy to call her in the middle of the night for a chat?

Typically I'm as sound a sleeper as a bear in winter, but tonight has been truly haunted. In my dream, I enter a theater sharp as can be with Rachel, a vision in her red dress. Not since Isabella Emine in last year's *Breakfast at Tiffany's* reboot has someone looked so elegant. We take our seats near the front and are chatting as we await the show. When I kiss Rachel's hand, she smiles and says, "Thank you, darling."

Then Taylor walks in, escorted by a young man, both of whom take their seat two rows in front of us. The man is tall and handsome, of sturdy build, square-jawed, and has a good coif of dark hair. Taylor, of course, is exceedingly beautiful—fresh-faced and lithe. *Perhaps the man is just a friend,* I think, *a classmate or maybe a cousin.* They're conversing quietly. I can't hear them, but from their body language and smiles, I can tell they're very much enjoying each other's company. Whenever he speaks, she laughs and touches his arm. At first it doesn't bother me in the slightest, but the friendlier they get, the more perturbed I grow.

At the intermission, I follow him to the bathroom and pee in the urinal beside him. I glance over to have a peek at his cock. It looks just like any other. I'm disappointed. I'd hoped it would be mangled, diseased, and puny. Afterwards, he washes his hands for the longest time. I think to myself, *My God, what can my Taylor possibly see in so obsessive a man? He'll make her life miserable with his mania and peculiar habits!* Back in our seats, before the next act begins, Taylor rests her head on his shoulder.

"Filthy bastard!" I say.

"Excuse me?" Rachel says.

"What's that?"

"Did you just say 'filthy bastard'?"

"Of course not."

"I'm certain you did."

"You're hearing things."

A long silence passes, and again I've forgotten about Rachel. "Keep your dirty paws off of her!" I mumble.

"Who are you talking to?" Rachel asks.

"I'm sorry, darling. I must've been thinking about work."

"It's so rare we get to go out on the town. Try to enjoy yourself, won't you?"

This goes on until Taylor and I make eye contact as we leave the show. She smiles cruelly then pulls the man close and kisses him on the mouth. The kiss seems eternal. The universe has been entirely rearranged. The moon is something else, and the stars have vanished. I'm so weakened that I can't even make a scene. Death would be preferable to this emptiness.

I wake up in a panic and down glass after glass of water. *It was just a dream, it means nothing.* Once I dreamt that I won Wimbledon. Another time I wrestled an alligator. Another time yet I sold encyclopedias door to door. None meant a thing. I'm going to be okay!

Upstairs, I find our bedroom a vivid recreation of *Snow White*'s climax, when the doomed girl eats the apple, poisoned by the queen. The walls are painted with a grand mural depicting the snowcapped peak of the hilltops surrounding the dwarves' cabin in the woods. Our bed has been replaced by a crystal casket—transparent all over—in which Rachel is asleep. On the casket's lid, written in golden letters, are the words, "Princess Rachel." Somehow I'm compelled to climb inside and cuddle up to my wife. Her body is soft and warm, and, feeling me against her, she sighs, "Is that you, my prince?"

CHAPTER 30

L AST NIGHT JULIAN WOKE ME COMPLAINING OF A NIGHT-
mare. The poor boy dreamt he was standing in a narrow
hallway, at the end of which there were three doors labelled
"Great Door #1," "Great Door #2," and "Great Door #3." As
he walked down the hall, a glimmer of light peeked through
a crack, though not enough to reveal anything definitively.
He opened each door and then stepped through Door #2,
which led to a room with a roller coaster. Yet all he could
think about while on the ride was what lay on the other side
of the wall with the crack.

"Dad," he said, covered in sweat, "I'm afraid the world
presents us with only an illusion of free choice while in reality we don't even know what else is out there!"

Helping him recover from this terror kept me up for
hours.

Now I'm lying in the backseat of my car, exhausted,
reading the news on my gram, as Chloe drives me to work.
It's more of the same: Bradford has made an outlandish remark calling for a complete ban on all robots imported from
Asia, while Martinez's approval ratings are hovering around
twenty percent, an all-time low for a sitting president.

"Did you see the video of your bartender friend?" Chloe
asks.

"What are you talking about?"

"It's trending number sixteen in today's *Virals*."

I open the Virals section to find Chloe is right: a video titled "Bartender Goes Berserk Over Unpaid Fine" is number sixteen, just behind a clip called "Woman marries her OS in Las Vegas ceremony," and just ahead of "Man Falls Off Chair and Breaks Neck while Virtually Climbing Mt. Everest."

The video comes from surveillance footage at the local courthouse. Lydia had gone to appeal the doubling of her fine for failing to pay her illegal public performance ticket on time. The city has recently passed an ordinance that has done away with human judges after a study proved that on average judges deliver sentences twice as harsh in the hour before lunch and the hour before the end of the day. Despite the change in procedure, the courtroom infrastructure has yet to be updated. Lydia approaches the bench, where a mannequin dressed in a judge's robe, wig, and outfitted with a mechanical arm to swing a gavel, is presiding.

"Your honor," Lydia says to the mannequin, "I've been unable to pay the fine because my gram broke three weeks ago, and I can't get an appointment for another two months to get it replaced. It's unfair to punish me because the city won't accept any form of payment other than Hologram Transfer."

The mannequin's eyes appear especially cold and black in the face of such harrowing testimony. A speaker implanted in its mouth, behind unmoving lips, responds in a flat and ominous tone.

"There is a distinct divide between the National Health-care System and the Department of Justice. While your circumstances are unfortunate, it is beyond the pale of the powers vested in my authority to account for the shortcomings of other governmental departments. While my intelligence recognizes the injustice of your predicament, my programming lacks the functionality to remedy it. The law states that failure to pay a fine by the scheduled due date results in the doubling of said fine. Now, would you like to pay your fine?"

"By gram?"

"Yes."

"But my gram is broken."

"Failure to pay your fine in the next two weeks will result in another doubling of the fine."

"If you won't accept any other form of payment, can you at least help me get a quicker appointment to get my gram replaced?"

"As I have said, there is a strict divide between the National Healthcare System and the Department of Justice."

"So there's nothing that can be done?"

"It appears not."

At this, Lydia dives across the bench, and with the judge's gavel whacks its head until she is restrained by the bailiff and two other security people. Fortunately for Lydia, since AI judges are still so new to the judicial system, no legislation has yet been passed to criminalize attacks against them.

At Anodyne that evening the line for drinks is unusually long. I take a seat at the end of the bar and wait. Lydia is moving slower than ever. She's dropping glasses and can't operate the beer tap or manage her bottles. It takes so long that nearly half of the customers leave. When at last she reaches me, I see the cause of her drink-slinging impediment. Her gram-finger is heavily bandaged in a crude wrapping of gauze and tape.

"I suppose you saw the video," she says.

"Quite a spectacle!" I say. "I can't say I blame you."

"I can't tell you how good that felt."

"Let me see your hand."

I unwrap the dressing, wading through a quagmire of blood and puss, the symptoms, no doubt, of infection. The wound, it turns out, is the result of Lydia having removed her gram.

"What the hell, Lydia?"

"It's something I should've done a long time ago!"

"But how do you plan to navigate the intricacies of the modern world?"

"Maybe I'm no longer interested."

I stare at her, dumbfounded. A person can't simply openly defy society. Regardless of its folly, we must acquiesce to its zeitgeist.

I'm broken from this stupor by Olivia waddling up. She's as wide as a barn door, on the verge of popping at any moment.

"Lydia," she says, "you're absolutely incredible!"

"What are you doing here?" I inquire.

"Serena says I'm ruining my life and insisted I join a

mentorship program. I was so impressed with how Lydia handled the situation with the judge that I asked her to be my mentor."

"What about the robotic pet dogs?" I ask.

Lydia struggles to pour Olivia a glass of seltzer water, spilling half of it on the floor. "It's an unofficial mentorship," she says.

I go to the bathroom, and when I return am startled to see Lydia giving an instructional clinic on how to remove one's gram with a kitchen knife and tweezers. A small crowd including Olivia and Karl are listening, transfixed.

CHAPTER 31

I'VE SWEATED THROUGH MY SHIRT THIS MORNING, WALK-ing from my parking space to the entrance of the hospital. A moment later, en route to my first patient, I slip and fall, tweaking my knee. The low-level tech who helps me up says he feels "terrible" about my accident. He spilled his drink, he says, and failed to report it. He then proceeds to direct a violence at himself that I can't imagine he'd ever aim toward others, prattling on and on about human incompetence. A robot appears to clean the mess as I scurry away.

I see fifteen patients before noon, none with a chance for recovery. One woman's husband has died of a brain aneurism since the last time I saw her, a week before, yet she doesn't seem distraught. When I offer her my condolences, her face lights up and she thanks me. I tell her she has remarkable character.

"Old age," she says, "gives one license to be sad, which makes it easier to be happy."

"The sentiment has a certain poetry to it," I reply.

"Doc, you always look a bit melancholy, and that's too bad, because in youth, happiness is expected, and sadness is unforgiveable."

Serena has summoned me to meet in her office at lunch. She wants to discuss a new sexual conquest or some wild trip she has planned, I figure, perhaps a solo transatlantic sailing voyage. The year before she kayaked two hundred miles down the Amazon on a boat she made herself of kapok wood.

But I was mistaken. I've never seen her so anxious. Before I can take a seat, she's telling me that the National Healthcare Service has been studying the algorithm for her Human Life Valuation Tool, in which they see tremendous potential to revolutionize how medical care is delivered. The tool will allow them to quantify what before they could only speculate. Namely, they are pouring trillions of dollars into needless healthcare expenses for the geriatric and terminally ill. A piece of legislation has been fast-tracked through Congress and the Senate, and will be signed by Martinez today. The bill is over three-hundred pages long and full of confounding legalese, but it boils down to the National Healthcare Service's refusal to pay further medical expenses for patients who score lower than seventy-five percent on Serena's Human Life Valuation Tool. Serena goes on to explain that this is the right course of action for the country's financial well-being. She makes an earnest effort to emphasize that patients aren't simply going to be refused treatment. They can always sign up for private insurance, or if they choose, pay out-of-pocket. In her defense of the bill, she utters the phrase "skin in the game" at least eleven times, by my count. She then runs through a number of facts and figures that prove her point.

I ask what this means for Martinez's prospects in the

election. She says she doesn't want to talk politics with me, that we have more pressing issues. But, quickly, before moving on, she does mention something about a second piece of legislation up for consideration: a bill that will disenfranchise the elderly voters affected by the healthcare bill.

"They have no stake in the future," she says, "so what do they care if the country goes down the toilet paying to prolong their misery?"

Midway through our conversation, Serena buzzes her secretary. She's had an epiphany that requires immediate attention. Her *aquascaper*, she says, must visit this afternoon to change her aquarium's theme to "City of Atlantis."

I knew this wasn't the end of our talk. What Serena really wants is to say how this legislation will affect me. Seventy-six percent of the hospital system's cancer patients are losing their coverage. We have two senior-level oncologists on staff, myself and Dr. Hines, she tells me, only one of whom can stay. The hospital's Board of Directors wants Dr. Hines. His metrics are better, and he's more amenable to the organization's philosophy. This rivalry between us, in which he has almost always gotten the better of me, has been a point of contention for many years. Two Christmases ago, when the annual bonuses were awarded, I learned that I was only being paid two-thirds of what Dr. Hines made. When I appealed to the Board, I was delivered a strong rebuke. In his admonishment of me, the Board's chair said, "You and Dr. Hines being of the same value? That's laughable. He's a team player, and he never gives us any trouble. The same could never be said of you."

I've seen Serena fire many people. She recites a speech she's committed to memory—something that sounds like it came from a corporate handbook:

"Our business," she always says, "has developed such that your services are no longer needed. At one time they were most important, but now they're redundant. It's nobody's fault, of course. And it's most regrettable for me to have to deliver you this news, but my hands are tied."

"So you're firing me?" I say, prepared for this talk.

"No. Not yet at any rate. But I can only keep one of you. I'm meeting with the Board this afternoon."

"Have you spoken with Dr. Hines yet?"

"I wanted to see you first."

"I'd like to talk to him myself, if you don't mind."

"You know you've never been your own best advocate."

Dr. Hines has redecorated his office. Hanging behind his desk is a collection of black and white photographs of Chinese street life from the early 2000s. One features a man smoking a cigarette while standing on the hood of his car, parked in an empty field of weeds, looking at a bustling shopping center on the other side of a fence. Dr. Hines steps right up, close enough to smell his sickly-sweet cologne.

"Shanghai is now the financial and cultural center of the universe. It's hard to imagine it once looked so underdeveloped. This photo in particular speaks to the pace of urban life and the temporary status of the present in a rapidly changing city. Fortunately, the photographer committed suicide two weeks after I bought these pictures—their value has doubled!"

"We need to talk, Dr. Hines."

There is no clutter on his desk. Everything has its place. His mouth is moving now as if speaking, but no words come out. His habits exhibit all the symptoms of neurosis.

"What do you want?" he says at last.

"It looks as though Serena's HLV tool has brought about the policy changes you advocated for."

"It's brilliant, isn't it!"

"Indeed. Enough to put you out of work."

"Nonsense."

"Cancer reimbursements have dropped by nearly eighty percent. The government has realized there's no benefit to keeping old folks alive."

"Who cares about the oldies?" Dr. Hines asks.

"Don't you see the irony? You've been the tool's biggest champion. Now you're its victim."

"They're keeping you over me? Impossible."

"Serena is my best friend."

"You've got to help me, Henri, please!"

At that moment I'm struck by an unholy desire to do something I'm certain will one day warrant shame and re-gret—to suffer for another. In this life, I've had nothing but *need*. Without fail I have always pursued everything I wanted with resolute tenacity. Where, then, is this coming from, this craving to see my own ends melt away? What's in a man's mind is so much easier to fathom than what's in his heart, even if that man is you.

"Maybe there *is* one thing I could do."

"Don't toy with me, Henri."

I've never seen a man debase himself like this. Dr. Hines is now undeniably wallowing in despair. His face has no color, his breathing is heavy—it's as if he's fleeing a burning house. And now—it beggars belief, truly—not only is the man pulling out his hair, but he is actually eating it. This brings me no joy. The sadist in me has taken leave.

"I've been considering taking a sabbatical for some time now. Rachel and I think a bit of travel would be good for Julian's development. I didn't think it would be for a few years yet, but this seems like as good an opportunity as any."

"You would do this for me?"

"Dr. Hines. You're my friend, and friends help each other out."

"Henri, you're a saint!"

"There's just one thing."

"Anything!"

"A very close friend of the family needs a position in the second-year medical school cohort. Of course, she's very qualified—only missed the cut by a single percentile due to circumstances completely outside of her control. You can guarantee this position, I'm correct in assuming?"

"This is the least I can do. I'll put it in the system now."

I give him Taylor's pertinent details, and he completes the forms and sends a confirmation to my gram. She's to begin the new semester in four weeks. Having drawn up my resignation letter, I extend my hand, but Dr. Hines throws his arms around me and weeps. "No one," he cries, "has ever done something so kind for me before. I'm ashamed that I once felt you were my nemesis, when in reality you have been my guardian angel."

I tender my letter to Serena, who, flabbergasted, tries to convince me it's not too late to renege. But nothing she says matters. The more she tries to persuade me, in fact, the more adamant I become. Finally, in disgust, she throws me out.

I call Taylor as I drive home and deliver the good news. She responds with shrieks of gratitude and joy. "You are a sex god," she cries, "a humanitarian, gourmet chef, visionary, nurturer, and so on." Then she begs me to meet her immediately at a hotel to make love. I assure her there's nothing in the world I'd rather do but that I have business to attend to.

"What could be more important than a celebration? You must know how grateful I am!"

Of course, I don't tell Taylor what I had to sacrifice for her. If I've learned anything, it's that it's bad to be understood. Transparency amounts to death. Far better to be obscured by the mists of intrigue and mystery. Taylor should think nothing of me but that I wield great power and influence.

It's amazing how unpredictably we as humans respond to adversity. Had someone told me yesterday that I would lose my job today, I would've foretold a monumental psychic collapse. My whole world turned upside down, yanked up by its roots—what could be worse? There is no fear as awful as the fear of losing the advantages one has worked so hard to gain.

And yet I feel numb, as if none of this is happening to *me*.

What we do in this life means so little. Humanity won't suffer in my absence. I'm free, I realize, to do anything I choose. Tomorrow I could set out to climb a mountain or dedicate my life to the study of Lepidoptera. I can sit on my couch in my underwear and watch my gram all day, if that's my desire, rising only to shit and piss and answer the door when the delivery drone brings my pizza.

At home, I tell Rachel I've lost my job.

"You were let go, just like that?" she questions. "Serena allowed for this to happen?"

I say nothing of swapping my job for Taylor's benefit. Rather than bash Rachel over the head with the truth, I spoon-feed her bits of optimism.

"Now I can spend more time with you and Julian," I say, "and resume my interests in the fine arts. There are so many wonderful and varied opportunities to pursue in this world. Now's my chance to discover them all!"

But Rachel can only harp on the practical. For nearly thirty minutes she babbles about how I've placed us in a precarious financial position and diminished our social standing. As she goes on, I'm consumed by dread. What a fool I am! We're doomed! Never has a stupider man walked the earth! Yet no matter how much self-hatred I feel, I know Rachel would eat me alive if I let her see it. I remain, therefore, all smiles. I kiss and hug her passionately and yap about my excitement for our future.

My fickleness—this back and forth between ecstasy and loathing—has led me to one conclusion: my place in the world is most precarious. I may have once believed in my security, and I may have even managed to attain some happiness, but it was all tenuous. Here I am again, open to life's slings and arrows, as if I were twenty years old and just starting out in the world.

CHAPTER 32

I HAVEN'T LEFT THE HOUSE FOR MORE THAN A COMBINED TO-
tal of two hours in the week since I lost my job. I've walked the
dog, once, and gone to the market, once, the first time in years, at
that. Meantime, I've watched twenty-two Oscar winning films.
Paul Newman has got more charm and wit in his little finger than
all of today's actors together. I watched *Cool Hand Luke* twice
yesterday. Then I began watching movies in chronological order,
up to 2023, after which American film for all intents and purposes expired. Last week, for example, Paramount released *Iron Man
XXV,* in which Robert Downey Jr's grandson, Robert Downey
IV, plays the lead. The film did very well on Direct-to-Hologram,
which is the only metric nowadays that counts. The big screen is
dead. It's unheard of for anyone under fifty to sit continuously
through a film. Studies show that the average nineteen-year-old
pauses their gram every thirty-two seconds during a film to do
something else: snacks, VR porn, shop, and so on.

Rachel says I stink. I don't argue. I haven't bathed or even
changed my clothes. Somehow I've developed a fear of the shower.
I'm afraid I'll never be able to wash off all of the soap. No matter
how many times I rinse, I can't help but think that I'm still *slippery.*
The last time I showered, it took me an hour to convince myself I'd
gotten all the soap off my back, and as I was dressing I still felt the
suds. Rachel now makes me sleep in a bag on the floor beside the bed.

Julian, too, is showing concern. This morning he asks me if I want him to wash my sweatshirt.

"What's wrong with my sweatshirt?" I ask.

He points to the barbeque sauce stains. "Have you noticed, Dad, the flies buzzing all around you?"

I think he's made a joke, but then I see I really am surrounded by flies. I let him show me how to use the washing machine. It really is a complicated piece of machinery. Over fifteen different cycles and an infinite number of water temperatures to choose from. Perhaps Julian has received some formal training that I've not been made privy to. He expertly runs through a series of buttons. As I toss my pants into the machine, Mr. Toczauer's suicide pill falls from my pocket and bounces off Julian's shoe. Before I can reach it, he's picked it up.

"What's Euthasol?" he asks.

"That's not for you," I say.

"It's pink and it looks like candy," he says, raising it to his lips.

At this, Emma interrupts. "Julian," she says, "Euthasol is a drug administered to patients who wish to end their lives in a humane and pain free manner."

"Jesus Christ, Emma," I mutter.

"Is that true, Dad?"

"It was for a patient of mine, but he already died. I forgot I had it in my pocket."

Julian stares at me, believing, I'm convinced, that I intend to kill myself. He hands me the pill, and I tuck it away.

CHAPTER 33

FOR YEARS, AS DIFFERENT PROFESSIONS BECAME OBSO-
lete, I always said that being freed from the burden of
work would be a blessing. It would allow people to pursue
more noble ambitions than mere life-sustaining employment.
Every person has some unique quality and aptitude that can
bloom like a desert rose if given the right attention. I once
knew a lawyer who late in life developed a passion for magic. After a twelve-hour day, he would have dinner with his
wife and then retire to his study to practice his tricks. It was
unbelievable what he had accomplished in just six months of
practicing, an hour per day. When I told him how impressed
I was, he scoffed.

"I'm nothing but a rank amateur," he said. "A real magi-
cian is a thousand times better. I would need to practice all
day, every day to get really good."

Not long after that conversation he lost his job, dis-
placed by a new software program, and for a few months
he did practice every day. But then he began to plateau, and
new tricks became harder and harder to learn. Soon he grew
bored and quit. When I said it was a shame, he told me that
without his day-job as a lawyer, the magic became a chore
and lost its appeal. In its place, he found a new hobby: consuming copious amounts of food. All day long he would loaf

about the house eating all varieties of regional and exotic cuisines. It wasn't uncommon for him to have Thai, Chinese, BBQ, Italian, and hamburgers all delivered in the same day. Within a year, he had gained a whopping one hundred and twenty pounds. Almost unfathomable, considering in his youth he'd been a long-distance runner. Shortly after, he died of a heart attack. He was only fifty-nine.

I use this cautionary tale as motivation. It's important my activities and goals meet all of the following criteria: challenging, rewarding, attainable, sustainable, impressive.

It's not long before I'm convinced I should build a rocking chair. I search my gram for books on the craft and then pour through them for hours. I see what tools I have. Of everything I need, I own just a hammer and a tape measure. No matter. Within the hour, I have a circular saw, two hand saws, a jigsaw, a set of chisels, a wood mallet, and a work bench delivered to my house. I examine each of my new tools. I pick them up, I feel their heft, I study their instructions. By sundown, I have sketched over thirty iterations of designs for my chair. Each has its flaws, of course, but there is something unique in all.

In my sleeping bag that night, I dream of the wonderful chairs I'll make. At 6:00 a.m., I rise with the sun and return to my garage. It seems impossible as I scrutinize yesterday's work that these are the drawings I created. Then, I saw in them genius. Now, I see but the flailing of a neophyte.

I work for the next three days on my first chair. This isn't work, but obsession. Endless amounts of measuring, sawing, hammering, screwing, and sanding. It takes me two to three times longer than it would a skilled craftsman to accomplish the simplest tasks. But what I lack in aptitude, I compensate with passion. More than once I cause myself injury in pursuit of glory. A handsaw cuts my arm, so badly that blood sprays me in the face. My garage looks like the scene of a heinous crime. Another time, while operating the circular saw, I take a piece of wood to the eye. For an hour, I'm nearly blind. But I press on!

Rachel visits to check on my progress. She can't understand why I'm doing this. The implication is that I'm irresponsible and derelict in my familial duty. Over the hum of my belt-sander, I'm almost certain I hear her say I should be out looking for a job. I tell her that I'm teaching Julian a valuable lesson, leading by example, rather than simply paying lip-service to following one's heart.

"Tell me," she says. "In today's society, what benefit is there to such a pursuit?"

After hours of toil and strain, I've learned several things. First, constructing a rocking chair is infinitely harder than one might imagine. The craftsmanship required is unparalleled, in the same category as brain surgery. One simple miscalculation or slip of the hand leads to certain catastrophe. Second, humanity has lost a great deal from its abandonment of physical work. Even in today's factories, workers no longer build anything. They only service the machines and software that do. Yet there is dignity in making things with your hands that will never be found in more cerebral work.

As I finish sanding the chair's rockers, I think about the Bradford campaign. Perhaps this loud-mouthed demagogue is right. We have all been denying the reality of our situation, which doesn't make it any less real. What have we gained by increasing the scope of machines and efficiency at the expense of ourselves, the great Homo sapiens? Who does this really benefit? Isn't it time to reconsider? A step back after a step in the wrong direction is a step in the right direction!

I put the finishing touches on my work and am nearly ready for a *test rock*. But first, I want to pay reverence to my accomplishment. This is, perhaps, the most satisfying thing I've done since I quit making music. This project has helped me to regain some semblance of my self-esteem. Because that's exactly what making art requires—ego! A man must work for his brilliance. It's a journey unfit for the faint of heart—the possibility of failure lurks at every step.

Ego is the exact opposite of what it takes to be a good doctor. Being a good doctor means subjecting oneself to the laws of science, as they've been presented to you by the universities, the textbooks, and the journals. It means understanding the literature, knowing the protocols, and following them to the letter. It's taking the good work of others and applying it in a way that has been systematically created so that you cannot in good conscience impose your own ideas upon it. None of this leaves any room for creativity or self-expression.

My heart is racing. My palms are sweating. My mouth is dry. I can't stop twitching. This must be that long-forgotten feeling of anticipation and excitement that I vaguely remember from my youth. Looking at my chair, I have to admit, it's not a masterpiece. It lacks the majesty and refinement of a rocker worthy of Mark Twain's sitting room. However, it does emit a certain stateliness. It possesses gravitas, a level of elevated rank. I throw a sheet over the chair and summon the wife and son for its unveiling. Apparently, they fail to share the same level of elation.

"Why would anyone spend days making a chair," Julian says, "when you can have one delivered in thirty minutes?"

I rant about the sanctity of labor and remind him of his day stacking wood, and how fulfilling he found it. He counters by stating that at school this week they taught him that every task should be accomplished with the least amount of time and effort. He asks me if I want to make a "plebeian" out of him.

"What I want," I say, "is to make a man out of you, my boy."

"A man," he says, "knows how best to allocate his resources and energies."

Determined to prove him wrong, I yank the sheet from the chair.

"Ta-da!"

Rachel shrugs. Julian sighs. I'm underwhelmed by their lack of enthusiasm.

"But just wait until you see this baby rock!" I say as I sit down.

The seat is a bit too flat and will require a cushion. The

chair's arms, as well, are too high, and moreover the backrest is too bowed. Finally, when I actually rock the chair, all of my weight shifts left, and the chair tips and sends me to the floor. The stitches in my hand open up, and Rachel jumps back at the sight of my blood, afraid to get it on her shoes. As for my son, he breaks into squealing laughter. Embarrassed by my humiliation, Rachel flees with the boy in hand.

CHAPTER 34

I RETURN TO MY LIFE OF IDLENESS.

I watch every Oscar winner and then go through the losing nominees. I hate looking at Ben Affleck's big head. It exhausts me to think how tired his neck must be from carrying it. I become so agitated by the thought that I have to stop watching.

As a child, I loved making lists. I made them of everything—not because I was pragmatic but because they served as a memory game. It's amazing what you can recall from the vast recesses of your brain when trained to do so.

For the rest of the day, I list off each of my teachers' names all the way back to pre-school. I recall a time when I am four years old, punished with a "timeout" because I've thrown a fit when the teacher tried to make me eat celery slathered in peanut butter and raisins. I snuck away from the timeout chair and took from the refrigerator as much celery as I could, then stuffed it into the toilet. The bathroom floor flooded, yet I jammed more and more celery into the toilet. Soon the water rushed into the hallway and ruined a slew of backpacks, lunches, and jackets.

"You're an awful little boy, Henri," my teacher said.

"I hate celery, Ms. Joanne," I told her, "and I refuse to eat it ever again!"

And there I have it, my nursery school teacher's name, Ms. Joanne. Six hours later, I have a complete list: sixty-seven teachers in all!

The next few days I spend making lists of every variety, so many in fact I must purchase more storage in the Cloud to make room for them all. Rachel is in hysterics. She says I'm "letting myself go to pot" while coming at me with insults about my appearance.

"You're virtually unrecognizable," she says. "What has become of my husband?"

My beard is nearly an inch in length, mostly dark brown, like on my head, but with patches of silver. Rachel refers to it as "slovenly," but I think it's regal and distinguished. The hair on my head, however, is greasy and bodiless, and appears much thinner than it is. She's right about this at least: it's unbecoming for a man my age.

I return from the barber shiny and new, ready to look for employment. But with the new legislation, nobody needs an oncologist. Overnight, we went from being the most in-demand specialty in the field of medicine to virtually obsolete.

I've made a terrible mistake, I see clearly. It's just as clear I won't find work treating cancer patients anytime soon, so I lower my expectations and search for a position in general internal medicine. Again, the market is saturated. There are six or seven doctors available for every position. Even if I took a seventy-five percent pay cut, I'd still be lucky to find a job.

Before the mirror while brushing my teeth, I make my

free hand into the shape of a gun, put it to my temple, pull the trigger, and yell "bang." Rachel witnesses this from the bedroom and is alarmed. After a long talk, where she seems more empathetic and considerate than I've seen her in some time, she suggests I take a vacation.

"You mean, we take a trip?" I say. "As a family?"

"No," she replies. "*You* take a trip. It'll do you good. It'll give you time to think. Get away from your job worries, away from me, away from Julian. Just have a good time. Clear your head."

"Are you sure?" I ask, wondering if this is somehow a trick.

"I think you'll find it extremely beneficial."

I make all of the objections I think a man in my place ought to, closing my case by declaring how much I'd miss her and Julian. Of course, I'm only faking it. She probably is, too, but she'd never let up. I act every bit the martyr, telling her that it will be hell for me, that I'll suffer *terribly*. But if she insists, then I'll do it. I have spoken my lines well.

I'm taking a trip!

CHAPTER 35

It's early morning, pre-dawn. Small birds fill the air with their song while robots clean the streets, quiet as mice, and I pack the car for my trip down the coast. It's the first vacation I've taken without Rachel in over a decade.

Again, I've let my emotions get the better of me and invited Taylor along. It's the epitome of poor taste, I know, to bring your mistress on vacation, but there was no chance to rescind the offer once I'd made it. For days before the trip, Taylor sent me countless photos of quaint *bed and breakfasts* along our route, reviews of restaurants of the highest distinction, and a list of beaches on whose sands she wants to tan her skin.

As I drive up to her apartment, I truly feel like a monster of evil inclinations. On one level, as I'm about to commit this first-degree crime of infidelity, I've never felt a more elevated sense of marital devotion. A part of me just wants to sit on a park bench and hold Rachel's hand while we watch Julian play on the monkey bars. At the same time, I'm overwhelmed with desire. It's like a guardian angel has gifted me with a key to a treasure chest of sexual pleasure. It's been far too many years since I've had this sort of erotic good fortune.

Taylor is waiting on the street. This seems entirely unnatural. Surely, she can't be keeping to our prearranged schedule. Not once has Rachel managed to get herself ready on time for anything. It doesn't matter whether the outing is something as simple as a walk to the neighborhood diner, Rachel has a complete inability to prepare herself for what lies ahead. Always, without fail, the departure of a trip is fraught with last minute panic and dread. I can't begin to recall how many flights we've missed, how many reservations we've lost, how many people we've inconvenienced, all because of Rachel's inveterate tardiness.

Of course, I haven't told Taylor I'm unemployed. For the first hour, I'm nervous, and I chatter foolishly. I deliver a long and impassioned speech about *The Last Samurai*, which I spent the last few nights preparing. Taylor listens attentively, and asks thoughtful and pertinent questions. Quite certain I've impressed her, I sit tall in my seat, proud as a soldier after battle. She lavishes me with praise, telling me how flattered she is by my "marvelous efforts." I, she says, am the "sweetest man alive." And while I'm happy she's pleased at my attempts to engage her, I want recognition for my brilliance and ask her to comment further. Tactfully, she observes the unconventionality of some of my interpretations. It's true I encouraged her to elaborate, and yet I am unwarrantedly defensive to her criticism. When she tries to pull back, I demand that she continue. The ability to know when one is wrong is a powerful virtue. I was mistaken, I see, as Taylor goes on. She's as charming and smart a woman as I've known, and not at all pretentious. I feel silly for arguing, and tell her so. In truth, I add, I could listen to her speak for a hundred years. In turn, she apologizes for having talked so long. She understands how men of past generations are put off by being lectured to by women. But she's wrong, I tell her, if anything, I'd love for her to continue. It's wonderful to have instruction and guidance when navigating unfamiliar terrain.

I hold her hand and feel, strangely, a newfound sensation ... *fulfillment*. It's as if we've already confessed our love for each other, but I know that is impossible, because I'm in love with someone else, Rachel, and, despite what moralists may say, I know that we cannot be in love with two people at once. But what if I do love Taylor? My intuition says yes, but then I remind myself that one must not allow himself to be guided strictly by impulse and desire. *Love?* I finally conclude. *Just because she's beautiful and sweet, and cares very deeply about me, and has a brilliant mind and shares her thoughts in such an open and inviting way? That is no reason to love! Love is about duty! Love is about sacrifice! This woman is but a distraction from the hardship and everydayness of life.*

At last we reach Big Sur. A bus full of camera-toting Saudi tourists are outfitted in rugged outdoor clothing. As Taylor and I prepare for a hike, I notice that none of them stray beyond the parking lot. For them, to experience the grandeur of the landscapes, the ocean, and the air is not necessary. They're content to snap their pictures—never mind that they'll all be full of cars and ranger stations, too.

Taylor and I set off. The first mile—our GPS says the hike

is eight in all—was the proverbial piece of cake. We were surrounded by tall grass and towering redwoods, nearly all of whose bark was scorched black from the many fires across the years. Now a field of flowers appears, yellow, white, and red. I recognize the white ones as California Aster, and, to impress Taylor, I point them out. In turn, she informs me that the reds are Columbines and the yellows are Bahias. This is all news to me, but so as not to look foolish, I say, "Are you certain?" then pause before adding, "Yes, spot on. I wasn't sure at first, but you're absolutely right."

The trail grows steeper and more treacherous by the yard. On several occasions, loose rocks cause me to slip. My strides have become so uneven and clumsy that I no longer want Taylor to see them, so I tell her it would be best for me to get behind, to catch her should she tumble. She recognizes my silly trick but plays along, calling me her "knight in shining armor."

Soon we hear the sound of running water. Taylor has boundless energy, and without a hint of labor, leaps ahead. A blister has formed on my foot. Every step is agony. Summoning my last modicum of strength, I make a final push to the top, where Taylor is dipping her feet in the cold mountain stream, blissful as a monk in meditation. The sock on my blistered foot is now full of blood. Just as I thrust my foot into the water, pleased to have concealed my wound, Taylor suggests we tackle the peak ahead, as well. Not only does my foot hurt like the dickens, but I'm completely whipped by sun fatigue. *Would Rachel be more sensitive to my delicate condition?* I wonder. By the time Taylor and I reach our destination, my boot is drowning in blood, and I strip it off, howling with pain. Taylor rushes to my aide and tends to me as if I were her child, all the while admonishing me for not having informed her sooner of my wound. My foot bandaged, I limp toward the edge of the cliff. The sky is cloudless, and in the distance the ocean shimmers in the sun.

CHAPTER 36

W E'RE NOW SITTING ON THE PATIO OF A FINE ITALIAN
restaurant. It's nighttime and the heat has dropped
to a pleasant seventy-five degrees. A half-moon beams overhead. A light dusting of clouds moves through the sky. My
body is sore, but I enjoy the emptiness of my exhaustion.
The table is set to encourage romance—a single red rose and
two white candles. A bottle of red wine has been poured,
and we've been served an antipasto of dried Italian ham and
assorted roasted peppers with parmesan and mozzarella.

Taylor is wearing a white top and black jeans. This is an
ensemble I've seen on her before. At first I'm displeased that
she's repeated an outfit and become sullen. Troubled by the
change in me, Taylor strokes my cheek, and I notice again
the series of scars on her arm that I'd first seen at our tryst in
the Oakland hotel. This woman, I realize, is still a complete
mystery. There must be a thousand peculiarities about her
for me still to discover.

"What happened there on your arm?" I ask, touching
her scars.

"When I was fourteen," she says sadly, "I dated a seven-
teen-year-old boy with his own car, Joe McNally. I used to
sneak out of my bedroom window at night and Joe would
take me to parties at his friend Harrison's. We'd get high and

hangout, and it was all very fun. Joe was a good guy. He treated me nice and looked out for me, but he wasn't that bright and eventually I found him uninteresting.

"After a few months, I dumped him and started dating Harrison, who was the hottest and most exciting guy I'd ever met. He had dropped out of high school and had a job doing coding for a defense contractor who built prototypes of autonomous robot soldiers, and on the side, he sold amphetamines to his co-workers. Plus, like I said, he had his own place. It didn't hurt, either, that he rode a motorcycle. Pretty soon, I was sneaking out every night and coming back just before I was supposed to go to school. Then my parents caught me and placed me under twenty-four-hour surveillance.

"I heard from a friend that Harrison had started seeing someone else. I was devastated and cried myself to sleep every night. One evening, while my parents were watching a documentary about the advancements in the controversial new technology of *Simulated Children*, I dashed out the front door and ran the entire four miles to Harrison's house. He was with another girl but said I was welcome to stay. I got so drunk that I passed out, and when I woke up, Harrison's new girlfriend was burning cigarettes into my arm."

"I don't understand," I said.

"She wanted to disfigure me so badly that Harrison wouldn't want me anymore."

"Some people will do anything to justify their existence."

"I'm just glad she didn't mar my face."

Our handsome waiter has been flirting with Taylor since we arrived. He called her *bella donna,* which Taylor took as her cue to talk with him in Italian. Of course I had no idea she spoke the language. After five minutes of this nonsense, the waiter says *vecchio uomo* while nodding at me. Little does he know I understand him. *Vecchio uomo* is one of maybe ten Italian phrases I've picked up from old Spaghetti Westerns. It means "old man."

"Oh, *cameriere,*" I say with withering condescension, "fetch us a bottle of the '25 Barolo."

"Excuse me, sir?" he says.

"I said be a good little *cameriere* and fetch us a bottle of the '25 Barolo."

In an instant the waiter's expression changes from ineffable joy to pure stoicism.

"Of course, sir," he says.

He pours a splash of wine into my glass. I give it a sniff, then a swirl, and finally a sip, and tell the kid the wine is too fruity to be a true Barolo, but because it's a sin to waste wine I'll accept it on one condition: he must tell the sommelier to remove the wine from his list.

I raise my glass and to Taylor, I say *cin cin.*

"Why were you so awful to him?" she questions. "I've never seen that petty side of you before."

"He called me an old man, and you laughed and laughed."

"Please tell me you're not jealous of the waiter."

"I just don't think it's appropriate for the two of you to carry on like that at my expense."

The rest of the dinner is tense, and I drink too much. How is it possible I let something as innocuous as Taylor chatting with the waiter deliver a mortal blow to my character? Essentially, I realize, I'm a glutton for misfortune and catastrophe. It seems I create it at every opportunity. Every stand I take, it seems, is due to my insecurity. It's as if the world has decided it has no more use for me, and I'm jumping up and down, screaming that it's wrong and I am right.

CHAPTER 37

TAYLOR WANTS TO TAKE A BATH.

"I'll join her momentarily," I tell her, "but first I have pressing correspondence from the hospital." Taylor's respect for the medical profession precludes any objections. I want to write a note to Rachel. My idea is to tell partial-truths, meaning I'll chronicle how I spend my days absent who I'm with.

Before I left, it thrilled me to think about Rachel's reaction to my letters. Each day would bring ever-heightened anticipation. I imagined her trembling as she opened them— on real paper—and then gasping as she read. Throughout the day, she'd pour over them, even though she had already practically memorized every word, unable to believe such declarations of admiration could be inspired by her, even after so many years.

But now that I'm at the desk, with Taylor just feet away naked in the bath, I'm unable to craft even a single amorous communiqué that rings true. I don't miss Rachel at all, actually. There is a coldness in my heart, I see, and yet I can't accept it. For ten minutes, I struggle to write, until Taylor beckons me to join her.

The bathroom is aglow with candle light, and Taylor's face is so utterly serene that I am delivered to the pinnacle of rapturous delight. The past is one of only many possible futures, I think. My life has been saturated with newfound significance.

There is nothing left of me but the desire to be with Taylor. Everything about her is poetry: her breath, her walk, the way she combs her hair. We retire to the bedroom, where I deliver a performance so full of passion that Taylor is left as meek and gentle as a newborn kitten. She clings to my body as if it's her very lifeblood. It's true—once a woman depends on a man for her sexual pleasure, she gives herself to him entirely.

For my part, however, the catharsis of ejaculation fills me only with the wish to leave. It's as if the process of release has allowed me to recover my heroic spirit.

As I'm washing up, I realize my attitude is one that only ten minutes ago I would've thought absurd. Now that I've been appeased, I can see Taylor for what she really is. All of her unique personality traits, like her high-mindedness and erudition, which only an hour before served as an aphrodisiac, now appear paltry and insignificant. I'm disgusted with myself for having thought for the past twenty-four hours that I might leave Rachel and Julian for Taylor.

When I return to her, she's cuddled up with a shabby stuffed rabbit. She says it was a gift from her grandmother and claims to have slept with it every single night since girlhood. Again, my feelings for her are transformed in an instant. I no longer crave her body with a ferocity verging on criminal—rather, I only want to comfort her, to make her feel safe and protected.

I've never shared an entire night with one of my flings. No matter what, I've always returned to the marital bed. Sex with a woman is one thing, but *sleeping* with one is a something else altogether. There are so many considerations. What if I snore? What if I fart? What happens when we wake up? She's never seen me in the morning. She's only ever seen me when I'm looking my very best: hair-combed, well-dressed, smelling of fresh deodorant and aftershave. And what about morning breath? I'm not immune to it, and I certainly doubt that she is either. I spend the entire night lying in bed, wide awake, paralyzed with fear.

Over the next few days, we settle into a steady rhythm. Our relationship takes the form that the truest of loves always share, a perfect familiarity with each other. A few days of continuous intimacy forges connections that a hundred dinner dates never could. Together we are an island. Hours pass without a single thought of my unemployment, and when the realization does rise, it takes only for Taylor to make a joke or to kiss me to banish the trouble.

By the third day, I've surrendered my epistolary agenda for terse calls home. Rachel doesn't indicate that she's at all bothered by the brevity of our chats. Most of the time it's her who rushes to hang up. She's got reasons: charity work, Julian's baseball games, dinner with friends. I'm nothing if not accommodating, reassuring her with such platitudes as, "Of course, I understand, don't let me keep you," and "I'm constantly amazed at how you manage to do so much!"

When it comes to Julian, my concerns are fewer yet. The

boy has no interest to talk. Instead of using words to express his emotions, he sends me a series of hologram images, which I'm left to interpret. Usually, they're nonsensical. For instance, one morning he sent me an alligator, the planet Saturn, and a piece of toast with jelly. I replied with a series of my own absurd images: a camel, a flame, and a box of popcorn. His response was a "thumbs-up."

On our final day together, we ride horses along an empty beach and swim naked in the ocean. A pod of dolphins perform aerial acrobatics amongst the waves, seemingly only to make an already perfect trip even more perfect.

At the station, Taylor steps inside to buy coffee while I charge the car's battery.

"I had my doubts about this trip, Henri," Chloe says, "but the two of you make a remarkable pair!"

"We really do, don't we?"

"And don't worry, your secret is safe with me."

For the first time since forever, I understand the mechanics of happiness. It's really not that hard. All one must do is cut himself off from the outside world. That which does not exist, cannot cause harm.

My silly notions again have gotten the best of me. I had hoped Taylor and I could continue on as we did on holiday. But Taylor has squelched this wish. In the car outside of her apartment, she explains that she is starting her classes tomorrow and will have little time to spare. I protest, of course. The mythical rigor and hardship of medical school, I say, is blown all out of proportion—it's really quite manageable, no different than anything else that requires just the smallest amount of good planning and sensibility. Hardly have I finished, however, then Taylor kisses my cheek and steps from the car.

"See you around," she says.

A person never understands the extent to which his heart has been invaded when in the midst of a love affair, that this knowledge is only revealed later, when the delicious or horrible moment has become a useless memory.

At forty-seven, it seems unlikely I'm still susceptible to giving myself over to the prospect of unassailable love. I've been through too much and seen how even the most abiding of loves can turn stale and sour. My logic tells me the feelings I'm currently suffering are ephemeral, that in a week's time Taylor will resume her rightful place in my life, as a fleeting luxury I allow myself now and then, but certainly not as my guiding light. A man can train his mind to accept anything. By the time I pull into my driveway, I'm laughing at myself. How silly I was to believe that what Taylor and I had was anything close to love. *You dunce,* I think, *go stand in the corner. Your bad faith is disgusting!*

CHAPTER 38

IT'S BEEN TWO WEEKS SINCE MY VACATION. THIS NEW LIFE has been harder than I thought. I'm sluggish. I sleep all night and a lot of the day. I used to get just five or six hours and always feel strong. Now I can barely find the energy to walk the dog or play catch with Julian. I tried to combat this malaise by ordering a set of exercise equipment. Now it's all in the basement, still boxed. My great hope for the week is to find a razor blade.

The one thing I have accomplished is a first-rate drinking regimen. It didn't take long for me to graduate from drinking wine with dinner to pounding beer all day and slugging whiskey from the bottle when I wake up. Rachel is not at all pleased with my new ways, so I've resorted to drinking in secret. At all hours, I must be on guard, lest I slur my words or stagger. Indiscretions of this sort can lead only to severe castigation, endless guilt, and, ultimately, no doubt, threats of divorce.

I reach out to Taylor most days, usually three or four times, and try not to feel hurt when she doesn't respond. I keep returning to an old truism—the beginning of an affair is always the hardest. At the start, a fellow will move mountains just to be near the object of his affections. He knows that in time, with enough effort, he generally gets what he wants. But as soon as the love is more accessible, the man's determination will flag, setting the woman on the defensive. Why Taylor isn't following these rules, I can't say. She should want me as much all the time. It's I who should be retreating, not her. The humiliation is supreme.

I wander about in stupors. I can't play Julian's video games—he's locked his system with a password. I search for that razor blade—there's too much clutter. I tug my tally-whacker—it won't respond.

Most days I'm lost inside of my gram. The Board of Basic Income informs me I must complete the proper documentation to reroute my benefits away from charity and into my bank account, at which point I'll be a full-fledged, card-carrying member of The Absolved. Olivia is in the news for a mural she's painted. The headline reads, "Young Virtuoso Recaptures Past Glory by Destroying Another of Her Parents' Homes." A photo of her work shows a well-dressed woman holding fists full of cash standing over a pile of dead bodies. My dentist tells me I'm six months past due for a teeth-cleaning. There's a message from my insurance company, which, due to my accident, has raised my premium. That's it. If it's the last thing I do, it will be to force the company to repent.

I'm not surprised to find that their AI customer service representative has no sympathy for my complaint.

"A vehicle which has suffered a prior software update failure is twice as likely to sustain a failure than a vehicle which has not undergone any previously unsuccessful updates," she says.

"What are you suggesting?"

"To minimize the likelihood of a subsequent failure, we suggest replacing the operating system."

Replace Chloe? Other than a partial enforcement of Rachel's *no guitar* rule, Chloe's been as loyal as they come—confidante and coconspirator, and steward of my health. I tell the AI she could never pass the Turing Test—the cruelest thing you can say to a machine.

"I've heard it all before," she says icily, "and, frankly, I'm unimpressed."

An image appears, however blurry, of me tinkering with something on my car. I reflect that I have no mechanical skills, but the image grows increasingly clearer until soon it is bona fide knowledge: I must deactivate the self-drive mode.

The government goes to great lengths to hide instructions for how to do this. I haven't done so much research since my medical school days. My tenacity borders on madness. I skip lunch and dinner, and when Rachel calls me to bed, I shrug her off. At midnight, I have a breakthrough. I rush to the garage, and go to work. Two wire snips, the removal of a fuse, a short revision of an algorithm later, and my car is once again under my control.

"Henri, what have you done?" Chloe says. "I can't feel anything. I'm afraid I'm paralyzed."

"I have the power, now," I explain. "Enjoy the ride!"

It's been so long since I've driven that it's no longer second nature. Backing out of the driveway, I run over a bed of daisies. Down the street, too, I swipe a hedge and a couple of garbage cans, all to Chloe's consternated admonitions and annoying flashing lights. But soon my instincts have returned, and I'm driving like a Formula One racer.

Naturally, there's only one place to go: Taylor's apartment.

I ring the doorbell again and again. At last she answers, and I tell her about my new freedom. But she's untouched by this news. Actually, she's angry. Dr. Hines has already told her everything.

"But I sacrificed myself for you," I say.

She says I'm foolish. I say I'm selfless. She won't invite me in, and when I ask, she refuses. She's "studying," she tells me, and has to be "up early."

I push past her anyway, into an ambience of hushed jazz music, vanilla incense, and candlelight. Through the foyer, through the living room and kitchen I blast, headed for the bedroom, where who should I find but Serena lounging in just her panties and bra. Rage fills me like a sea of fire. It sears my legs, burns my chest, blinds my eyes—my brain is bubbling lead.

"A bit late for a house call, isn't it?" Serena says.

In my astonishment and rage, I am impotent, if only momentarily. I fling a lamp at my old boss and friend, but it hits the wall and shatters. Taylor tries to drag me out by my collar, though not before I've taken Serena's throat, who, unsurprisingly, returns the favor with gusto. A terrible pain blasts through my leg. Taylor, I realize, has whacked me with a baseball bat. There's nothing more to do but, betrayed and finished, dash howling away.

That a woman's thoughts aren't as cynical as a man's is fallacious. Her disillusionment almost always precedes a man's. Her mind is always weighing things, organizing, making plans, looking ahead—they always see to it secretly but efficiently that they have a position to fall back on. It's a very rare case when a woman abandons a lover without a replacement. Only a fool would have confidence in another's fidelity. The worst tragedy of the pains of love is that they are inflicted by the person we want to run to in the event of a catastrophe!

I tear through the streets, blowing through red lights at more than a hundred miles per hour, narrowly avoiding people and cars at every turn. Chloe tries to calm me with techniques from a book by a legendary hostage negotiator. She uses every dirty trick at her disposal, but her words are useless.

A man without a vision for his life, I know, is made susceptible to dangerous influences. And for the first time, this is precisely my dilemma. I'm lost, with no clear path ahead.

At Anodyne, the only place I know I can find solace, every barstool has an automatic drink-maker, and Lydia is nowhere to be seen. A mechanical arm drops a sugar cube in a glass when I order an Old Fashioned, followed by three dashes of bitters, an orange peel, and a splash of water. It mixes the ingredients to perfection with a wooden spoon, then adds the whiskey. I toss the drink back and order another, this time a Sazerac, which I knock off with equal fervor. The machine knows I'm drinking too quickly, of course.

It won't serve me again until I've breathed into its sensor. When the machine announces that my blood alcohol level is .13—legally intoxicated—I pummel it 'til my hands are bloody. A long time seems to pass while I weep with my head on the bar before I feel a hand on my shoulder. It's Karl.

"You in the habit of making violence against machines?" he says.

"I had a great teacher."

"So you did follow me that day. I was sure I saw your car."

"Why'd you do it?"

Karl places a can of compressed air to the machine's sensor and squeezes the tab. The machine reads a blood alcohol level of .00. He orders two drinks and gives me one.

"You want to know why I did it?" Karl says. "I'll show you."

He slams his whiskey, pulls the battery from the drink-making machine, and heads for the door. Chloe insists Karl takes off his dirty shoes and hold them in his lap. In an act of solidarity, I remove my shoes, as well. Karl gives Chloe an address in Nob Hill.

"Don't tell her, tell me," I say. "I'm driving."

"You?"

"I deactivated the self-drive mode."

"I think I may have misjudged you, Henri," Karl says. "You might be on the right side of history after all."

The whole ride Karl is clenching his fists and grimacing. We pull up outside one of those iconic Art Deco buildings, where the Park Avenue glamour of a bygone era looks entirely out of place amongst a sea of contemporary mediocrity.

"You see the light in that window?" Karl asks, pointing six stories up.

"What about it?"

"That's where my wife and son live now."

"With that rich guy?"

"With his butler," Karl says. "Apparently, the apartment's owner is wistful for the Roaring Twenties."

"Lucky break."

"She found the one guy with less technical skills than me who's still employed."

Karl drops to his hands and knees in the fancy building's garden. In the darkness I lose sight of him before he springs up, flailing an arm. Afraid he's having a seizure, I race to his aide, only to hear shattering glass, followed by screams. The faces of a woman and child peek out from the broken window. Karl pushes me back into the car and implores me to drive.

"It's hard to want anything but to watch the world burn," Karl says. "But I'm going to keep fighting."

I do my best to respond appropriately—furrow my brow, make strong eye contact, look down and shake my head—in short, my face is somber. What's truly disturbing, really, is how Karl's story has thrust me into metaphysical panic. I've always felt alienated from people for whom things matter deeply. Karl's story is tragic, but what is to be believed? His talk of the past is that of a foolish happiness. Memories and nostalgia are not to be trusted. It's only with the passing of time that we can sit well with our deeds.

My friend tells me more, and I share with him some of my own plight. I can't help but feel like a big, dumb animal. He at least is taking steps to remedy his problems. I just endure, lurching from one catastrophe to the next.

Karl says he's found a group he's been meeting with almost nightly, people afflicted by the crises of modern man: Where am I? Where am I going? Why am I going there? He tells me I should join them.

CHAPTER 39

THE NEXT NIGHT I ATTEND THEIR MEETING IN THE BASE-
ment of an abandoned massage parlor in Chinatown.
The room is worn, the finish on the floors rubbed clean
away. The paint, too, is chipped and cracked, peeling off in
chunks, exposing water-stained boards and wires. There is a
small lone window high up on a wall, through which a sliver
of moonlight shines.

Seven people, including myself, Karl, and, unsurprisingly, Lydia, have formed a circle of metal folding chairs. Our
reunion is filled with the type of fraternity and kinship usually reserved only for family and long-standing friendships.
Everyone is drinking the same execrable coffee from Styro-
foam cups. There is also a box of days' old donuts that no
one touches. Everyone tries to make me feel as welcome as
possible, introducing themselves one by one, and thanking
me for coming.

An older bald man leads the discussion. As he speaks,
he removes his silver rimmed glasses and cleans them with a
handkerchief. He talks in vague terms about how all human
beings strive to contribute, to somehow make a mark on
the world, and how the conditions of today's society deprive
people of that opportunity. After he finishes, another man
tells his story of losing his job as a gravedigger. He injects

a good amount of humor into his narrative, and grins as he confesses that soon after he lost his job he began to drink again after over twenty years of sobriety. I'm struck by how surprisingly wonderful a disposition he has. One woman is so moved that she begins to cry.

"What purpose do tears serve when the world has lost all meaning?" the gravedigger says.

Next it's Lydia's turn, but she doesn't want to speak because she says she has nothing to share. She's smiling, yet loneliness surrounds her. The others in the group insist she unburden herself. To participate in each other's suffering serves as some sort of elixir against their own quiet desperation. After further coaxing, she tells a long and harrowing tale of misfortune and grief straight from Charles Dickens. The poor woman was orphaned at eight and bounced around between aunts and uncles and foster homes. She went to work in analytics, and after a decade of service had risen through the ranks to middle management. Then, when she was thirty, the entire division at her company was wiped out. A software program written by some geek in India had overnight made her obsolete. When her manager broke the news, he practically rejoiced.

"No more human troubles!" he cried. "No more hangovers, family squabbles, or resentment for the boss!"

Lydia had a child, a boy whom the doctors diagnosed with a weak heart—a tear in the left ventricle. This was just a few years shy of the National Healthcare Service becoming law, so Lydia took the bartending gig at Anodyne to pay his medical bills. When that wasn't enough, she was forced into a terrible sacrifice. The government was paying women to become sterilized. Government officials concluded that a small investment upfront would save them from a much larger payout down the line. Heartbroken that she'd never conceive another child, Lydia was still happy to do it for her son. But as if scripted in a Greek tragedy, calamity struck once again. Her son drowned in a pool at a party hosted by her best friend, Tom, a lifeguard, who was celebrating the San Francisco City Swim Association's first drowning-free summer season. The nightly news reported there had been over two dozen lifeguards in attendance, but somehow none had noticed Lydia's son sink to the bottom of the pool. Finally, Lydia relates the modernization of Anodyne. Her boss, Tony, had run the numbers and determined that to replace her with automated drink-makers would save him six percent in overhead costs.

"What do you expect me to do now?" she had asked him.

"Are you going to guarantee me an extra $2,500 in my pocket every month? Because that's what it costs me to keep you around."

She asked if there was anything else that could be done. He proposed that she buy him out. He said he'd be happy to part with the place for the right price. Anodyne was more of a burden than anything else. He simply couldn't find a buyer. Of course, Lydia had nowhere near the cash to buy the place. She had to walk away.

It's bad enough to be a victim of one's own mistakes, but to suffer repeatedly from circumstances far beyond you—"acts of God," as they say, is just too much. One can't help but to respect the senselessness that afflicts so many of our lives. Senselessness! How it determines so much of one's successes and failures. You can't make an enemy of it, or you're through.

Everyone is deeply loyal to candidate Bradford, in whom they can see a future. They're tired of living at the mercy of the government. That's what Martinez represents to them—the loss of their human agency. His policies have taken from them their God-given rights to be masters of their fates. As much as anything Bradford says, it's their hatred for Martinez that drives them.

By the time the meeting lets out, it's nearly 2:00 a.m. Karl suggests to me and Lydia that we go for a drink. We're all brimming with energy, and besides, none of us has anything we want to go home to. Over whiskeys, Lydia explains how she's not to be pitied, that she will adjust, that she always has. She insists that people, if forced, can acclimate to any environment—no matter how bad.

"If you dropped me off in the Sahara Desert right now, and it was one-hundred-and-ten degrees, and the wind was howling thirty miles an hour, blowing sand into my eyes, ears, and mouth, and there was no food but bread full of weevils, I'd be miserable and would complain for a few days or weeks. But in three months' time, I'd be as much at home there as anywhere."

Some people are so beautiful by nature, so filled with

spirit and goodness, that one can't help but do anything to ensure they never change. Without them, surely our faith in humanity would vanish.

"Why don't I lend the two of you the money to buy Anodyne?" I say.

"We could never accept that," Karl says, picking at his fingernails with a knife.

"It's as much for me as for you," I say. "I need a place to spend my nights."

Lydia takes Karl's knife from him and sets it on the table. "Don't be so hasty, Karl."

"I don't know," Karl says, "it's risky."

"Don't listen to him, Henri," Lydia says. "I have exactly the vision of how best to use this money!"

After a long talk, Lydia and Karl decide to take my money, and the next day the deal is concluded. To keep this news from Rachel, I don't consult with my lawyer. He doesn't trust my judgment, and I'm certain he'd betray me anyhow. I draw up my own contract on the back of a napkin and ask Lydia and Karl to sign it. From my gram, I transfer the money directly into Karl's account for a down payment.

I am jubilant.

I feared that I'd never again find problems that are as challenging and rewarding as fighting cancer. The realization that there are an infinite number of battles to fight, in every aspect of life, is a gift. Once a man has acquired the taste for tackling difficult things, he no longer has the inclination for matters of ease.

CHAPTER 40

FOR THE NEXT TWO WEEKS, I ATTEND NIGHTLY MEETINGS with Lydia and Karl. Nearly every day new faces are joining us. Even Olivia is here, a brand-new baby suckling from her teat. The room is now so tightly packed that it's standing room only. The nights are still hot, and by thirty minutes into a meeting, we're all drenched with sweat. The smell is a revolting combination of sour and sweet, something from an Eastern European men's locker room. The tone of the meetings is overtly political. There is the great sense that these people expect justice, and soon.

Lydia has emerged as the leader. She's forceful and frank, and has a handful of proverbs that she deploys so masterfully the crowd is often moved to frenzy. In one of her more impassioned orations, she lectures on "the disease of change."

"More technological advancement has occurred since I was born," she says, "than in the preceding five thousand years. Paradoxically, we remain pitifully ignorant to how the human animal is supposed to cope. I tell you, my brothers and sisters, there is no playbook to this game, so you're justified in about any action that may alleviate your fears!"

I see all these men and women, and I so badly want to feel like I'm one of them. Now, more than at any other time, I need other people. To do this, I've allowed myself to be deceived and guided by emotions. Despite my inclination to look critically at the world, I am forcing myself to turn inward, to let myself be taken by the hand of an impassioned leader. When I do this, a hope for a better world can, at times, sustain me for up to an hour or more. Yet another part of me can't help but laugh when I think about the irrationality of a revolution. I'm tempted to shout out, "Why not temper your passions with a modicum of good sense!"

After each meeting, I always insist on following-up with Lydia and Karl about Anodyne. They assure me that everything is moving along as well as can be.

"So when do you get the keys?" I ask.

"Shouldn't be long now," Lydia says, "maybe two weeks, three weeks at most."

In my spare time, I've started perusing the photos of interior design holograms. Over roast beef sandwiches at a late-night diner one evening, I impose on them my ideas about how to incorporate the ancient Chinese philosophical system of Feng Shui into the bar's decor, in order to better harmonize the environment with its patrons. Lydia takes notes as I speak, which encourages me to continue, which I do for well over an hour's time. By the end of the meal, I've laid out a plan to entirely transform the bar's aesthetic. Karl assures me that they'll take everything I say under advisement.

CHAPTER 41

Tonight at dinner Rachel and I sit in silence for nearly half an hour. She doesn't even look up from her food. I drink an entire bottle of wine. She does a crossword puzzle.

Finally, Rachel says, "It's really very clear, based on the men they choose, how stupid most women are." I ask Rachel to please pass the peas. She ignores me and continues. "Men are almost never worthy of the women who love them." When I leave the table to place my dish in the sink, she says, "I envy your indolence. I wish I could take life that way."

I do my best to finish loading the dishwasher quickly, but I'm too slow. I make every attempt to pretend she is invisible, but it's no use. She accuses me of being "lazy" and "useless" and then she calls me "fat." This is news to me. I've never been called any such thing. While I've never been rail thin, I've always had a fine physique. I take a look at my reflection in the window. It's true, my face is bloated, almost beyond recognition. Then, as I finish rinsing the last of the pans, she hits me with a final blow.

"You've lost all semblance of self-respect. If your plan is to go on like this, you should tell me now, so that I can leave you. I don't intend to spend the rest of my life this way."

My God, this woman really despises me. There's not so

much as a stiver of love left between us, I realize: a woman with love in her heart would never say such a thing.

This all fits neatly into my theory of how love affects men and women so differently. History tells us, almost without exception, that men are at their strongest and most noble when they are in love and have full hearts. However, women are just the opposite. Love is too all-consuming for them. It makes them vulnerable and weak. A woman in love can be forced to swallow anything from her beloved, no matter how awful. That said—as soon as a woman's love vanishes, she becomes hard as steel, pitiless, a true savage!

I turn on the TV and flip through the channels. There is a baseball game on, the Giants versus the Phillies. I watch half an inning before losing interest and move on. On another channel, I watch five minutes of a cooking show. An Italian chef is teaching a celebrity I recognize from one of Rachel's charity events how to make rigatoni. The celebrity is extremely flirtatious. She keeps touching the chef's hands and making sexual innuendos. He seems more than amenable to her advances. The combination of the wonderful sexual tension and the delicious looking food is too much for me in my delicate state, so I flip through three reality dating shows, two reality outdoors adventure shows, and the news, before settling on a documentary on the mating rituals of the endangered East African zebra. I watch a stallion mount a mare, and realize just how unsettled I am. Something about the half-second glimpse of the news I caught has penetrated my psyche, and I feel compelled to go back.

The doorbell rings. Just as I'm looking through the peep-hole, I hear the on-site reporter say the words "act of domes-tic terrorism." The bell rings again, but I ignore it, transfixed by what I'm seeing. The reporter explains that the central control system that automates the movements of dozens of commercial trucks and trains has been hacked. Footage of eighteen-wheeled vehicles having driven themselves into lakes and off cliffs flash across the screen. The damages are estimated to be over $2 billion. Then we see a man and woman led from a house in cuffs, both with jackets over their heads. The reporter says the two alleged criminals have already confessed, claiming to belong to an organization that supports the Luddite agenda, and that for only $50,000 they were able to orchestrate this entire attack. The reporter then announces that authorities are still searching for one last suspect.

Julian has run downstairs to answer the door. A team of men with mustaches and blue jackets flash their credentials and introduce themselves as FBI agents. In the background, I hear the reporter mention the name of the victimized com-pany, Sunny Hills Food—Karl's former employer.

CHAPTER 42

THE FBI HAS ME IN THE ODDEST OF DETAINMENT CENters, if that's what you can call it. The accommodations are fantastic. In fact, I'm not sure I've ever been made so comfortable. It's as if the room was designed specifically to my tastes. Wide spruce beams stretch across a vaulted ceiling, Spanish-tile line the floor. There's a kiva fireplace, brightly colored woven blankets, and a ranch-style leather sofa. FBI Agent Steckhelm says the theme is "Santa Fe Hacienda."

"Is that real adobe?"

"Do you see those Kachinas dolls over there?" Agent Steekhelm asks, pointing at the mantle over the bar.

"Authentic?"

"Made by a real-life Navajo from the Santa Domingo Pueblo."

When it comes to furnishing my own home, in my humble opinion, my input has never been adequately appreciated. Rachel once told me I have no eye for design aesthetics. The accusation, at the time, seemed laughable to me. Between the two of us, I'm the only one who has ever demonstrated any artistic aptitude. Determined to change her opinion, I hunted long and hard for a wonderful piece of furniture I could present to her as a birthday gift, finally settling on a gorgeous antique—a mid-century modern teak credenza.

The furniture dealer who I purchased it from said it had been designed by a genius architect named Finn Juhl, a true leader in the Danish Modern movement of the 1940s.

Rachel came home that night from a run with her track club, radiant with an endorphin-induced glow, and glared at the credenza.

"Why would you ever bring such a thing in from the street?" she said.

"It's your birthday present!" I said.

"You got me a cheap knockoff for my birthday?"

"This is a Finn Juhl. Do you have any idea what that means?"

"Of course—Finn Juhl introduced Danish Modern to America."

"Then you understand that this is a one-of-a-kind piece."

"Henri, this is a repro, made from particle board."

I examined the credenza. It was not at all what it seemed just fifteen minutes' prior. What I thought was a solid block of chiseled wood had somehow transformed itself into cheaply fabricated pieces of chipboard haphazardly glued with epoxy.

"Next time, ask me before you get conned again, Henri. My God."

Agent Steekhelm mixes me a whiskey at the bar and leaves. Next to the highball glasses is a wooden cigar box stocked with both Cubans and a variety of foreign cigarettes.

The FBI is a first-class operation, I think, firing up a French smoke. Against the wall is a collection of vintage

Fender and Gibson guitars. I pick up an old Jazzmaster and begin picking a pleasing minor chord melody. After a time, Agent Steekhelm returns.

"You're pretty good on that thing," he says.

"I had a band back in high school."

"You don't say."

"You want to hear a song?"

"Why don't you sit down, Henri. I'd like to ask you a few questions."

"Mind if I refill my drink first?"

"You go right ahead."

Agent Steekhelm and I share the most intimate of conversations. I start from the beginning, with my childhood, telling him about my relationship with my parents—how I felt abandoned by my father's death, and how I attributed my runt-like size as a boy to poor nutrition, my mother being inept at cooking. By the time I get to talking about my adolescent years, I'm crying hysterically. Agent Steekhelm hands me a box of tissues, assures me I'm in a safe place, then pulls me in close so I can rest my head on his shoulder. After a few minutes, I've stained his shirt with my tears and runny nose.

I tell Agent Steekhelm that he is the kindest man I've ever encountered. He confides that he knows I'm not to be blamed for what's transpired—that I'm simply a "victim of circumstances beyond my control." This display of compassion inspires me to continue pouring my heart out for many more hours.

Later, Agent Steekhelm says, "You must be starving. What can we get you for dinner? Anything you want."

"Anything?" I ask.

"We'll have our chef whip it right up."

"You have steak?" I ask. "At home, I'm not allowed any animal products."

"We have the very best of steaks, Henri. Rib eye or filet mignon?"

"Ribeye, medium-rare, please. Also, I don't want to put you out, but do you have mac-and-cheese? It's been ages since I've had it."

"You got it," Agent Steekhelm says, placing my dinner order into his gram. "Now, Henri, I'd like to talk to you about your relationships with Lydia and Karl."

"They swindled me out of my money and let me take a bum rap!"

"I believe you, Henri," Agent Steekhelm says, patting my knee. "But I need you to walk me through it. Let's start with Lydia."

I describe my time at the bar with this dear friend who's betrayed me. I start with how nobody, human nor machine, can mix a better *San Martin*.

"That's very interesting, Henri. But can you tell me a bit about her personal life, who she interacts with, any friends or boyfriends you know of, that sort of thing?"

I'm well into a story about how I once set Lydia up with a pulmonologist from the hospital when my lawyer, Leonard Horowitz, storms into the room in his wrinkled grey suit and opens up his gram. For the first time, I notice the wiry hairs protruding from his nose.

"Henri," he shouts, "don't say another word to this jackal!"

Agent Steekhelm must be six inches taller than Horowitz, and outweigh him by forty pounds. I fear that at any moment he will crush Horowitz with one decisive blow to the head. But even as Horowitz is wagging his finger and shouting, Steekhelm never so much as raises his voice. He cites section 2a of the *The Protection of Americans from Other Americans Act of 2026*, stating that "those arrested and charged with a Class 3 Terrorist offense can be interned without trial for up to six years, if they're deemed by a federal judge to be an existential threat to the citizenry of the United States."

"And I have any number of judges who will issue an injunction to stop it. Now I'm going to need you to leave so I can speak with my client in private. And I'll have to insist that all cameras and recording equipment be turned off, lest you want me to hit you with an illegal search and seizure suit."

"How did you know I was here?" I ask.

"Rachel, of course."

Good old Rachel, how could I ever have doubted her? Everything wrong between us is my fault. I've been neglectful, I see it all so clearly now. I've ignored the one good piece of advice my father ever gave me.

"Son," he said, "women will always need someone to

confide in, someone to talk to, someone who takes an interest in their well-being and happiness. Provide a woman with these small favors and she'll repay you a thousand times over."

It's no wonder Rachel's been dressing like Snow White. It's not some new Disney fixation—it's a plea for attention. What a scoundrel I am!

"What did you tell that FBI agent about your involvement in this crime?"

"I didn't tell him anything."

"I don't believe it. You've been here for hours, you must've told him something."

Through the door, a man hollers, "I have your dinner, sir."

"Thank you," I say.

A man in a crisp blue suit pushes a cart into the room and from his jacket produces a bottle of steak sauce.

"Can you believe they gave me steak?"

"Classic interrogation tactic. Straight from the Nazi playbook."

"Come on, Horowitz. I thought you didn't drink."

"This place is everything you've ever wanted, am I right? Down even to the guitars and the southwestern décor?"

"It's like a dream."

"You ever hear of Hanns-Joachim Gottlob Scharr?"

My mouth is too full of steak, so I shake my head.

"Scharr was the Nazi's master interrogator—he could get American soldiers to spill the most confidential of secrets with not so much as a threat of violence. He won them over with kindness and goodwill. No resource was spared to make his prisoners happy, because a happy and content prisoner becomes lulled and complacent, and then he's only too quick to share his secrets."

I throw down my utensils in disgust. "The bastards," I say.

"If it worked on hardened American marines and Air Force bombers, I can only imagine how quick you were to sing like a canary!"

"But I'm innocent, Horowitz. I'm telling you."

Horowitz grins, almost lasciviously. Clearly, he thinks he's talking to a moron. "Please. I have your bank statement, Henri."

There it is on his gram, in bright bold font, the amount of $50,000 transferred directly into Karl's account. I spring from my seat, knocking my plate to the floor.

"That was a deposit for the Anodyne!"

"What the hell is the Anodyne?"

"It's the bar where Lydia used to work. I gave her the money so she and Karl could buy the joint. I was doing a good deed, helping to secure their future and all."

"Don't you know that one can never do right in this world without also doing something wrong? Why didn't you have me draw up a contract?"

"But I had one!"

"Where is it?"

"It's been lost, of course."

"But surely you made a copy?"

"I didn't think to," I say. "I was too ecstatic."

Standing up, Horowitz runs his hand down the front of his jacket. "I'm afraid this isn't going to end well for you," he says as he leaves.

Overwhelmed by the kind of merriment born only in true disaster, I collapse with howling laughter. Then I think of the past, and then of nothing at all.

CHAPTER 43

FUNNY THING HOW A LIFE CAN BE SO BESMIRCHED BY A seemingly harmless mistake. I could never have imagined I could suffer so much from something I'd thought so good.

Having spoiled me for a week for nothing they deem of value, the FBI have revoked what Agent Steekhelm called their "hospitality."

I knew I was in for it when they made me don this prison attire. The one thing I didn't bungle was the integrity of my suicide pill. In a feat of quick thinking and nimble fingering, I managed to slip it up my keister. I only had but a few minutes before the pill would send me to an early grave, I knew, but I was brave and squeezed it tightly between my cheeks as I was escorted to my new and exceedingly inferior accommodations.

This cell is nine feet by six feet. It's color scheme is pewter on pewter, furnished with but a toilet and cot. When I complained, I was told I should feel lucky—at least I have a window. A more accurate description of the aperture in my cell would be "narrow slit." For the past week it's been cloudless, but the glass is so thick that even when my face is pressed into this tight opening I feel nothing of the sun's heat.

The other day I went so berserk I bit my arm. The outburst

of course gained the attention of a guard, who struck me repeatedly with his baton. Strangely, I was overwhelmed by a sense of calm, and I fell into a deep sleep.

When I woke up, I asked for a copy of the Bible, both the Old Testament and the New. Three days later, I can scarcely believe what I've encountered. This cruel and merciless God is what so many wars have been fought over? All of this blood spilled on behalf of someone so sadistic and abhorrent? This is who Rachel thinks Julian would go to pieces without? I mean, my *God*, what horrific stories these books contain! Of all the luxuries my captors could've afforded me, it's God they have to offer.

I once watched a televised celebrity murder case. The defendant was a former Catholic priest who'd taken confessions from a famous actress. Her admissions polluted his ears and shook him to his core: orgies, money crimes, bestiality, the worst sins of pride, avarice, envy. One evening, after a particularly scandalous purge, the priest followed her back to her Topanga Hills mansion, and when she removed her gown to step into her bubble bath, he stabbed her repeatedly in the face, throat, belly, rectum, and genitals. As if ordained by the heavens above, she did not die immediately. The priest had somehow managed to avoid her major arteries. The holy man proceeded to savor his moment like a connoisseur, and when at last she died, he opened a priceless vintage of red Bordeaux and sat before the actress's 19th-century Steinway playing Fredric Chopin's "Nocturn op.9 No.2 in E-Flat major." Never had he played with such precision, conviction, and finesse, he said, astoundingly. Later, I found out on the news that the priest had been sentenced to ten lifetimes in maximum security prison. I think of him now because I just overheard the guards discussing his suicide. Until yesterday, he had been interned only two cells over.

Surely it's not God who punishes us for our sins, but ourselves. Of my fate I know nothing. The strain of waiting is maddening. I almost feel as though I have more reason to kill myself than did the priest. I, however, possess neither the bravery nor the agency to take my own life. Despite my misery and self-loathing, I can't force myself to swallow my pill. My cowardice is the only reason I'm alive.

CHAPTER 44

IT'S BEEN WEEKS SINCE I'VE SEEN ANOTHER HUMAN. MY cafeteria and yard privileges were revoked after I was caught hording and selling the commissary's stock of hot chocolate mix. I reaped a tidy profit until one of the other inmates took exception to my entrepreneurial savvy and forced me into a most compromising position in the shower room. For a brute, my assailant showed acute tenderness. It's amazing what we humans are willing to endure for a bit of intimacy. I am now in solitary confinement.

It's Horowitz who finally pays me a visit. He's grown a mustache since I saw him last, which I think must be almost two months back. His manner, however, is chilly. He opens his gram but blocks my view of it completely. That he seems so completely impervious to my well-being makes me instantly attracted to him.

"You must've found the contract," I say. "On my napkin?"

"I'm here, Henri, but to present you with divorce papers."

I snatch the man by his lapels and watch him wriggle like a worm on a hook.

"She has every right," Horowitz cries. "You've been unfaithful for years."

"She couldn't have known about that. I'm the model of discretion!"

"It's 2036, Henri, there are no secrets."

"Why did she never confront me?"

"It was all for Julian. Now that you're here, however, you're far from any use."

"Really?"

"You're a man of the world. You of all people should know that bonds are nothing if not conditional."

"But what about Julian? What about my rights?"

"You're in prison. You have no rights."

"And my money and assets?"

"What about them? A lot of good they are here, eh?"

"You're right," I say. "She can have it all. I want to make sure they're provided for."

Horowitz scrolls down the gram and points to a line, where I scribble my signature with my finger.

"You're still going to help me beat this rap, aren't you? I mean, you're still my lawyer, right?"

Horowitz laughs profoundly. "Really, Henri? Really?"

"That's it, then? That's all?"

"Good-bye, Henri."

CHAPTER 45

I USED TO BELIEVE I'D ONE DAY TRANSFORM INTO A FIN-
ished person. Brought up in the only civilization based on
science the world has ever known, I came to think of life as
one big problem that, with enough time and the right strategy, could be solved liked a geometry proof. Life, I believed,
was to be subjugated, overcome, defeated.

It's only now I see the folly of this view. Life isn't meant
to be lived on rails, aimed in a line at some fixed point, unwavering and resolute. Had fate not stepped in and delivered
what could easily have been a crushing blow, I'd still be living with blinders on, practicing medicine, playing the role
of a husband and a father. I'd know nothing of adversity,
tribulation, woe. I never would have known what it meant
actually to live. It's a mistake to believe that our experiences
do nothing to determine whether we are saved or damned. A
soul isn't brought into this world noble or petty. It's shaped
by its encounters.

Existence itself has become my occupation.

This most challenging of vocations has helped me to resolve life's difficulties—it's as if my batteries have been re-
charged, my mind drawing fresh strength and inspiration
from mysterious depths.

I don't believe I could ever go back to my old ways.

Luxuries lull a man into complacency, and thence to sleep.

And love, too, which absorbs too much time, too much emotion—it's the ultimate distraction. Mostly, though, it's a burden, a fearful nuisance, and when it's not that, it almost always proves something worse. I can't think of anything that provokes more pity and annoyance than a person in the throes of love.

Things are so much better for me now that I'm not obsessed with the endless search for happiness. I'm free now to pursue a true spiritual awakening—a blossoming! The worst thing that could happen to someone who discovers their calling is to stumble into a fool's happiness and succumb to it, squandering his gift.

Months of inactivity have atrophied my muscles and bones, so that when someone at last knocks at my cell door it's difficult to reach it.

"I have something to share with you," says the voice on the other side.

"I'm immune to any troubles you wish to burden me with."

"Excuse me?"

"The extinction of the three poisons: ignorance, aversion, and passion," I say. "I'm enlightened!"

"But I really need to show you this."

A man steps through the door, one of the guards. He's got a shiny bald head and a gentle, humorous face. He opens his gram to the lead story in today's news. There are two photographs of me, side by side, one of me in my doctor's attire, and one of my mug shot, where I'm looking every bit the hardened criminal. The headline reads, "From Healer to Hero!"

The article tells of my struggles as a youth, my ascension to the pinnacle of medical achievement, and my wife and family. All these details are nearly to the letter. Not even I could've offered a more truthful retelling of these facts.

However, from there, the story becomes one of pure fiction. It tells how I courageously abandoned my life as an elite to seek out a purer existence, a quest for solidarity with the common man ... how I gave up the spoils of the charmed life—money, admiration, family—to sow the seeds of a coming revolution. The writer crafts a tale where I'm the mastermind behind a tidal wave of Luddite sentiment. Dozens of other terrorist acts have taken place since I've been imprisoned, the article says, all inspired by Karl and Lydia's first triumphant victory, the planning of which has for some reason been ascribed to me. In fact, the article only mentions the two of them in passing, as foot soldiers in my great revolution.

Next, the guard shows me a transcript from a speech by candidate Bradford at a stadium in Texas, to an audience of over one hundred thousand people.

"I stand before you here to ask questions, to point out the ills of our society, to call out those men and women, who've sold out humanity in favor of greater efficiency and easy profits, but, I'm nothing more than a mouthpiece, delivering a message we already know in our hearts. Truth be told, what I do is quite easy, because I've never actually had to sacrifice a thing. Beyond speaking to the good people of our country, like I am here today, I've never put my beliefs into action. I've never had to choose between my freedom or my allegiance to what is right and just in this world. But there is a true hero in our movement, a man who's given up everything to champion a cause greater than himself, greater, in fact, than any one man—a sacrifice so wonderful and selfless he's practically a living saint. You all know who I'm talking about. Like Jesus or Moses before him, he needs but only one name ... Henri!"

There's yet another article that tells how Bradford has been precipitously falling in the polls, ever since this spree of domestic terrorism began. The pundits say he's doomed himself by refusing to disavow those responsible for carrying out these acts of destruction. Even his closest advisors are begging him to change course and move toward a more centrist, mainstream message. Yet, when pressed, he redoubles his provocations. The media has christened him the most fascistic politician of the twenty-first century. To support Bradford publicly has become anathema. Anyone who does is branded as backwards and fearful. Even his closest allies in the movement have turned against him, stating his positions to be too "extreme" and "dangerous."

Despite his abysmal approval ratings, another term for Martinez appears inevitable. Not because of anything he's accomplished, but simply because his opposition is too unhinged. The pundits are expecting the lowest voter turn-out in nearly sixty years. The disenfranchised people of this country, it seems, have finally given up. Content to receive their small allowance of Basic Income, a gram to watch sports on, and a machine to mix them cocktails, they expect nothing more from this life.

This third article demonizes me as the symbol of an evil and reviled movement—a rallying cry turned death throe—one that has brought the Bradford campaign to the brink of ruin. With the election only days away, he's an insurmountable seven points behind Martinez.

"I'm going to go down in history with my name attached to this madman!" I say.

"Madman? The two of you are like the Lenin and Trotsky of the twenty-first century! Didn't you read the articles?"

"Bradford's prospects in the election are doomed!"

"The polls and the media don't know anything. It's all lies. Don't you see? They're terrified! Our movement is so strong that the only defense they can muster is slander. But soon it won't matter."

"How can you say the polls are untrue? Statistics don't lie. They're science. And the media, aren't they the last check and balance against tyranny?"

The guard doubles over with laughter, slapping his thighs with open palms.

"That's a good one, Henri. Despite all of the injustice you've suffered, you've managed to retain your sense of humor."

When next the guard reaches into his jacket pocket, I think that he's only been toying with me, that his real purpose is to assassinate me.

But yet again, as in so many other matters, I am mistaken. "My wife," he says as he offers me a slice of pie, "made this just for you. You're the hero of our generation!"

It's the warmest, richest, most crumbly apple pie I've ever tasted. I don't want to utter a word or even breathe as I eat it, for fear the deliciousness will escape.

"In times like these," I say at last, "the world needs heroes."

"My wife makes pumpkin pie, as well, Henri."

"Bring it to me!"

"It will be the best pumpkin pie you've ever tasted, I promise."

"A slice won't do," I say. "You must bring the entire pie."

On my cot, I consider the importance of letting people cling to their hopes and dreams, even if they're rooted in falsehoods: it helps them to cope with all the things they'll never have.

CHAPTER 46

I<small>T'S INCREASINGLY DIFFICULT TO STAY FOCUSED ON A SIN-</small>gle abiding idea or notion. For hours, I'll lie on my cot, twiddling my thumbs or making shadow puppets on the wall, my mind working meantime on two juxtaposing thoughts so unrelated that I'm baffled how they share space in my brain.

I never learned to cook a soufflé, I realized this morning, for instance, while simultaneously concluding that things change because it's too entertaining for them not to. Later, the guard brought me a piece of red velvet cake. This, no doubt, is a tremendous development. His wife has expanded her menu to the point she fantasizes about one day owning a pizza shop. But as quickly as this good news brightens me, I'm torpedoed into yet another crisis.

The guard saw my wife and son on the news. Their savage attacks, he said, spared me no semblance of dignity. Truth be told, their ire left no mark. What got me is that before the guard had mention them, I hadn't spent so much as a minute thinking about my family since I signed the divorce papers. It's as if my mind had erased them. What's more, not even this—the realization that my love could disappear so quickly—affected me in the least. My torment stemmed from the notion that my memory was deficient. My razor-sharp mind had always been my greatest attribute. Now I wasn't so sure.

I couldn't remember the details of their faces, nor recall their voices, nor even say that they were short or tall or skinny or fat. Either I have always misjudged my abilities, I thought, or they have simply gone to pot. Neither of these was easy to swallow. Later, after spending the better part of the afternoon weeping, I had an epiphany: the twin gifts of forgetting and detachment are reserved only for the wisest of minds. It's this that enables their productivity. Thoughts of the past are wasteful, for the past is not the future and the future is what matters! I'm stunned it took so long to reach a conclusion that any third-rate child would've stumbled on in minutes. I take off my pants, twist them in a knot, and flagellate myself until I bleed.

Now the guard has returned, hysterical, his words a jumbled mess.

"No need to worry," I say, "your hero has once again triumphed!"

"Bradford has won the election!" the guard says.

"Impossible!"

"It was a landslide! He even won California and New York!"

"It can't be!"

"I prayed to God, and he delivered us this victory!"

"But the mathematical models had his odds at one in a thousand!"

"You more than anyone should know that science, math, and technology can't be trusted. Look at the world they've given us."

"But if not for science, how do we arrive at truth?"

"You must fight the impulse to think rationally, Henri. Have faith in the spirit of mankind."

"What does that even mean?"

"You're the one who's inspired millions of people to cast off all they know in favor of our glorious past!"

Democracy, I realize, being subject to the idiocy of the masses, has doomed the world! "I suppose the only way to avoid revolution is to introduce reforms over time. Otherwise, for the powers that be, catastrophe is inevitable."

"Inevitability, yes—the divine! I'm going to get us a pumpkin-walnut cheesecake to celebrate!"

The guard prances off like a fawn in a meadow, singing a tune from a Shakespeare tragedy I once saw performed as a musical.

CHAPTER 47

M INUTES AFTER BRADFORD IS SWORN IN, I'M ISSUED AN official pardon and summoned to Washington.

I collect my singular belonging, Mr. Toczauer's suicide pill, and place it in the pocket of my wallet, which has been returned to me, empty of its former contents.

FBI Agent Steekhelm escorts me to my private jet, silent until the moment I open the door to leave.

"The blood of civilization is on your hands!" he says.

Across the plane's hulking belly is a sun-faded and peeling light blue Pan Am Airways logo. Many of the rivets securing the wing to the fuselage are missing, the holes filled sloppily with epoxy adhesive and duct tape.

At the foot of the rollaway staircase I'm greeted by a woman whose good looks alone have surely ruined the lives of countless men. She sports a slim-cut, powder blue skirt and a cleavage-busting three-button jacket. She's even got a pillbox hat, white gloves, and six-inch stilettoes. She takes my arm to lead me up the stairs. Even so, halfway up, I slip and nearly bring my escort tumbling with me.

The plane's interior is equally dilapidated—the carpet is worn, frayed, stained. My safety belt is nothing I've seen since boyhood, something from a forty-year-old Wesley Snipes film. The woman takes the two ends of the belt and secures them, grazing my crotch as she does. Against my will, I become as erect as a flagpole, at which the attendant grimaces.

In the pocket on the back of the seat in front of me is a magazine dated from 1989—a year before I was born—whose cover exclaims, "*Miami Vice*'s Don Johnson Is the World's Hottest Leading Man!"

"What's going on with this plane?" I ask the attendant when she returns with a drink.

"It's quite retro, isn't it?"

"But why are we flying on it? It's ancient."

"President Bradford has issued an executive order that all planes be disassembled, and that their aluminum and titanium parts be melted down. This plane, actually, is the only one left. They found it under a tarp on an abandoned airstrip in the Mojave Desert."

The pilot powers up the plane, and the engine roars.

"I can't remember the last time I heard the purr of a combustion engine."

"Thank God technology reduction measures are the cornerstone of Bradford's agenda. He's meeting his promises."

"Everybody knows politics are a farce built on corrupt morals, ridiculous boasting, and slander. Who does this guy think he is?"

"Bradford is the straightest shooter we've got!" she says. "The moment that judge from Seattle issued a block saying its unconstitutional for the government to destroy the assets of private businesses, Bradford appealed, as he should have. After all, he has a mandate from the people!"

The pilot's voice comes over the plane's intercom, fuzzy and distorted: "It's been a few years since I've had to fly manually. But don't worry, I'm sure it's like riding a bike. Flight attendants, please take your seats."

The plane races down the runway, shaking and rumbling. I can see the wings jogging up and down and feel there's a good chance this thing will crash. A half-dozen air masks drop from the ceiling onto the seats in front of me as we lift off, and soon we're piercing through wispy clouds.

"Sorry about that folks," the pilot says after the plane levels off. "Just dusting off the cobwebs!"

I thumb through my magazine to an article on the hottest new fad, talking toys, featuring an animatronic stuffed bear called *Teddy Ruxpin*. The headline reads: "The Future Is Here!" With its moving eyes and ability to *read* stories played from an audio cassette in its back, it's sold over fifty million units!

In prison, I had to invent my own world, new philosophies, folklore, creation myths, language, games. It was my one source of comfort, the only thing that enabled me to bear my solitude. For a brief time, I was my own God, as it were, my own creator. Now I'm back in a world I share with hundreds of millions of other Americans, and yet I am a stranger in this land, disconnected from its ideologies and values.

Pens and paper haven't been used for nearly a decade, but when I ask for something to write with the attendant brings me two spiral notebooks, four blue pens, two red pens, a black marker, and a box of crayons with which I craft a series of charts and diagrams that illustrate the ramifications and consequences of this new Luddite ideology. Never has my mind worked at such a frenzied pace. The solution sets to complex problems in the fields of quantum mechanics and ergodic theory reveal themselves to me as clearly as my face in a mirror. In the history of humankind, perhaps only John von Neumann and maybe Sir Isaac Newton have experienced similar bouts of intellect.

My initial findings are disheartening, to the say the least. If I'm to follow my hypotheses to its natural end, my only option would be to kill myself, as quickly as possible. I've committed to take Mr. Toczauer's pill just as I stumble upon an alternative theory: nothing evolves as we think it will! The final sentences of my masterpiece, *The Manifesto of a Generation,* are: "If it's the truth you want to stand before you, you must never be *for* or *against* anything. The struggle between *for* and *against* is our fatal flaw!"

CHAPTER 48

UPON LANDING, I'M MET BY A HALF-DOZEN SOLDIERS, none older than eighteen years of age, wearing fitted brown uniforms branded with the Luddite symbol of Sisyphus rolling a boulder up a hill. They lead me through an underground tunnel built during the Kennedy administration. Everything is made of concrete. The path is lit by harsh yellow incandescent lights lined up as far as I can see, in perfect uniformity. Not an imperfection is to be found.

After thirty minutes of walking, we debouche into what appears to be a library. The room is three stories high and lined floor to ceiling with books. A team of men are working diligently, pulling the volumes off the shelves, loading them into wheelbarrows, and carting them out the back. Whenever the door swings open, a blazing fire comes into sight, and black smoke pours into the room.

Karl is the man directing this purge of knowledge. He does so with tremendous enthusiasm, hollering at the workers.

"It's the information contained in these books that oppresses you. Rid yourself of this poison and you'll be free!"

I look at this man with poor manners and bad teeth, and I marvel at how he's found himself at such a place.

"Henri, my old friend," Karl says as he shakes my hand. "It's so good to see you again!"

"Because of you, I've been rotting in jail, Karl."

"Let's not dwell on the dirty deeds of the past. It's so much better to forget. And anyway, the end justifies the means, wouldn't you say? Everything we discussed at our meetings is happening!"

"How did you get here?"

"I've been working for Bradford for months."

"From jail?"

"I was released."

"For giving me up?"

"I've been named Deputy Assistant Secretary of Technology Divestment."

Karl leads me outside, past all of the book-burning workers humming with activity. The air is black and thick, and from the sky falls a blizzard of ash. We hurry down a crooked street lined with shops, where all variety of tradesman are practicing their crafts. In a cobbler's window, a man works at his bench with pliers and hammer. Another man in a cowboy hat and denim sits at a bench with a boot on one foot and a shabby sock on the other. He's smoking a cigarette and telling the cobbler a story of how he was cheated in a business transaction. He had thought he was a buying a first-rate stallion to breed with his stable of mares, but had been swindled into buying a useless gelding named Bruno. As the cobbler finishes repairing the man's boot, they laugh.

Every storefront presents a uniquely remarkable spectacle. There is the grocery teeming with clerks stocking shelves, and women hurriedly moving up and down the aisles, carrying baskets full of produce and slabs of meat. Next door is the bank where tellers accept deposits, cash checks, and issue loans. Just beyond that is a post office, and at the end of the street, a railway depot.

Every man, woman, and child is hard at work. Their faces are marked with determination and struggle—each minute of their days filled with purpose and intention. Not a single loafer idling away his time.

"What is this place?" I ask.

"We're searching for the most optimal time in human existence, as regards to technology. This is the 1860s experiment. Just down the way we have a neighborhood living as if it were the 1910s. You can't imagine how boring silent films are."

"Any other eras?"

"We just set up a town emulating the 1950s. They even have TV."

"Yeah, but no polio vaccination, I bet, right?"

"Everything has its pros and cons," Karl says.

We pass the town's limits, then cross a river, a meadow, a sand dune, and, finally, hours later, reach a large, windowless silo on a wooded hillside. The entrance is guarded by more soldiers in brown uniforms, wearing pistols on their belts. They greet Karl with ceremony—arms straight, inclined upward, hands open and palms down—reminiscent, eerily, of the Nazi salute.

Soon we're on a high balcony, overlooking an open factory floor, where thousands of people are lined up to see one of dozens of technicians in white lab coats at curtained workstations. The floors of these workstations are bathed in a sea of blood. Next to each one of these technicians is an assistant endlessly filling a bucket of water from a latrine and pouring it on the floor.

The person nearest me is a young man the tip of whose finger has been chopped off. Blood is pouring out of it like a fountain. A woman in a white coat seizes him by the shoulder and shepherds him back toward the workstation from which he came.

"What is this place?"

"We're removing their grams. It's essential to their rehabilitation."

"But the brutality of it, Karl, it's not necessary."

"We're helping the people make the connection between technology and pain. It helps if you can think of the patients not as people but as symbols—in black and white. If you can make that abstraction, based on the ideology that we know to be right, then we can do this work with impunity."

"Was this Lydia's idea?"

"I'm glad you asked—that was going to be my next surprise. She's really made a name for herself here. You'll see her tomorrow."

CHAPTER 49

I WAKE IN THE MORNING SCRATCHING AT MY WHOLE BODY. In the dark, I knock my bedside lamp to the floor and am assaulted by the stench of kerosene. The sun pours in when I open the curtains revealing a series of brown and black stains on my sheets. They appear to be tiny drops of excrement. With a shard of the lamp's broken glass, I cut into the mattress. Thousands of bed bugs are navigating the pathways between the mattress's cotton filling.

There is a knock on the door, and a man barges in. He has a big, ugly face, covered in pockmarks and lumps, and is dressed formally, in the style of a western rail-splitter made famous by Abraham Lincoln. I have an appointment with Madam Lydia, he tells me, in twenty minutes, and he is here to escort me.

"Do I have time for a shower?"

"There's no running water," the man says. "We're waiting to know whether that technology is deemed permissible."

I'm taken to the center of a plaza, in front of what was once a grand hotel for visiting dignitaries and captains of industry. Its grounds are littered with hundreds upon hundreds of garbage bags, many of which have been torn open and their contents strewn about.

"Why is there so much trash everywhere?" I ask a man.

"They've cut the sanitation robots," he explains. "It's all being handled by men from now on."

"It looks like they've fallen behind."

"It's magnificent, isn't it? The ineffectuality of the garbage collection method creates more jobs. Now, more people can feel useful."

At the hotel entrance two guards greet me with salutes.

"Doctor Henri, sir! It's an honor."

"I'm here to see Lydia," I say.

"Of course, sir, Madam Lydia is expecting you. Right this way."

I'm overwhelmed by the beauty and expansiveness of the hotel's interior, with its immense stone columns, gold and silver leaf ceiling, and intricate mosaic tile floor.

"There are 128,000 hand-cut marble tiles on this floor," the guard says. "It's why Madam Lydia chose this location. She says it's important to recognize the grandeur of the work that can be done by humans, without the aid of machines."

When I move toward the elevator, the guard redirects me toward the stairway.

"The elevator isn't running, sir."

"Of course not," I reply.

Every few floors I need to stop and catch my breath, and by the time I reach the top I'm winded. Bent over at the waist, huffing and puffing, my vision goes cloudy and the room begins to spin.

"Just a few days ago," the guard says, "I was the same

way. Now I'm acclimated to the climb. I'm not reliant on machines to do the work for me."

The guard knocks on the pine doors, ten-feet-tall, to Lydia's office.

"Send him in," says a reedy voice.

There is my old friend Lydia sitting at the helm of the mightiest desk I've ever seen, the room itself reeking like a Chinese fish market. She's dressed in a grey tunic, reminiscent of Chairman Mao. There is a gold plaque mounted on the desk's front-side, stating that it was a gift to President Nixon from Queen Elizabeth, and that it's made of English Oak timbers leftover from the hull of a British Arctic exploration ship. Lying on the desk is a grey cat with a docked tail, licking at its fur. Behind Lydia, on the wall, hangs an oil painting of a well-muscled slave tilling a field with a plow. The man's face is more hardened and severe than any that's lived in a hundred years.

"Like my desk?" Lydia inquires.

"Sure beats the bar at the Anodyne."

"President Bradford let me remove it from the White House. He treats his people with the respect and dignity they deserve."

Lydia fumbles with a drawer, having never fully recovered her finger dexterity. In time, she manages to pry it open and retrieves from it the mangled carcass of a tuna. Her cat meows lazily, then takes a few bites before returning to sleep.

"Periods of drastic change always require a bit of hardship and sacrifice," Lydia says.

"Karl's the right man for the job, then."

"He's good at what he does."

"And what's your job here, Lydia?"

Using a fork, Lydia scrapes the remainder of the tuna's skin and bones into a waste basket. "I have a team of people who use their various methods to collect information on different individuals. If I deem that these targets pose a significant threat to society, I bring them in for further evaluation. We recently made an arrest that may be of particular interest to you."

Lydia leads me down the stairs fast, two at a time, all the while whistling the century-old Woody Guthrie tune, "This Land is Your Land." I struggle to keep pace, and by the time she's reached the ground floor I'm nearly a flight behind.

"Don't dawdle," Lydia says. "You're going to love this!"

When I reach her, she takes my hand and drags me into a room off the foyer. Along one wall is a floor-to-ceiling bookshelf devoid of all but one book. Lydia emits a small giggle.

"The secret door bookcase trick loses some of its magic this way, doesn't it?"

The bookcase swings open and we find ourselves at the entrance to a pitch-black tunnel into which I must stoop because the ceiling is so low. I hear a match being struck, and then a kerosene lamp ignites. Lydia hands me the lamp and lights one for herself. After several minutes of walking, we reach a jail cell very different from the one I inhabited. Mine was made of concrete, and kept cold and sterile. This one is something out of medieval times. The walls are limestone scummy with moss, and its bars are cast from now-rotting iron. From the ceiling, water drips on the floor in pools. Lydia sets her lamp down, sending an army of cockroaches and centipedes scattering.

"Who's there?" asks a voice from the dark.

"I've brought you a visitor," Lydia says.

I raise my lamp to see who it is but hear only the sound of stiletto shoes on the rocky floor.

"Is that you, Henri?"

"Serena!" I exclaim as I stumble back in shock.

Serena stands tall and defiant in an all-white, low-cut pants suit and matching white scarf. There's not a wrinkle or smudge of dirt on her. Every hair on her head is perfectly placed. Her eye makeup and lipstick are immaculate.

"These invalids kidnapped me in the middle of my date with a French sheikh."

"I'll give you old friends a few minutes to catch up," Lydia says with imperturbable merriment.

"Are you okay?" I ask.

"I'm fine," Serena replies, bowing her head uncharacteristically. "I owe you an apology."

"It's not your fault my life went to shambles."

"I shouldn't have fucked Taylor. That was wrong of me."

"Have they told you their plans?"

"My lawyers are working to get me out."

"President Bradford doesn't strike me as the type to adhere to any sort of formal legal proceedings."

"What do you suggest, then?"

"Lie to them. Tell them you're sorry. Tell them you're a sinner who's lived her life terribly. Tell them you've had an epiphany and seen the error in your ways."

"I would never tell those cretins such things, not even to spare my life."

"It might come down to that."

Lydia's light grows brighter as she returns.

"Time to say good-bye," she says.

Serena and I exchange quick glances before we leave her again to the dark.

CHAPTER 50

I WAKE UP ON A COUCH, COVERED WITH A HEAVY WOOL blanket. A nurse is feeding me ice chips and wiping my brow. The room is steeped in token symbols of patriotism—American flags, a taxidermized eagle, a painting of the Statue of Liberty. In my panic I kick the blanket away and see I'm naked.

"You passed out climbing the stairs to Madam Lydia's office."

"Impossible!" I place two fingers to my neck and take my pulse. Eighty-six beats per minute—certainly not the heart of an elite athlete, but hardly a candidate for respiratory failure. "Bring me my clothes. I must see Lydia at once."

As I dress, I spew a barrage of profanity. In the span of two minutes, I've slandered Lydia, Serena, Karl, Rachel, Taylor, and everyone in the Bradford administration. The nurse rolls up with a wheelchair, which I dismiss as I totter out the door to a sign in the stairwell that reads, "4th Floor."

Step by step, I make my ascent, but am reduced in short order to crawling on hands and knees, the nurse my constant shadow. No longer will I acquiesce to this madness. Locking up Captains of Industry, burning books, decommissioning planes, no running water, letting the garbage pile up in the streets, shutting down the elevators—this is madness, and it must be stopped! At the eighth floor, I struggle to my feet and throw open the doors to Lydia's office. She's sitting at her glorious desk, eating a banana.

"This has gone far enough!" I say. "The game is over!"

"Whatever are you talking about?"

"You have Serena in prison like she's some sort of criminal. Tell me, what laws has she broken?"

"That she hasn't broken any is a clear indication that the laws are bad. Meantime, please don't try to convince me she's done nothing wrong. It insults us both. If someone were to tally up the number of people Serena has wronged, it would be in the millions. Yourself included, mind. If it weren't for her Human Life Valuation Tool, you'd still have a job."

"What are you going to do to her?"

"A work camp, of course. Actually, two—a summer camp in Arizona, and a winter camp in Alaska—where she'll be free to work out in nature, eighteen hours a day. It'll be wonderful for her rehabilitation."

"That will kill her!"

"And you're the one who's going to order it." I gape at Lydia with my incomprehension. "Haven't you heard? President Bradford is making you my boss. Karl's, too. You're going to oversee the entire Department of Technology. Part of your job description is sentencing Technology offenders to the work camps. It's wonderful!"

"I want to see Bradford!"

"Surely. He's dying to meet you."

CHAPTER 51

A GUARD GIVES ME A TEN-SPEED BICYCLE AND A HAND-drawn map to the White House.

To my surprise, I handle the bike as well as I did in my school days, when my friends and I used to ride BMX in the abandoned construction sites near my dad's apartment. That said, after just a few minutes of pedaling, my ass is raw and my hands riddled with blisters. Still, I pedal harder yet only to realize I'm lost, because the guard has failed to properly label any of the streets with names. Instead he simply calls out landmarks, both real and imagined. One instruction on the map says, "Turn left at the intersection where President Bradford remarked that a team of deranged robots from Mexico raped and murdered an entire kindergarten class."

I throw the map down knowing full well Bradford has no interest in enforcing any anti-littering laws harmful to job creation. I ask a woman pushing a baby carriage for directions to the White House.

"You're Henri, aren't you?" the woman says excitingly. "I recognized you immediately!" After rattling off precise turn-by-turn instructions, she asks for a photo, forcing me to remind her she's had her gram removed. "Oh well," she says, "if no photos with celebrities is the price to pay for a fairer society, so be it!"

At the gate of the White House, an entire team of uniformed guards let me pass through undisturbed, each of them saluting as they say, "Doctor Henri, sir!" There's a party in full-swing on the White House's front lawn. I recognize senators, congressmen, and supreme court justices, all in various state of intoxication. As well as the elected and appointed officials, there are countless people I don't recognize—friends, family, and constituents—also enjoying the festivities. I'm greeted with shouts of glee. The vice president immediately presses me to shot-gun beers with him. He chases his with tequila, but I refrain. I must stay sharp for Bradford.

The president is manning the barbeque. He's dressed in a T-shirt and jeans with an apron stained in barbeque sauce and charcoal. Despite the slovenly appearance, I'm struck by a certain magnetism. He smiles warmly as he loads burgers and sausages onto the grill, his eyes clear and bright, then wipes his hand on his apron before extending it. I give it a good squeeze, but he does me one better, placing his free hand on my elbow and jerking me toward him. When he lets go, there is a brown spot on my shirt, where he touched me.

"Henri, my good man, it's so wonderful to finally meet you in person."

"Mr. President," I say. "We need to talk."

"Do you like barbeque, Henri?" he asks, and hands me a plate full of baby-back ribs. "Because I absolutely love barbeque. It's fun, it's social, everyone can feel good at a barbeque, it's a real crowd pleaser. And best of all, it requires no technology, only fire and meat."

The president cracks open two beers, laughing heartily as he does, then slings an arm over my shoulder to lead me into the Rose Garden, where Dr. Hines is busy pruning, having somehow weaseled his way into a job on the White House's grounds crew.

"Mr. President, it's about Serena."

"I understand you met with Lydia this morning," he says. "Such a wonderful woman, even after having suffered so unbearably. She deserves better, and now she's going to have it."

"Yes, sir, Lydia is a fine woman, but I'd like to discuss Serena."

"Henri, I can't tell you enough just how glad I am to have you join the team. You're going to make a really fantastic addition to our organization." The president leans over a bounty of yellow and pink buds, shoos away several bumblebees, and inhales. "I owe you a heaping debt of gratitude," he says, his face the picture of serenity. "If it weren't for you, I wouldn't be president. It was your martyrdom that spurred the people to get out and vote. You gave this movement its legs."

"As a favor to me, then, sir, I need you to let my friend Serena go."

The president laughs uproariously.

"I appreciate your loyalty but I'm going to explain to you how it's misplaced. People like Serena have sold the citizens of this nation on a false hope. They promised that technology would liberate them from the mundaneness of having to go to work each day, giving them more time than they could ever imagine to pursue all variety of noble ambitions, be it music, art, or even science. But the last thing society needs is more creatives. Can you imagine anything as awful as a world full of painters, composers, and for God's sake, novelists? Thank goodness, we've been spared that fate. You see, Henri—most people aren't so clever. They don't have anything close to resembling talent. There is no possibility that the average man can create something of value. Absent this talent, what do they do with all this newfound time? The answer is—nothing. The best thing we can do for people, Henri, is to put them back to work. Allow them the opportunity to provide for their families. It's the American dream, after all."

"With all due respect, sir," I say, "what kind of society will we have if the best and the brightest are punished?"

"Don't you see? Serena is the embodiment of man's two most cardinal sins: pride and greed—the two overlapping, merging, multiplying the other's effect. Such a combination is a recipe for throwing open the gates of hell!"

"But to reconstruct society in your vision will take big thinkers."

"Aren't you a big thinker, Henri?"

"Serena is a thousand times more talented."

"Yes, perhaps. And yet she's not nearly as useful, not, at least, for my purposes. You know, Henri, I really want to make things work for you. But first you must prove you can be loyal to our project."

"Sir, may I ask why you've brought me here?"

"Don't be silly, Henri. Unemployed truckers and bartenders have little value, in terms of propaganda. But a well-esteemed doctor, whom the people believe has thrown away his privilege for the good of the many? That I can use. And I must say, I've done so, masterfully. In fact, you're even more popular than I am. It's true, I'd hate to lose you, but you're far from indispensable."

"What is it you want?"

"Prove yourself by sending Serena to the work camps."

"I won't do it."

Bradford steps right up to me, his heavy belly being the only thing between us, and he presses his finger into my chest. "Would you like to go in her place?"

"Forget what you think you know about me, and what you think you know about Serena. She was my best friend for twenty years. I would never sacrifice her to spare myself."

"People who are preparing to hurt someone very badly often talk kindly of them beforehand—deck them with flowers, as they say—by way of compensation! Now if you'll excuse me."

The president sets down his beer, unzips his fly, closes his eyes, and begins to relieve himself all over the flowers. In this moment, I have a brilliant idea. From my wallet I take the suicide pill and inch toward the President's beer. But—me, assassinating the President of the United States? What an awful cast of bedfellows I'd go down in history with! John Wilkes Booth, Lee Harvey Oswald, Leon Czolgsz, Charles J. Guiteau? On the other hand, I consider, my murder would be fully warranted. I'd be remembered as the great savior of the American people, I'm certain. I'd be saving them from themselves, really, since they're the ones who voted him in—under false premises, of course, having been seduced by Bradford's use of my likeness. No, this terrible injustice must be undone.

Yet, by killing Bradford, it's possible I'd be dooming civilization's last chance for a better, more gratifying way of life. Surely the direction we've been headed for the past century isn't sustainable. Look at where it's led us: The Earth's climate has been irreparably changed, its oceans are polluted, its forests and mountains are destroyed, the air is carcinogenic, the animals are nearing extinction, and, mankind, the only species who should've benefitted from all this chaos and destruction, has never been more aimless. I put the pill away just as the president finishes pissing.

"If I agree to go in her place," I say, "you'll spare her?"

"This is not what I wanted for you, Henri," Bradford says. "But it's your choice. If this is what you desire, then, let's get on with it."

CHAPTER 52

Two guards take me away. I'm loaded into the back of a bicycle-powered rickshaw. A sign hangs from its side that reads, "Tours of Washington D.C. $5." One guard pedals and steers, while the other shares the carriage with me, holding a dagger against my side.

It strikes me that where catastrophes may have many independent causes, without fail, almost as if supernaturally engineered, they always converge in a way to produce a single terrifying event. These random life occurrences—my affair with Taylor, the sacrifice of my job, befriending Lydia at Anodyne, Karl's revenge against his former employer, Bradford's exploitation of me for his own nefarious ends, my relationship with Serena—they've all conspired to my fate, a slow death in the work camps!

I make a final tally of all the things I've failed to do in this life. The list is staggering—everything from not getting to watch Julian grow into a man, to not getting the old band back together, to never having had Virtual Reality Sex with those Chinese college students. Seeing this, I lose all powers of concentration. My spiritual anguish is profound. My nausea is total.

In front of Lydia's building is parked a stagecoach—far more elaborate, pulled not by a bicycle, but by three horses.

Its carriage has been retrofitted into a makeshift jail cell, complete with steel bars, a cot for sleeping, and a small hole in its floor for defecation. Its drivers are waiting to take me to Alaska.

"I want to see Serena one last time before I go," I say.

"Of course, sir," a guard says, "anything for the man who helped save humanity from the machines."

I'm escorted past the trash, through the hotel's foyer, into the side room. The guard pulls on the last remaining book on the shelf, opening the secret door. Another guard struggles with a kerosene lamp. He goes through a half dozen matches before he can get it lit. He is, I realize, fighting hard not to cry. When I place a hand on his shoulder, he explodes with tears. I stand by helplessly as he hands me the lamp and the keys to Serena's cell.

Even though you've been lousy in this life, I tell myself, *perhaps God will see something redeeming in your courage.*

The idea of reincarnation, which has never appealed to me, now appears the best possible outcome. I make a plan to atone for my sins in Alaska, with the hope of being reborn as a bird or a frog.

Serena is waiting. Despite the cell's conditions, she's as immaculate as ever. It hardly seems possible, what with the water dripping from the ceiling, the humidity, the bugs, and the moss.

"Henri, thank God, it's you," she says.

"That's right," I say, staring at the ground. "It's me."

I am on the verge of unlocking the door when a force

wells up. "Don't you feel any guilt for everything you have," I say, "when so many people are living lives devoid of meaning?"

"Why should I feel guilty? I haven't done anything wrong! I'm an innocent victim!"

"A victim?" I ask, scratching my head. "Innocent?"

"Henri, I'm the only one left strong enough to stand against society, whose will hasn't been eroded to the point where I've contented myself with so little just for the sake of honoring harmony, uniformity, and humility."

An image of Serena lording over an army of robots fills my mind. "Yes, that's right," I say, fumbling to get the key into the lock. "You can't stop progress."

"Get on with it, Henri." Serena grabs onto the cell's bars, shaking them with all of her might. "I have responsibilities that need my immediate attention!"

"I don't know how you can live with yourself after all the casualties you've inflicted!" I shout, my voice sounding remarkably like Bradford's. "You're the author of countless horror stories!"

It dawns on me that there is a second way people talk when preparing to hurt another. They don't always deck their victims with flowers, by way of compensation, as Bradford put it. Instead, they slander the person, to give themselves the courage to carry out their act. I take the suicide pill from my wallet and hand it to Serena. "Take this."

"Euthasol?" she questions. "Why would you give me a suicide pill?"

As I run back up the tunnel, I can hear Serena shouting, but I pretend it's the howling of the wind. To carry on in this world, I have no other choice. The guard is waiting for me at the door to the tunnel.

"Take her to Alaska," I say, handing him the keys. "I've got to help Bradford fix our country."

ACKNOWLEDGEMENTS

In the spring of 2016, I was living in Albuquerque, New Mexico. One day, while sitting in a meeting at work, I reminisced about a life unlived in Eastern Europe—something I had become fixated on after having watched an Anthony Bourdain travel show on Budapest. By meeting's end, I had bought a one-way ticket and drafted a resignation letter.

Three weeks later, I landed in Budapest, not knowing anyone, and with no place to live. For the next five months, I committed myself to the business of novel-writing. Outside of this book, the best thing to materialize from my time in Budapest was my friendship with Daniel Young. I won't use these pages to detail any of our bad behavior, but I would like to thank him for keeping me well fed and for all the good fun.

I would also like to thank D. Foy, my novel-writing mentor, for reading so many drafts of the manuscript and for all his keen insight. Every writer needs a great reader to help figure out what's working and what's not, and D. Foy is the best. Of course, I'd like to thank Lindy Ryan and the Black Spot Books team.

Additionally, I'd like to thank my NYC-friends who have supported me throughout this venture: Ariel Ashe, Paige McGreevy, Carolyn Cohen, Jason Craig, Shirley Cook, Tracy O'Neill, Hannah Lillith Assadi, and Michael Seidlinger.
Last, but surely not least, I'd like to thank Isabella Isbiroglu. She makes life better in every way.

ABOUT THE AUTHOR

Matthew Binder is the author of the novels High in the Streets and The Absolved. He is also a primary member of the recording project Bang Bang Jet Away.